TRUSTING FOREVER

*USA TODAY* BESTSELLING AUTHOR

LEA COLL

# GET THE MOUNTAIN HAVEN SERIES 40% OFF!

*Get ready for a romance that'll make your heart melt! Seven books, beautifully written stories of rugged men and the women who own their hearts. Off-the-charts chemistry guaranteed! Get 7 books for 40% off for a limited time on Lea's Shop.*

# CHAPTER 1

## HANNA

"You're welcome to stay with me as long as you need," Sebastian said as we stood next to the elaborately decorated Christmas trees at the newly renovated Matthews Inn. Music drifted down the grand staircase from the ballroom upstairs. Guests mingled around us, drinking cocktails.

Sebastian offered me his guest room while I searched for an apartment, and it coincided with the few weeks before Christmas when he was busiest at the farm. I'd help with Ember in exchange for a room. It was a good deal if your heart wasn't on the line. "My parents won't be happy, but I don't have a choice unless I want to move back in with them."

"This is our busiest time of the year. We'll need help in the shop," Lori, Sebastian's mom, said.

Sebastian's family owned the neighboring Christmas tree farm where, over the years, his brothers had built cabins to live on the property and run the business. Sebastian was the last one to make that move.

"I'm happy to help." I was pleased Sebastian was finally relocating closer to his family. I suspected it was because he needed more help with his daughter, Ember, whom he was raising by himself, and wanted her to spend more time with his family.

"It will be easier to watch Ember if you're living with me," Sebastian said to me.

My heart skipped a beat, then galloped in my chest. I longed for my best friend to see me as something more than a friend. I'd settled into the friend role a long time ago, but the idea of living together made me feel excited and panicked at the same time.

Would he finally see how I felt about him? Then I panicked for a different reason. What if he asked me to watch Ember so he could go out with another woman? It would be torture, but I couldn't say no.

His brother, Talon, raised a brow. "A live-in nanny?"

Sebastian sighed. "She's my friend and roommate. Don't be a jerk."

I'd held the role of Sebastian's best friend since we were kids. He either never saw how I felt about him or didn't see me in that way. I suspected it was partly both.

"Whatever you say," Talon said.

Holly stepped forward, holding an ornament she'd hand-painted with an image of the inn, and I tuned out the conversation. Was moving in with my best friend a good idea? When he'd gotten his ex, Brandy, pregnant, I'd backed away to allow them to work it out. When she left him to raise Ember, I helped as much as I could. But my attraction to him hadn't waned. Over the years, I'd hoped he'd finally see me as more than a friend, but maybe it was time to come to terms with the fact he never would. Maybe it was time to move on.

"Can we dance now?" Ember tugged on Sebastian's hand.

Sebastian looked at me over her head and grinned. "We can do that."

There was something in his eyes, a combination of sexy

single dad and reliable best friend, that had my nerves going haywire.

We took the stairs to the second floor, where the guest rooms were located. Each door held a wreath, and at the end of the hallway, another tree stood in the window. Marley, who'd recently inherited the property from her grandmother, had done an amazing job decorating the inn for the holidays and restoring it to its former glory.

The music grew louder as we climbed to the third floor and entered the ballroom. Guests danced in the center of the room, and a crowd gathered around Alex, the cellist who was playing on the makeshift stage.

"He's amazing," Marley said.

Ireland dipped her head to say, "He was invited to play the national anthem at Madison Square Garden."

The couples in our group paired off to dance, and I wondered what I was doing here. It was Ember who'd begged for my attendance.

Ember tugged on my hand. When my gaze met hers, she said, "You should dance with Daddy so he's not alone."

Tingles erupted down my spine. I shifted my gaze from her to Sebastian. "Is that so?"

He held out his hand to me, and my heart raced in my chest. "You don't want me to be lonely, do you?"

I smiled, placing my hand in his. "We can't have that."

His palm felt warm against mine, and my body was tingly all over with the anticipation of being close to him. We'd gone together to a dance or two in high school, and I'd always hoped it would lead to more, that he'd feel something between us, but if he did, he never let on.

He led me into the center of the dance floor and drew me into his arms. My cheeks flushed, and I felt a little lightheaded as he pulled me close and grinned at me. "I think Ember manipulated us."

I smiled up at him, catching the amusement in his gaze. "I think so, too."

He dipped his head slightly and lowered his voice. "I can't complain."

I had so many questions. Did he want to dance with me? Was he enjoying this as much as I was? The entire room smelled like evergreens from the number of trees around the perimeter of the room. There was a large one in the center of the dance floor, decorated with large ornaments and ribbon. It was quite possibly the grandest tree I'd ever seen.

"Do you have any trees left on the farm?" I asked him, nodding my head in the direction of the numerous trees.

He chuckled, and it rumbled through my chest, making me feel off-kilter.

I wanted to move closer to him. I wanted to put my hands around his neck and press my body against his. But this was a formal dance, and Sebastian was my friend, not my date.

"I don't get involved in the planting or the growing of the trees. That's mainly Knox and Heath. What I do know is that Heath will do anything to make Marley happy."

"That's sweet." I couldn't imagine a love like that. This feeling I'd been harboring for Sebastian all my life was based on our friendship. I had no way of knowing what would happen if we took that step, and it was scary.

Sebastian led me around in a circle, and for a few minutes, he blocked out everything else, along with the sound of the cello and the twinkling of the lights. "I recently found out Marley and Heath dated a bit in high school. They kept their relationship a secret, but I have a feeling it was quite serious."

"They dated in high school?" We were younger than both of them, and I didn't hang in the same circle as the Monroe brothers. They were athletic teens, and the girls naturally gravitated toward them.

But Sebastian was different. He didn't play sports, other than tennis, and he wasn't interested in girls. He liked school. We'd hang out a lot at his house under the guise of studying. And that's what we did, but I spent more time gazing at his beautiful face and analyzing every word that came out of his mouth. He was an innocent schoolgirl's crush.

My parents were never concerned about us hanging out together, and maybe that should have been my first clue that he wasn't interested in me. If no one else saw the potential for anything, why would Sebastian?

"You have any plans for the new year besides spending time with me?" Sebastian flashed a charming grin, his dimple popping, and my entire body heated.

I wished more than anything I was living with him for real. That we were a couple, that he'd do anything for me, like Heath did for Marley. But that wasn't a possibility for us. Once you were in the friend zone, there was no getting out of it. "Not really."

My life was predictable. I taught language arts at the elementary school in Annapolis. I blogged my thoughts and ideas for education on the side and sold various worksheets and programs online. I didn't make a lot of money, but I loved working with children, and I enjoyed my job. Recently, I wondered about moving from a teaching position to a reading specialist one. I was reluctant to leave the classroom, but I wondered if I could do more good in a specialized position.

"You don't have a dream you want to pursue or an interest you haven't spent time on?" Sebastian continued.

*Just you.* I'd been singularly focused on Sebastian since we met in eighth grade. It was right before he hit puberty, grew tall, and filled out. I kept waiting for him to notice girls, but he hadn't. The downside of that was, he hadn't noticed me either.

"You spend so much time with me and Ember. I worry about you."

This time, my cheeks flushed for a different reason. I was

embarrassed. "You don't need to worry about me. My New Year's resolution is to start dating again."

Sebastian stilled, and we stopped moving in a circle, even as the other dancers flitted around us, laughter and conversation surrounding us. "Are you serious?"

I shrugged as nonchalantly as I could, as if I hadn't just given up on Sebastian finally noticing me. My heart pounded in my chest. "I'm eager to get back out there."

He started moving us again, this time slower, and I felt his gaze on my face. "I didn't realize you were eager to meet someone."

My mouth suddenly dry, I said, "I'm twenty-seven. I want to get married and have a few kids. You know I've always wanted a family."

Sebastian swallowed hard. "I didn't realize it was something you wanted in your life right now."

"I'm not getting any younger. Women have a biological clock, you know, and mine's ticking." I wasn't being entirely truthful. I did want a family and kids, but I wasn't feeling pressured to have kids now. It was more that I wanted to stop pining after my best friend, especially since we were going to be living together.

I saw the sympathetic looks his family gave me. Everyone knew about my crush. Did Sebastian? Did he feel sorry for me? That didn't sit right with me. I felt hot all over and slightly clammy.

"Are you okay?" Sebastian asked.

"I think I need some fresh air." I looked around, desperate for a way to escape his scrutiny.

Sebastian's gaze roamed the room, and I was positive he was checking to ensure one of his brothers or his mom had Ember, and then he gripped my hand tightly in his and led the way across the floor.

"Where are we going?" I wanted to tell him that I needed

space from him. That he couldn't just take me wherever he wanted to.

He squeezed my hand and said over his shoulder, "To get you some fresh air."

I followed behind as he pushed open a door I hadn't noticed before. The cool air hit us as we stepped onto a deck that overlooked the back of the property. White rocking chairs and heaters lined the space, and the railing was wrapped with garland and lights.

Sebastian shut the door behind us, shrugged off his suit jacket, and wrapped it around my shoulders. His familiar scent of spice with a hint of evergreen engulfed me.

"I didn't know this was here," I said as I held the jacket closed.

"Heath showed it to me when he gave me the tour," Sebastian said as he scrutinized me. "How are you feeling?"

"It was hot in there." I'd wanted space, but now he was here, standing closer than before. It was hard to draw in a deep breath.

Sebastian put his hand on my shoulder and ushered me closer to the railing. "Look, it's snowing."

I held one hand out as fat flakes fell from the sky and into my hand. Enraptured with the white fluff on my palm, I said, "It's beautiful."

I shivered, and Sebastian moved closer, his chest a wall of heat against my back. I wanted to sink into him and watch the snow come down. But it didn't seem appropriate. Not when he was just a friend.

He lowered his head so that he could watch the flakes land in my hand. "I should call Ember out here."

But neither of us moved. It was as if time was suspended. The music filtered through the windows, but out here, it was just us and the falling snow. There was a hushed quality, as if we shouldn't speak.

"Thank you for coming tonight," he whispered across the shell of my ear, causing me to tremble.

I turned slightly so that I could see his face. "Ember invited me."

Sebastian glanced down at me, concern etched in his brows. "Are you sure you're okay with living with us and helping me out with her after work and on the weekends?"

"I love Ember. You know I don't mind watching her."

Sebastian pulled me close to him so that I was leaning against his body. "I'm so lucky to have you in my life."

His words flamed my desire for him, which always simmered just below the surface. There was a part of me that longed for Sebastian to do things for me because he wanted to spend time with me, and he was attracted to me. Not because he felt obligated as a friend.

"I feel the same way. The only thing is, I haven't told my family I'm living with you. They're going to ask what my plans are for the future."

"We can tell them we're roommates. It's convenient since I'll be working late during the holidays and tax season."

"And I need a place to live." I'd searched for other arrangements, but I needed a roommate to afford the apartments closer to my school.

"It's a mutually beneficial arrangement."

"It's a win-win," I said, but the words felt flat to me. I was Sebastian's best friend, the first person he called when he needed help with Ember, but I wanted to be more. I wanted him to see me as a woman, not just as a friend.

"Now, what were you saying inside about your New Year's resolution?" His words tickled my ear.

"It's time for me to meet someone. I need to make a real effort this time." I tended to go out with a few guys and then give up, claiming there were no good men out there. Mainly because I'd already met the one I wanted to give my heart to. If only he felt the same way. But I couldn't wait around any longer.

It was pathetic to harbor a crush on Sebastian for so long. Now I was living with him and taking care of his daughter; the pitying looks would only increase.

"I don't want you to get hurt."

"That's part of dating, right? You put yourself out there and hope the other person feels the same way." I was still leaning on Sebastian, his warmth heating me more than his suit jacket. I didn't want to pull away from him physically or emotionally, but it was time.

The only thing that made me hesitate was that I hadn't told Sebastian how I felt. But I was worried it would ruin everything. Our friendship, my relationship with Ember and his family. I couldn't risk it.

I stepped away from him, turning to face him, the cool air nipping at my exposed chest and legs. I tightened his jacket around me as if I could ward off the cold. My heart raced in my chest. "If you're home in the evenings, I might go out with friends or even on a date."

Sebastian stiffened. "You don't work for me. You are free to go out."

He wasn't paying me to watch Ember, but he was giving me a place to live rent-free. "This arrangement will work for both of us."

Sebastian stayed quiet, his gaze assessing me, almost as if he were trying to figure me out. If he didn't already know I liked him, I wasn't going to tell him. It wouldn't lead to anything but heartbreak and awkward moments.

He needed me to take care of his daughter, and like always, I'd do that for him. But I wouldn't wait around for him to notice me anymore.

# CHAPTER 2

## SEBASTIAN

Shortly after our talk, we came inside so that I could check on Ember. She was happy to hang out with her extended family and generally didn't need me at events like this. I personally disliked social events. I preferred to stay home and watch TV or play games, especially now that Hanna was living with us.

But I was off-balance ever since Hanna mentioned her New Year's resolution. When I invited her to stay with me, I hadn't considered the fact that she might be actively dating. Surely, she wouldn't bring a man over with Ember in the house.

I was getting all worked up over nothing. Hanna had never been serious about anyone before. She'd go on a few dates, they'd be awful, and she'd get frustrated and vow to never date again. Then things would go back to normal.

I approached Knox, who was leaning against the bar. "How are things between you and Hanna?"

My gaze sought her out on the dance floor with the other girls. My heart warmed at how she held Ember's hands, dancing with her in a circle. Ember was laughing, clearly having a good time. "Good."

He tipped his glass back. "Are you sure about that? I heard the girls talking about Hanna's New Year's resolution to start dating again."

I let out a breath, forcing my voice to remain steady. "It's frustrating listening to her go on those dates. All she meets are jerks, but that's what happens when you do the online dating thing."

Knox raised a brow. "So, you're not upset about it?"

I sifted through my complicated feelings on the idea of Hanna dating and finally settled on part of the truth. "I don't want her to get hurt."

Knox tapped his finger on the glass in his hand. "You don't have any other feelings about her dating?"

"What other feelings would I have? We're friends, and I worry about her." I cleared my throat, hoping Knox would stop digging.

Knox shot me an exasperated look. "She's liked you for as long as I can remember."

My brothers teased me about her having a crush on me, but I thought it was just their usual ribbing. I didn't take them seriously. They couldn't imagine a man and a woman being friends, but we'd proved that it was possible. "You say that, but—"

Knox leaned forward. "You don't believe us?"

"Has she said anything to the girls?" I asked, not ready to answer his question.

"Not that I'm aware of. But everyone can see it." He shifted closer to me and lowered his voice. "Do you like her?"

I shook my head, my heart picking up the pace inside my chest. "I like her as a friend."

"You've never thought of her as more than that?" Knox asked.

"I don't know. Maybe?" Why was he pushing this? There were a few times when I thought about touching or kissing her, but I didn't want to lose what we had. She was my best friend, especially when Brandy walked away, leaving me with Ember. Hanna was my lifeline. I couldn't do anything to mess that up.

"You should figure it out before a smarter guy snatches her up. She's beautiful"—he pointed to where she held Ember's hand above her head, twirling her—"and obviously great with kids."

Now we were both watching her as she danced with Ember; both had bright smiles on their faces. Every time I saw Hanna with Ember, I wished that she was her mother. Sometimes, I think Ember did, too. She was an important female figure in her life. "She's all of those things and more."

"If you're telling me it's nothing more than friendship, then I'll leave you alone. I'm just worried that you're going to regret your decision not to make a move. If you have even half a chance at what I have with Sarah, or what Emmett has with Ireland, you have to go for it. Love like that doesn't come around often."

My heart squeezed in my chest. "I don't want to ruin what we have."

Knox raised a brow. "So, you're fine with her dating other guys?"

"I don't like it." I just thought I'd have more time. She'd move in with us, and we could figure out if there was something worth pursuing. But she was changing things up and moving on with someone else. "But she's made her choice."

"Maybe she's given up on you." There was more than a tinge of disgust in his tone.

My jaw tightened. "I've been busy with Ember and work."

"And maybe that's the problem. She's tired of waiting for you to make a move."

I sighed, a sense of melancholy settling over me. "If she's dating other guys, then she's already made up her mind when it comes to me."

"Can you blame her?"

This conversation was irritating. I thought I was playing it safe by waiting until I was more settled and Ember was older. Now that Hanna was living with me, I thought I'd have time to show her what she meant to me, to explore if there was anything between us. But it was too late.

She was the total package—beautiful, smart, and caring. It was ridiculous to think she'd want me, the nerdy Monroe brother, the one who wasn't particularly athletic, despite my habitual workout routine.

She was obviously looking for something else, some*one* else. I didn't fit into her picture of the future, no matter how much I wanted to.

Knox sighed, shaking his head. "For what it's worth, I don't think it's too late. You're living with her. You have a unique opportunity to make her yours."

"What are you talking about?" I asked sharply, my gaze flying to his.

"Look at Ireland and Emmett. It took them being snowed in together to give each other a chance. Remember how Heath moved Marley in, knowing she wouldn't be able to escape? It made things easier in a way. You're in proximity, forced to spend time together. I don't know their stories, but I can assume you run into each other in various stages of undress. There are opportunities to spend time together without the pressures of dating." Knox smirked.

"You're saying I still have a chance," I said as I looked at Ember.

A man approached Hanna. Her eyes were bright, her smile wide as she responded to him. Then she laughed at something he'd said. I doubted it was that funny.

"I think so," Knox said, but I was already striding across the ballroom floor, eating up the distance between us. I wasn't usually bold with women, but if I wanted a chance, I was going to have to be different than I'd always been. I moved between them, pushing the man back, using Ember as the excuse. "How's my girl?"

"I love to dance," Ember said as she twirled in circles, her dress flitting around her legs.

"I can see that."

"She's yours?" the man asked, and I couldn't place him. He was about the same height as me but more filled out. I almost thought he was one of the brothers who owned a competing Christmas tree farm, Pine Valley, but I couldn't be sure.

"That's right," I said, not caring if he meant Ember or Hanna. For his purposes, they were both mine and off-limits.

He looked at Hanna one more time, as if waiting for her to argue, and then he nodded. "It was nice talking to you."

Once he was gone, Hanna leaned closer and asked, "What was that?"

I dipped my head toward Ember, who was now dancing and laughing with Addy. "I was checking on Ember."

"I was talking to him."

I grunted because there was zero chance that guy wasn't coming onto her, whether she realized it or not. I felt a hint of guilt that I'd overstepped, but then I remembered my discussion with Knox. I was going after Hanna, and I wouldn't let anyone get in my way.

Hanna tipped her head to the side. "Seriously, what's gotten into you?"

I kept my eyes trained on the girls. "I just realized some things."

She raised a brow. "And what's that?"

"I've been holding back my whole life, letting other people step in and take what's mine, and that stops now."

Her forehead wrinkled as if she had no idea what I was talking about. But that was okay. She'd get it eventually. I meant every word I said.

Knox approached, an amused expression on his face. "I need to get Addy to bed. Want to extract them at the same time?"

"You got it." We'd already learned it was easier to leave parties and gatherings together so that neither girl felt like they were missing out on anything.

Knox waved them over. "Come on, Addy. Ember's leaving, too."

"That's right," I said to the girls when they groaned.

"We don't want to leave," Addy whined.

Knox made a show of pulling out his watch and checking the time. "It's way past your bedtime."

Addy's lip protruded. "So? We were having fun."

"You better be good. Santa's watching," Knox said.

Addy's eyes narrowed on him, and then she sighed. "Fine."

I held my hand out to Ember. "You want to ride with us?" I asked Hanna.

"I might as well. I'm tired, too."

I smiled, pleased she was coming home with me.

We said our goodbyes to my brothers and my mom, then we headed outside to my truck, the same one all my brothers drove, with the Monroe Christmas Tree Farm logo on the door. I opened the rear passenger door for Ember and helped her inside. By the time she was settled, Hanna was buckled in.

I wished I could be more of a gentleman, but taking care of Ember made it difficult.

On the short drive home, Ember chatted about the party. When we pulled up to the cabin, the lights on the porch twinkled, making it feel inviting.

When I opened the door for Ember, she said, "Carry me."

I couldn't resist her when she was warm and sleepy. She would only be this young for so long. I was already worried about the day when she'd ask for a phone and want to date.

I lifted her, and her arms wrapped around my neck.

Hanna closed the door behind us, a soft smile on her face.

Did she think me holding my daughter was endearing? I hoped so because she was going to see a lot of that kind of thing over the next few weeks. I wanted to impress her in other ways, but if I knew her weaknesses, I could capitalize on those, as well.

She led the way up the porch and opened the front door with her key. I admired the way her dress clung to her curves as she pushed the door open, and we stepped inside.

I patted Ember's back. "I'm going to put this one to bed."

"No," Ember said, even as her face was buried in my neck. She'd be out within a few minutes of me putting her down.

"Can you wait for me? Maybe we can watch a movie." I wasn't ready for the night to be over.

Hanna smiled as she made her way up the steps. "Sure, I'll just change into something more comfortable."

I wanted to be the one who unzipped her dress, but we weren't there yet. My plan to win her over would be an uphill battle, with her plan to date other guys.

I wasn't sure if Knox's comments about her liking me were accurate. He could be wrong, misinterpreting friendship for a crush. I had never been sure about Hanna's feelings for me.

There were moments I thought she might feel the same way I did, but then it could have been just friendship. How would I know for sure?

I helped Ember get on her pajamas and brush her teeth, then I tucked her into bed. Her eyes closed immediately, and I kissed her forehead. Love for her filled my chest.

It was hard being a single dad, but I had my family, and now Hanna, to help. For the first time, I didn't feel like I was doing it alone. Moving to the cabin was the best decision I could have made. It was perfect timing since Hanna's roommate had moved out, and she couldn't afford to stay there. I shrugged out of my jacket and tugged off the tie, wondering if I should take the time to change like Hanna had or if it was better to stay in my formal attire.

I wanted to be comfortable, so I unbuttoned my shirt and threw on sweatpants and a T-shirt. It wasn't going to win me any great awards in the looks department, but I needed to feel like myself for this evening to go as planned.

Downstairs, Hanna had turned on the gas fireplace and was standing by the bare tree. "You didn't decorate?"

She'd changed into soft-looking red pajamas with white trim. Her hair looked freshly brushed, and her face was devoid of the makeup she wore at the party. I wondered if she was wearing a bra underneath.

I moved closer to her. "We haven't had time, and honestly, I'm not a fan of the holidays. The farm, the shop, all of it turns me off from the season."

Hanna frowned. "Doesn't Ember want to decorate?"

"She does. I just haven't felt like it with the move and then working long hours on the farm after my regular job." I felt the weight of the season on my shoulders, and instead of trying to give Ember what she wanted, I'd shied away from it.

Hanna smiled, and it was so bright it hit me square in the chest. "I can help you decorate tomorrow."

I felt some of the tension release between my shoulder blades. "Ember will love it, and I'd appreciate your help."

"I was hoping I'd catch some of the magic of the season by living here. I've heard Ireland, Sarah, and Marley talk about how much they love the farm. It gets my mind off the reality of being homeless."

I brushed a strand of hair off her shoulder. It was a move I never would have done before, but I was doing things differently. I couldn't get the picture of her and that other man talking out of my head. She could be dating someone else very soon. I didn't have much time. "You're not homeless. You can always stay with me."

I meant that literally. I didn't see why there would be a rush for her to move out and get her own apartment. Not when she was comfortable here.

"Are you sure?" She turned slightly until we were standing close, too close for friends.

"I wouldn't have said it if I didn't mean it." My heart picked up the pace inside my chest.

She swayed toward me slightly as she looked up at me. "You're too good to me."

"I wouldn't say that," I murmured, wondering if she would mind if I lowered my lips to hers. I'd finally know how she felt about me. If there wasn't any chemistry, then I'd know once and for all. Standing this close to her, I felt electrified, as if her skin was giving off little sparks, and mine wanted to get closer to spark a flame. I had a feeling we could be explosive together.

Anytime I felt this way in the past, I shoved it aside, thinking I wanted something to be there that wasn't. What could be more convenient than falling in love with your best friend?

"Did you want to watch a movie?" Hanna broke the intimate moment by stepping around me and toward the large sectional.

"Sure," I said, trying not to feel disappointed that I'd missed the perfect opportunity to test the waters.

I tried to remember what occurred in those Hallmark movies Mom always had playing on the TV at her house. Someone was always drinking hot cocoa, and I had the fixings because Mom made sure we were stocked with that and decorations for the holidays. "Would you like hot chocolate?"

"I'd love some." Hanna followed me into the kitchen, and I couldn't help but feel like she belonged here, in her pajamas, with her hair loose around her shoulders. And it wasn't because she'd always been in my life. She fit here. I'd never felt the way I felt for her with someone else. Not even Ember's mother, who was more of a one-night stand that turned into several.

I filled a pot with milk and turned on the heat. I grabbed the bag of hot chocolate mix out of the pantry and measured out what we'd need into two mugs.

"I'm so happy for Marley. The party was amazing. I think the inn reopening is going to be great for her and the area."

"I think so, too. For a while, Heath and Knox wanted to buy it, mainly to stop any development. I wasn't sure we could afford to buy it, much less renovate the inn and reopen it. This is the best-case scenario. Marley revisited her past, made peace with it, and is now reopening her family's legacy. She also reconnected with Heath."

"It sounds like Marley reopening the inn was for the best." Hanna leaned against the counter, the soft glow of the light illuminating her tan skin, making her blue eyes brighter, almost as if she were lit from within.

"It brought her and Heath together again, and that's worth everything." My voice felt rough with emotion. Ever since my father had had a heart attack a few years ago, I'd found myself wanting to be closer to my family. To cherish every moment with them. You never knew how long you had. I wanted Ember to experience what it was like to grow up in a big family, since I hadn't been able to give her any siblings.

Hanna tipped her head to the side. "You think so?"

"You don't?" I asked, curious to understand what she thought about love and relationships. It was a topic I'd avoided over the years. Occasionally, Hanna had confided in me if a date had gone bad, but otherwise, we didn't discuss it.

"I didn't realize you were such a romantic," she said softly.

"I'm—" I almost said I'm not, but then I realized she liked what I'd said. I needed to show her more of that side of me, the one who wanted to be close to my family and was happy for my brothers for finding the love of their lives. "I guess I am."

Her lips twitched. "I had no idea. I kind of like it."

It wasn't a declaration that she liked me, but it was a start. I knew I had a long way to go, but I'd take advantage of every opportunity to draw her closer. “I was overwhelmed with everything involved in raising Ember on my own, but now I can see that meeting their significant others was the best thing that could have happened to them.”

They’d mentioned several times that their women were drawn to the farm and the magic of the holiday season. Since we were a few weeks away from Christmas, I could use that knowledge and Hanna’s desire to enjoy the season to my advantage.

“Can you spend the day with us tomorrow? I make pancakes on Sundays, and then we spend the day in our pajamas.”

A smile spread over her face. “I already promised to help with the tree. That sounds nice.”

I’d keep her involved with me and my family, and she wouldn’t have any time to peruse dating apps. At least not until after the holidays, and hopefully, by then, I’d have made progress. But just the thought of telling Hanna how I felt had my heart thumping in my chest. I’d lived in fear of losing her, and that hadn’t gone away. If anything, it had only intensified. The stakes were high, but I didn’t want to lose my chance with her.

# CHAPTER 3

## HANNA

I woke up slowly, reveling in the soft flannel of Sebastian's guest room sheets. For someone who didn't like the holidays, he'd outfitted the bed in a festive holiday print. Although, I had a feeling it was his mom who'd provided the linens.

As long as I'd known Sebastian, he'd been apathetic about the holidays. He did what he needed to for Ember, but he maintained that working on the farm sucked all the excitement for the season out of him.

I could understand that, but I wanted him to remember what it was like to be a little kid opening presents on Christmas morning again, the anticipation, the excitement, the joy when you got exactly what you asked for.

I rolled over and tucked my hands under my cheek. I'd wanted Sebastian Monroe for as long as I could remember. I'd been asking for him under my tree since we were teenagers, but my wish hadn't come true.

I sighed. Would this finally be my year to find someone who could love me back? I felt pathetic pining after a man who'd never see me as more than his friend. But on the other hand, he'd been so sweet last night. The memory of him ushering me out of the ballroom and onto the balcony, giving me his jacket, and holding me while we watched the snow fall made my heart squeeze.

When I'd mentioned how nice it would be to have lights on his tree, Sebastian had immediately agreed to grab them, and we strung them on the branches together. He didn't think Ember would mind missing out on that task, since he normally did it when she was sleeping.

I'd appreciated that he'd done it for me, and not just Ember. It meant he was willing to open his heart to the season. If he was willing to do that, maybe he'd see the unwrapped present that was right in front of him.

I'd promised myself I'd make a good-faith effort to find someone who felt the same way about me that I felt about them. It was time for me to move on from this ridiculous crush.

My door flew open, and Ember jumped on the bed, her curls bouncing in the air. "Wake up, sleepyhead. We're making pancakes."

I heard heavy footsteps on the stairs. "Ember, I told you not to bother Hanna. She's sleeping."

"I was awake," I said to Ember as she came to a stop on her knees at the foot of the bed.

"See, Daddy, she was already awake," Ember said as he came into the room and leaned a shoulder on the doorjamb, his lips twitching into a smile.

"Even if that's true, you can't just run into someone else's room. You have to knock first and ask if it's okay for you to come in."

Ember tipped her head to the side, and her curls fell over her shoulder. "Miss Hanna, is it okay if I come in?"

I couldn't help the laugh that slid out. "Of course."

"It's a little too late now," Sebastian mumbled as Ember jumped off the bed and ran out of the room.

"Don't jump off the bed. You could get hurt. You want to have a broken leg for Christmas?" Sebastian called after her.

I had a feeling he said that line to her often, and it had little to no effect on her.

Sebastian shook his head. "I'm sorry about that."

I sat up in the bed, and his gaze dropped to my white tank top, where my nipples were probably visible. I'd forgotten I'd taken off the flannel top sometime during the night because I was hot. I reached for it and drew it over my shoulders, buttoning it. "I was already awake when she flew in here."

Sebastian shook his head, and I wondered if it was to rid himself of the vision of my chest, or if he'd noticed it at all. "Let me try again. Would you like to come downstairs and help us make pancakes?"

I smiled. "I'd love to."

"Please take your time getting ready. You're a guest here. I don't expect you to cook or hang out with us all the time."

I untangled myself from the blankets and stood on the soft carpet in front of him. "I'd like to join you for breakfast. It sounds like you have the perfect day planned. Pancakes, pajamas, and Christmas tree decorating."

He scowled. "I forgot about the tree decorating."

"We don't have to if you don't want to."

He sighed. "Ember will love it."

"I'll just freshen up and be down. It's pajama day, after all."

He grinned, and his dimple popped. "Sounds great."

I'd made it my mission to make him smile as much as possible because I adored his dimple. He was the only Monroe brother who had one. He said his father had one, too, but I didn't see it often. Larry was a gruff man, who was firm with his boys and sweet to his wife.

Sebastian pushed off the doorway and stood straight. He paused for a second as if he wanted to say something, his gaze scanning the room, and then he shook his head again and turned to leave.

For the first time in a long time, I was looking forward to a Sunday. My roommate spent all her weekends with her boyfriend, now fiancé, and I took advantage of the quiet to grade papers. It was a good life, but I was lonely.

I washed my face, brushed my teeth and hair, then slipped on my slippers and a bra before heading downstairs.

I loved Sebastian's new cabin, the home he'd created for his daughter. It was warm and inviting, and despite his grumpiness over the holidays, I was positive I could get him to see how amazing the season could be.

Last night, Sebastian's home appeared to be neat and organized, but this morning, the counter was covered in flour.

"We're making pancakes." Ember beamed from her seated spot on the counter. She was mixing the ingredients, and more flour was escaping than staying inside the bowl.

"I can see that," I said, amusement tinging my tone.

"We're messy cooks," Sebastian said.

He grinned, which showed a spot of flour on his cheek and on the gray shirt he wore. His pajamas consisted of blue-and-green plaid flannel pajama bottoms that hung low on his hips. He looked delectable this early in the morning.

I'd spent a lot of time with him and his daughter but never early in the morning like this. Not when everyone was rumpled from sleep, his hair standing on end, and his clothes covered in flour.

He preferred organization, but I liked that he could be messy with his daughter. He was capable of letting go.

Maybe this was the key to really getting to know Sebastian on a deeper level. I couldn't believe it took moving in with my best friend to see the real man beneath the façade of the rigid and serious persona he presented to everyone else.

He stretched his arms over his head, and his shirt rode up,

revealing defined abs and those V-shaped muscles I'd heard about but never seen on a man before. I licked my dry lips and squeaked in surprise when his amused gaze landed on my face.

"Like what you see?" His dimple popped, and my cheeks flamed hot.

"Those are very nice pajamas," I managed to croak out as he helped Ember down. He rounded the island, grabbed a wooden spoon out of a container on the counter behind me, and leaned in to whisper in my ear. "That wasn't what I was talking about, and you know it."

My face heated, and I hoped that Ember hadn't heard him or noticed my reaction.

Sebastian was my friend. He'd never flirted with me before or asked if I'd noticed his body. What was happening? It was like my carefully crafted life had suddenly been tilted on its axis.

Maybe he was just teasing. I'd seen the way his brothers constantly teased each other. But I wasn't his sister, and his ribbing hadn't felt like that kind of back-and-forth. It felt more like flirting.

*Is Sebastian Monroe flirting with me?*

My heart was pounding in my ears as I sat on a stool to watch as they poured batter into the pan.

I felt hot all over and kept shifting in my seat.

When the pancakes were poured, Ember asked to watch cartoons, and Sebastian said she could. She raced out of the room, and a few seconds later, the sound of the TV drifted into the kitchen.

"Are you okay?" Sebastian asked, his gaze shifting to me.

My face flushed hotter. "Of course."

He smirked. "You seemed a little flustered."

"It's going to take some time to get used to living together. I've never had a male roommate before."

Sebastian's brow raised. "We've been friends forever. What is there to get used to?"

"As long as we've been friends, I've never stayed the night." There was that one time when I fell asleep on the couch and woke up to my head in his lap. I'd gotten out of there as fast as I could and never stayed that late again.

It had felt too good and only solidified my crush.

His thigh muscles were hard, and the hand he'd rested in my hair sent tingles down my spine. He hadn't woken up when I put on my shoes, grabbed my coat, and slipped out. I had no idea if he'd known about our compromising position. Neither one of us had ever brought it up.

Technically, it was innocent. He wasn't spooning me or touching my breast, but it felt intimate. My body had been a live wire the rest of the day, and I couldn't get the feel of his thigh muscle against my cheek out of my head.

Sebastian's smile widened. "There was that one night when you fell asleep on the couch and ended up in my lap."

"I didn't think you remembered that," I mumbled, my skin feeling too tight.

Sebastian flashed me a smile. "I remember everything about you."

"Why are you bringing it up now?" My voice had a whiny tone to it that I wasn't proud of.

Sebastian sobered, moving to stand next to me. He was blocking me from Ember in the living room. I was forced to look up at him, and his familiar evergreen scent wrapped around me. "I want you to feel comfortable here."

My throat was dry, and I could barely form any words. The problem was, being this close to him was waking up everything inside of me that longed for more. I wasn't sure I'd survive it. And the worst part was I had no way of knowing if he felt the same way. But the casual way he leaned a hip against the counter and leaned in close to me told me he didn't feel the same. How could he be this close to me and be so relaxed? Whereas every muscle in my body was pulled taut.

"I need some water."

Sebastian gazed down at me, assessing, then flashed me a wink as if he knew exactly what my problem was, and it wasn't being thirsty for water. Then he pushed off the counter and went in search of a glass. He turned his back to me while he filled it with ice and water, then turned and placed it in front of me.

I guzzled it down, desperate for a way to cool my body down.

"Is that better?" he asked, his tone filled with amusement.

Irritation flowed through me that he didn't feel the same draw I did. How could only one person sense chemistry? Maybe I was making it up in my head. I wanted so badly for there to be a connection between us that I was making it up. I was losing it. "I should look for apartments. I don't want to crowd you."

He sobered. "We have plenty of space, and it's easier for you to help me out if you're here. If money's an issue, I can pay you. You are providing a service, after all."

"You're letting me live here rent-free so I can save up for an apartment. I don't need anything else."

"While you're here, food, utilities, and anything you need are on me. You're doing me a huge favor. I don't trust just anyone with Ember."

He trusted me, and while that felt good, I wanted him to feel the spark between us, to want me as badly as I wanted him. I wanted him to kiss me, to chase the fire simmering just under the surface. But I was the only one who felt it.

That realization sucked because it was hard to imagine how he didn't feel the same. Yet, it was achingly sad because that was the truth. I blinked away the tears of frustration. I had to get through the next few weeks, and then after the holidays, I could look at apartments.

"Seriously, you're welcome to stay for as long as you like. I like having you here."

"It's only been a day." I'd moved my things in yesterday, and Sebastian had helped me put the few pieces of furniture I had into a barn on the property. It was the perfect solution to my problem—except for this pesky one-sided attraction.

If I was going to live here, I needed to get over it. And the best way to do that was to date other guys. It was more than obvious that Sebastian wasn't interested. If he was, he would have made a move years ago. He wouldn't be so relaxed in his kitchen while I was burning up inside.

Sebastian turned away from me to check the pancakes and then flip them. But all I could focus on was the way his pants hugged his ass and thighs.

I took the opportunity to place the glass of ice water against my forehead, hoping it would cool my imagination.

Sebastian turned around, and I slowly lowered the glass, hoping he hadn't noticed. I was too young for hot flashes, and it was cold outside.

He tipped his head to the side, as if he were studying me. "Are you sure you're okay?"

"It's a little hot in here," I croaked and then hopped off the stool to refill my glass.

Sebastian moved close so that his front was touching my back. He reached over and pushed the ice button because I was frozen in place. Then he chuckled and leaned down to whisper into my ear. "I wasn't sure you knew how to get ice."

Then he pushed the water button, and we both waited for the glass to fill. When it was full, I quickly turned, realizing he stood unbearably close.

He flashed me a smile with his dimple showing and said, "If I haven't said it already, I love having you here. It's like a slumber party with my best friend."

He moved to the stove, and I was finally able to draw in a deep breath. I drank the water, hoping it would simultaneously cool my throat and the blood pumping hot and heavy through my veins.

I moved to the stool and wondered how I'd survive the next few weeks. I could hide in my room and escape to the library in town with an excuse that I needed to grade papers. Start volunteering at the local animal shelter. I needed something to keep me busy and out of Sebastian's cabin.

"Don't forget, you promised to help decorate the tree and spend the day with us. Later, we'll go over to the main house for dinner. Mom will want you there."

"I hadn't realized."

He turned and braced his hands on the counter, leaning in. "You don't mind, do you? I want you to have the full Monroe experience while you're here."

My entire body flushed again. Either I was going through early menopause, or it was Sebastian having this unexpected effect on me. Maybe I was just hyperaware of my attraction to him now that we were living together. It had to ease up over time, wouldn't it?

Then my mind wandered to thoughts of what he meant by *the full Monroe experience*. Was he talking about the family or him? If he'd dated over the years, he'd never discussed it with me. So, I didn't know if he was a one-night stand kind of guy or more of a relationship guy. Either way, I hadn't witnessed it for myself. I forced myself to ask the question. "What does that entail?"

His dimple flashed again as he smiled wide. "I want to give you a tour of the farm. Maybe you can bring Ember to the shop and help there. We could rent a carriage from the neighboring farm and show you around. There's a pond past Heath's house, and all the paths are lit with lights. Maybe tonight, after dinner?"

"That sounds lovely." Why had I so easily agreed to a carriage ride through the woods? I was supposed to be keeping my distance.

"Perfect." He winked at me and then removed the pancakes from the stove, stacking them onto a plate and pouring another batch into the pan.

I went to the fridge, intending to get the maple syrup, but stood in the open door, allowing the cool air to drift over my skin. Unfortunately, my nipples were hard points and clearly visible through my bra. This is how I reacted to Sebastian Monroe. How had I ever thought it was a good idea to move in with him? It only highlighted my crush and the contrast with how he felt about me.

A slumber party with his best friend? That's not what I was feeling. Not even close.

He didn't feel the same way, and as crushing as that realization was, nothing had changed. I needed to move on, and quickly. Or this situation was going to get awkward fast.

# CHAPTER 4

## SEBASTIAN

My plan was working.

Hanna seemed flustered. She kept talking about how hot it was in the kitchen. I turned down the heat, but her skin was still flushed, and she'd pulled her hair into a messy bun on the top of her head. It only made me want to run my nose along the column of her bare neck and suck on her sensitive skin.

She had me all twisted up inside. I hoped she felt the same.

We ate pancakes at the small round table in the kitchen, and the girls watched TV while I cleaned up the mess.

Hanna had offered to help, but I wanted to take care of her. I wanted her to feel pampered while she was here. It was the least I could do for the assistance she was giving me. A live-in nanny who was also my best friend? It couldn't be a better situation for me, other than the attraction that only seemed to worsen while she was here.

When the kitchen was cleaned up, I watched them on the couch. I heard the soft murmur of their voices the way Ember had cuddled into Hanna's side, as if she'd always lived with us.

My heart squeezed at how close they were, how much I felt for Hanna, and how much I wanted this to work.

There hadn't been any talk of dating, so I hoped she'd tabled that idea until January. I needed some time to work on this situation between us, to show her how life could be with me, on the farm, and how good I suspected we could be together.

"Can we decorate the tree now, Daddy?" Ember asked.

"Let me grab the decorations." I disappeared down the steps to the basement, hoping the cool air would feel good. But Hanna followed me a few seconds later.

"I figured you needed help," she said when she found me next to a stack of boxes labeled *Christmas.*

Mom had provided each one of us with a few boxes of decorations for our houses. I figured she hoped we'd catch the Christmas spirit. When I lived in town, I decorated a small fake tree for Ember's benefit.

I sifted through the boxes and handed her one that was light. Then I stacked a few in my arms and followed her upstairs. Her pajamas hugged her ass, and I wasn't seeing any panty lines. Was she naked underneath, or was she wearing a thong? I was dying to know what kind of secrets she was hiding under her clothes. *Au natural,* lace, or satin?

I nearly groaned out loud. It was torture having her here. Why had I told her about pajama day? I should have gotten dressed and pretended it wasn't our Sunday tradition. Because seeing her soft and messy made me want to dirty her up.

I stacked the boxes next to the tree, where Ember was already pulling decorations out of a box. I grabbed a container of hooks and placed them on the floor so they could be added to the ornaments. Then I disappeared into the basement for the last few boxes.

I took the opportunity to take a few seconds to calm down. If I was going to have a chance with her, I needed to pull myself together. I couldn't be getting a hard-on because she was walking around in flannel pajamas. Technically, there was nothing sexy about her outfit. Unfortunately, my dick wasn't getting the message.

When I returned to the family room, they'd already put up several ornaments on the tree.

"We reserved the top of the tree for you since you can reach it easier," Hanna said as she hung a Cinderella's castle over one of the lights, illuminating it blue.

"That's so pretty," Ember said, admiring it.

I pulled out my phone and snapped a few pictures.

Hanna turned while my phone was raised and asked, "What are you doing?"

"I wanted to commemorate decorating the first tree in our new house," I said, pleased with how domestic the pictures looked.

Hanna moved to the side, out of camera range. "I probably shouldn't be in the pictures."

I snapped a few of Ember because she turned to face me and smiled. Then I sent them to Mom, adding one of Hanna and Ember at the last second.

Hanna frowned. "Why are you sending pictures of me to your mom?"

"She'll love it, and you belong in our pictures. You're part of our family."

Hanna shook her head. "I'm a friend."

I raised a brow, silently pleading with her not to make a big deal out of it in front of Ember.

"You're my other mother," Ember said, giving Hanna a hug. It's what she'd called her ever since Hanna suggested it one night while she was reading her a book. Ember had asked if she could call her something other than Miss Hanna, and she'd responded by saying, 'I guess you could say I'm your other mother.'

Hanna squeezed her tight. "I love you, sweetie."

My heart contracted at the scene. It was moments like this that I wanted to remember forever. I wanted more family events where Hanna was included, and not just as a friend, but as a member of my family, as my significant other, and maybe even as Ember's stepmother.

It was wishful thinking, but if someone asked what I wanted Santa to bring me this year, it would be Hanna. She was all I wanted, every day for the rest of my life. I'd add a few more kids and maybe even a puppy. I was open to whatever she wanted.

"Are you going to help?" Ember asked as she looked up from the box she'd been sifting through.

"You want to hand me a few and I can put them up high?"

Ember handed me a snowman, and I put him on a sturdy branch.

Hanna turned on a holiday music playlist on her phone. "You don't mind, do you?"

"Of course not," I said, noticing that Ember was nodding her head in time to the music.

"I wanted to make sure. You can be cranky about the holidays," Hanna said.

"I stay away from the shop this time of year because of the nonstop holiday tunes. I get tired of hearing the same songs. But I haven't listened to many this year."

Hanna nodded, ever conscious of everyone else's feelings. "If it's too much, let me know."

"Can we watch a holiday movie tonight?" Ember asked.

"We have dinner at Grandma's tonight," I pointed out.

"Yay!" Ember said. "I'm so excited that we can walk to Grandma's, and I'm near Addy all the time."

"I am, too." As a parent, I worried about whether I was making the right decisions. I'd stayed in town because it was close to my work, but now that Ember was older, being close to family was more important than ever. "I have fond memories of growing up on the farm, and I want you to have the same experience."

Ember looked up at me from where she was kneeling on the floor. "What kinds of things did you like to do as a kid?"

I chuckled, remembering how crazy my brothers were. "We liked to build forts with the couch cushions until Grandma told us to go outside. Then we'd use the sticks and rocks in the woods to build them."

Ember's wide eyes were fixed on me. "Wow. That sounds fun."

"Mmm. With my brothers, there was a lot of fighting over who owned the fort, who was allowed inside, and the best way to make it. Then we'd each make our own fort, fortify it, and try to tear each other's down."

Ember's eyes widened. "Why would you do that?"

I shrugged. "I don't know, because we were idiots. We played inside, too. But we had more fun tearing things apart."

Ember shook her head. "I don't get it."

"Me either," Hanna said with an amused tone as she ruffled Ember's hair.

This is how it would be if Hanna lived with us permanently. We'd let her sleep in while we cooked breakfast, then watch cartoons together and do a project around the house before dressing and going to my mom's for dinner. There would always be love and laughter. I wished I could collapse time and be there now. I wanted to ask Hanna for so many things, but I had no idea how she felt about anything.

I had to remind myself that she was planning to date other guys. I didn't have a lot of time to make her mine.

Glancing down at Ember, I wondered if she could help me. But it would be wrong to ask my daughter to help me get a girl.

"I want to make my presents this year," Ember said.

I frowned, panicking a little. "I'm not crafty."

Hanna smiled wide. "I can help you. I love doing crafts."

"Because you're a teacher?" Ember asked.

Hanna licked her lips. "I guess so. I love creating things."

It was on the tip of my tongue to ask if she'd create a life with me, but I berated myself for jumping too far ahead. I had to come up with a plan, and showing her what made our farm special was just the start.

I stepped aside and called the neighboring farm to secure the carriage for tonight, then texted Mom my plans.

When the tree was decorated, we stepped back to see how it looked, then we took turns posing for a picture.

Hanna gestured at my phone. "You should use one of these pictures for your holiday cards."

I frowned. "I don't do holiday cards. Mom handles that."

Hanna laughed, the sound light and carefree. "You're a grown man. Why would your mom be sending out your Christmas cards?"

Ember frowned at me, and I was reminded of all the ways I was failing my daughter. "Yeah, why, Daddy?"

I shrugged. "I assumed her holiday cards include the entire family."

"I'm sure Ireland and Sarah are doing their own cards this year. And Marley mentioned using a picture of her and Heath in front of the inn while it was decorated for Christmas."

I grunted. My brothers were getting a little too into the holiday spirit for my liking.

"Or you could use the picture as a gift for your mom. We could blow it up and have it framed."

"I like the idea of that," I said, hoping she'd get off the card idea.

She scrolled through the pictures. There were ones of just Ember, then me and Ember, and Hanna and Ember.

"We should do one of all three of us. We can use the timer on my phone." I took it from Hanna and set it up on a nearby table.

Hanna backed away. "Oh, I don't think I should be in the picture."

"What do you think, Ember?" I asked as I ushered everyone together in front of the tree.

Ember reached for Hanna's hand. "You have to be in the picture. It won't be the same without you."

I flashed a grin at Hanna, who sighed. We stood, Ember in front of me, my hands on her shoulders, and Hanna next to me. I wrapped an arm around her, pulling her into my side. "Now, smile big. Three more seconds."

When the flash stopped, I grabbed my phone. We looked like a family. We were smiling and happy, and I swore there was an extra twinkle in our eyes.

"That turned out great. Can you send it to me?" Hanna asked.

"Sure," I said, but I made a mental note to print it and frame it for her. I wanted her to have a memory of us together when she was dating these other guys. No one could compare to what we had. Or, at least, I hoped not.

Ember was my world, and Hanna was our future. I just had to convince her of that.

After the tree was covered with ornaments, we watched a holiday movie and then got dressed for dinner. It was the perfect day. I hadn't realized how empty our lives were until Hanna joined us. I loved Ember, but I wanted more for us.

On the short walk to the main house, Hanna said, "What cookies do you like to eat at Christmas?"

"Grandma makes all the cookies," Ember said as she skipped down the lane.

"Would you like to make some? I make them and distribute them to my coworkers."

Ember stopped and squinted at her. "That would be fun. What would we make?"

Hanna tapped her chin. "Hmm. How about sugar cookies and gingerbread? Those are my two favorites."

Ember smiled. "I like those."

"Do you mind if we make cookies sometime?" Hanna asked me.

"My kitchen is your kitchen, and that goes for the whole house. You don't need to ask permission. Just let me know what you need, and I'll order it."

"You order your groceries?"

"I don't have time to go to the store."

"I can shop while I'm staying here," Hanna said, and I didn't argue with her. I wanted her to be comfortable.

I opened Mom's door, not bothering to knock. The driveway was already filled with Monroe Christmas Tree Farm trucks. It looked like everyone was already here, including our cousin, Cole, who was staying at Heath's house for a while.

"There you are," Marley said as soon as we shrugged off our coats. "I have the best idea, and I need your help."

"With what?" Hanna asked cautiously.

We all knew how exuberant Marley could be when she got an idea.

"We want to do a couples' night here on the farm before Christmas, and since you're single, I thought you could help us with it."

I ground my teeth together. If I had my way, Hanna wouldn't be single for long. Although, with my track record, I might need longer than the few weeks left before Christmas.

"I was thinking we could do a speed dating thing or a bachelor auction," Marley continued rambling, her voice racing with excitement.

"Why would we do that?" Emmett grumbled.

The women were used to Emmett protesting all their ideas, but I had to agree with him; both ideas sounded awful.

"You realize this is our busy season?" I raised a brow, but

Marley waved me off.

"People are looking for things to do at the holidays, and we could provide that."

"I thought that's what the light display was supposed to be," I said carefully, not liking where this conversation was going.

Marley's eyes sparkled with mischief. "That's a great addition to the farm. But I thought since we held the movie nights for the community, it would be nice to have a date night event."

"I don't like the idea of a dating thing," Emmett said.

"I don't either," I was quick to add.

"I think it could be fun. We'd be drawing in a different demographic. It keeps the farm fresh in everyone's mind. People come for a tree and maybe shop at the store, but they leave and have no reason to return. This will be an additional event for them to attend." Marley's hands gestured wildly as she spoke.

I didn't mention the light display again because Marley wasn't listening to me or Emmett. I had a feeling she was used to the pushback she got from Emmett and was prepared to bulldoze through any objection we raised.

"It would be fun to do a bachelor or bachelorette auction. Men could vote on a date with a woman," Marley continued.

"Then they could have the date right here on the farm. We could set up a few romantic areas: the pond, the gazebo in the woods..." Ireland said excitedly.

"Oh, what about the hot tub?" Marley threw out, and I saw red.

"The hot tub is something we built, but no one uses," I said, my voice tight.

Marley's cheeks turned red as Heath threw an arm over her shoulders. "I don't know about that."

I gripped the back of my neck, willing my temper to stay in check. The thought of someone bidding on Hanna and then having a romantic date with her in the secluded hot tub in the woods was too much for me to handle. I was starting to see why

Emmett reacted so strongly to any suggestions for change. "This is the worst idea I've heard for the farm yet."

Marley flinched, and Ireland took a step back from the force of my words.

Hanna shot me a reproachful look. She was disappointed in me, but she couldn't see that a bachelorette auction was cheesy. "We're not a reality TV show."

Mom frowned. "I don't know. I love those dating shows. I think this would be tasteful and romantic."

I shot her an incredulous look.

"I think it will be all in good fun. We'll have several romantic dates planned for them so they won't have to wait to go on their dates. Isn't that what everyone wants for the holidays? Someone to spend their time with?" Mom asked.

"No one will be alone at midnight on New Year's. That could be our slogan. *Come to Monroe Christmas Tree Farm and find that special someone to spend the holidays with,*" Marley said.

I shook my head. "No. No. No. I don't like it."

Marley shot me an exasperated look. "I expect this kind of pushback from Emmett, but not from you, Sebastian. I thought you were the one who said we needed to make more money for the farm."

My jaw tightened. "That's true."

Marley smiled triumphantly. "And I'm a wiz at this marketing stuff. Leave this to me."

I clenched my teeth so hard I thought I'd crack a tooth.

"For what it's worth, I don't like it either, but no one listens to me anymore," Emmett grumbled.

"I'm with you," I said to Emmett.

Since Emmett was the oldest and the one in charge of the trees, his word held more weight. But ever since my brothers started pairing off, their significant others' opinions were becoming increasingly stronger, and Mom felt more confident supporting their suggestions.

"Who knew you were such a curmudgeon?" Hanna said rhetorically to the room at large.

I felt a twinge of shame. But then I remembered I didn't want Hanna being auctioned off.

"We can use the money to freshen the paint on the barn and do a few other cosmetic changes. I'd like to create a new sign for the entrance," Marley said.

"Who said we need any of those improvements?" Emmett asked with a wave of his hand.

"Is it the original sign?" Marley asked.

I frowned. "I think so."

Marley sobered. "I think it could use an upgrade. Little improvements can go a long way to increase the value of the farm."

I couldn't argue with that logic because she was right. The red barn was faded and didn't look as good as it could. And it wouldn't hurt to get a sturdier sign.

"I'll look into the prices for both, and get back to you with a few other ideas," Marley said to me.

"Fine."

She smiled brightly, as if she'd won that round.

"I still don't like—"

Marley held up her hand. "You don't like the bachelorette auction. Your opinion is noted."

She'd noted it and quickly dismissed my concerns.

Then a smile spread over her face. "Unless you have a reason why Hanna shouldn't be auctioned off? She's single and wants to start dating again. This is the perfect way to jumpstart her New Year's resolution and has the added effect of ensuring she won't be alone on the holidays."

"She won't be alone. She'll be with me," I said, realizing too late what I'd revealed to everyone in the room. I didn't want her to date anyone else. If I wanted her, I'd need to make a move sooner than I thought.

# CHAPTER 5

## HANNA

*She won't be alone. She'll be with me.*

Sebastian's words played in my mind on a loop. It sounded nice, but what did it mean? I wasn't a part of Sebastian and Ember's family. I was just a friend who was helping with childcare. I was an afterthought. Hanna was always reliable and there for everyone in her life. It was time for me to start thinking about what I wanted.

If I couldn't have Sebastian, then I'd create my own family, starting with finding someone I could see myself with in the future. "I think it's a great idea. I'd love to support the farm and possibly meet someone I could date."

Marley and Ireland beamed at me, but if anything, Sebastian's expression turned darker, and irritation flashed in his gaze.

"I'm the perfect candidate. I'm the only single female here," I said.

Sebastian moved closer to me and lowered his voice. "What are you doing?"

His proximity increased my awareness of him. The firm grip of his hand on my lower back, the smell of spice, and the tickle of his breath on my ear.

"We could ask Holly if she'd be interested in being involved. I don't think she's seeing anyone," Sarah said.

Talon's head snapped up from where he was looking at the screen of his phone. "I don't think that's a good idea."

Marley threw her hands up in the air. "You guys are literally impossible."

Heath drew her to his side and whispered something into her ear. She relaxed into him, and I wondered what that would be like, to have someone who had your back, no matter what.

"What are you doing?" Sebastian repeated in my ear.

"I'm trying to help the farm. You said you needed money, and it would also help me find someone. Do you want me on those dating apps?"

"I don't want you dating at all," Sebastian mumbled so softly I almost wasn't sure I'd heard him correctly.

"Why is that?" I asked, my heart beating an erratic rhythm in my chest.

"You're going to be busy, helping with Ember, your schoolwork, and the holidays. You don't have time to date."

"That's not for you to decide," I said as I crossed my arms over my chest. There was something about Sebastian's protests that was bothering me, but I couldn't put my finger on exactly what it was. "Why do you care so much?"

He opened his mouth and closed it.

"You don't want me to date?" I hissed as everyone broke away from the conversation and wandered into the kitchen for the plates of appetizers on the island counter.

When Sebastian floundered with a response, I huffed and walked away. I just couldn't deal with Sebastian's stubbornness right now. I thought the auction sounded scary, but fun, too. What if I met someone who was nice, and we had a good time on the date? I hadn't been out with a guy in a long time, and the thought of not being alone on New Year's held a certain appeal.

I was done being single. I wanted what Ireland, Sarah, and

Marley had. I wanted to be loved. I wanted to be the priority in someone's life.

I filled a small plate with crackers, cheese, and fruit and then moved to the table to eat. Marley sat next to me and handed me a glass of what looked like apple cider. "I thought you could use this."

"Is it spiked?"

Marley giggled. "It is."

I grabbed the glass and drank it. "This is good."

"It's Heath's recipe for Apple Zingers, made with cider and whiskey."

"It hit the spot. Thank you." I stacked cheese on a cracker and popped it into my mouth. I had one eye on Marley and the other tracking Sebastian as he filled a plate for Ember. Anytime I saw them together, my heart melted.

"So, are you in?" Marley asked me, drawing my attention back to her.

"For the bachelorette auction?" At Marley's nod, I said, "Absolutely. Let me know what I can do to help."

"I think we'll have it soon since there isn't much time before Christmas. I'll ask Holly, and maybe advertise for a few more bachelorettes."

"That sounds good."

"We'll charge the men to enter, and then the winning one will pay for the date, of course. I was thinking we could use the auction money and donate it to a local animal rescue in honor of our pups."

"What do you need my help with?" I asked.

Marley smiled wide. "Planning the perfect date."

"Sebastian is taking me on a carriage ride tonight around the property. That could be one of the dates. They could stop at a secluded location for a picnic."

Marley clasped her hands together. "I love it. You're a

natural at this." Then she surprised me by hugging me. "You're going to fit right in. I'm so glad you're living here."

"Well, it's only temporary. I'll help Sebastian get through the holidays and maybe tax season. Then I'll get my own place." I had a feeling Sebastian was going to be difficult when I tried to go on dates. I'd need to meet the guys off the farm somewhere, like at a coffee shop or a wine bar.

Marley smiled brightly. "That's plenty of time, and by then, you'll have fallen in love with the farm and us."

When she said *fallen in love*, my heart stuttered because I almost thought she was going to say *with Sebastian*. Did everyone know about my unfortunate crush? Maybe I was overreacting. Marley had only recently moved in with Heath. She couldn't possibly know about it.

Marley leaned in and said slyly, "I think it's making Sebastian jealous."

"What are you talking about?" My gaze flashed down the table to where Sebastian was sitting next to his daughter.

Marley fanned herself. "He doesn't want you to be auctioned off. Oh, maybe he'll bid on you."

I laughed. "Why would he do that?"

Marley's brow furrowed. "So that no one else can take you out."

"Why does he care so much? If he wants to remain single, that's fine, but I'm ready to share my life with someone."

Marley laughed and rested a hand on my arm. "I think he likes you."

I shook my head, and then my gaze snagged on Sebastian's concerned one. "No way."

She nodded. "Yes way. Why else would he protest so much?"

I frowned as I remembered how it had played out. "Emmett didn't like it either."

Marley waved a hand. "Emmett doesn't like any of our ideas. He shoots them all down."

I knew that was true. Sebastian was the level-headed one, the one who looked at the numbers. But I'd never known him to get involved in these kinds of decisions. He let Emmett take the lead and only interjected if his financial advice was needed. "If that's true, why hasn't it come up before?"

"I don't think he was ready. He was busy with Ember, and you were always there. He wasn't worried about you dating because you weren't."

I usually didn't discuss dates that went well with Sebastian. Was that because, on some level, I knew he was interested in me? My brain was starting to hurt.

Marley lowered her voice. "I don't know for sure. It's just my intuition. He was too upset not to be invested in you."

The idea warmed me from the inside out. "Do you think I should back out?"

Marley stopped me with a hand on my shoulder. "Absolutely not. Don't worry about anything. I've got this. He's not going to want you with anyone else, and the only way to do that is to be the highest bidder."

"I don't know."

"Trust me. After that little display in there"—she gestured toward the living room—"I think we've got this."

"Thank you for organizing it." Even if it didn't work out, it was a step in the right direction.

"We have to stick together with these stubborn men, or we'll never get what we want." She gestured around at the guys.

I laughed, feeling freer than I had in a long time. I loved the idea of being closer to the women here. "They are pretty grumpy about change."

Marley's eyes widened comically. "Right? They're literally impossible. Especially Emmett. I just hadn't anticipated Sebastian's reaction. That's why I think it's you. He never gets riled up about anything. At least not since I've been around."

"I have to agree. I've never seen him upset, unless he's talking about Ember's mother."

Marley growled. "What mother could just leave her child? Do you know what happened?"

"Not really. My understanding is that she didn't want the responsibilities that came with being a parent."

"I hope he doesn't let her near Ember if she ever comes back."

"You think she will?"

Her nose scrunched in distaste. "My mom did when I inherited the inn. People always return when you have something they want."

Sebastian told me that Marley had paid her mom a certain amount of money to not contest her grandmother's will. I knew Sebastian was financially comfortable, but neither of us had that kind of money to throw around.

There was something about Sebastian's brothers settling down with these women and creating a home here that warmed my heart. I wanted to fit in the same way, but that was wishful thinking.

Even if Marley thought Sebastian was jealous, I wasn't going to fall back into my crush. I needed to move on. If he wanted me, then he needed to make it clear. I wasn't going to wait around on him anymore.

My focus needed to be on me and getting back out into the dating world. What better way to do that than with a bachelorette auction and a pre-planned date? It sounded amazing. "What if no one bids on me?" I leaned over to ask Marley.

She tipped her head back and laughed. "There's no chance of that. I don't think you have anything to worry about. If anything, you're going to create a bidding frenzy."

"What are you two talking about down there?" Sebastian asked, his voice low and even.

"Oh, just about how many guys are going to be bidding on our girl here. I told her she's going to create a bidding frenzy."

This time, I watched Sebastian carefully, and sure enough, his eyes narrowed, and his jaw clenched. Was he jealous that I was dating and he wasn't? Or was it something more? Was Marley right, and he liked me?

Marley pointed around the room. "Y'all better be present that night to support the farm. I'm including all the Monroe brothers. Even if you're taken, you need to be present as representatives from the farm. We'll auction off Holly and Hanna, and I'll shoot out a sign-up form for more single women on our socials and in our emails."

Heath rested his elbows on the table. "Don't you think you're moving fast?"

"Look, we need to plan things during the season. That's our busiest time. We can't do this in the summer. We'll plan the perfect romantic date with the backdrop of the trees and twinkling lights. It's going to be perfect." Then Marley turned to me. "Do you want to pick the date you go on, or should we have the men do that?"

Before I could answer, she snapped her fingers. "Should we auction off the right to have the hot tub date?"

"This is too much," Sebastian said.

Marley's eyes narrowed on him. "This is my baby, and we're doing it, with or without your help."

"You want to auction off the hot tub for a date?" Emmett asked.

Marley nodded. "I think it will help us raise more money."

Could I get into the hot tub with a strange guy I'd never met before? Or what if it was someone I knew but didn't have a romantic interest in? It didn't feel right.

The thought of being in the hot tub with Sebastian had me thinking all sorts of naughty thoughts. Would he want me close? Would he touch me?

Flashes of bare, wet skin flitted through my head. After seeing a sliver of his abdomen this morning, it made me yearn for more. Sebastian was hiding a hot body under those conservative suits.

Lori finally held up her hands. "Dinner is ready to be served. Let's table this discussion for another time."

I let out a sigh of relief as everyone got up to help Lori carry in the dishes. Ember and Addy had gone into the living room to play a while ago, leaving us free to talk business.

Sebastian rose and stalked toward me. He braced a hand on the table next to me and leaned in. "Is this what you want?"

I blinked up at him, a little confused as to why he was so determined to clarify my intentions. "It sounds fun, and I wanted to jump into dating again. This seems like the perfect way to do it. You and your brothers will be nearby if anything goes wrong."

A rumble erupted from Sebastian's throat.

"Are you—are you growling at me?" I asked him, a little shocked.

He leaned in closer. "I don't like the idea of men bidding on you."

The intensity of his gaze and the way his muscles flexed was so distracting I wasn't sure if he'd asked a question. "I don't know what to say. Marley wants to raise money for the farm, and I thought you said you needed an extra stream of income."

He nodded. "That's true."

"She's just trying to help, and I want to do something, too."

"You think you can help the farm and my family by letting some stranger bid on you and then take you into a secluded hot tub?"

I stood, which brought me against Sebastian's body. He didn't take a step back. His warmth and scent surrounded me, and I couldn't look away from him. I pulled on every bit of confidence I had. "I guess you'll need to make sure it's not a stranger who wins."

With that parting shot, I moved around him and into the kitchen. I thought I heard him say, "What the hell is that supposed to mean?"

But I was so surprised by my words, I couldn't respond. I'd literally just challenged my best friend to bid on me during an auction. What the hell had I gotten myself into?

I helped carry in the glasses and assisted Ember and Addy with setting the table. Then I poured water from a pitcher into everyone's glasses. My plan was to stay busy and not fall into a conversation with Sebastian about the auction again.

But when I stepped close to him, I realized my error. He took the opportunity to pull me close, and I almost spilled the water.

Conversation was going on around us as if no one noticed that I was leaning against Sebastian and had stopped pouring water. Ember was leaning away from Sebastian to talk to Addy, who was seated next to her.

"We're not done with this conversation."

I forced myself to breathe evenly and managed to pour the water into his glass without spilling it. "I appreciate your concern, but I don't see how it's any of your business."

I'd dropped the challenge, and now I was pushing him to show me his cards. Did he like me, or did he not want me dating anyone else? I wasn't going to back down. If he forced the issue, I'd keep pushing.

Then I moved away to finish the rest of the glasses. His hand fell away, and I missed the warmth of his body. What would it be like to be here as Sebastian's girl and not just his friend?

As worried as I was about the chemistry between us, each time we'd gotten close, my heart rate picked up.

I was challenging him to tell me how he felt. But what if I didn't like his answer? What if it changed things between us? I loved his family as if they were my own, and I adored his daughter.

I'd hate it if we couldn't be as close as we'd been. It would break my heart. But at the same time, it wasn't healthy for me to be involved with him and his family if I wanted something more and he didn't.

# CHAPTER 6

## SEBASTIAN

I spent the meal grinding my teeth together so hard my jaw ached. Ember was too busy talking to Addy to notice that something was off with me. But I was hyperaware of Hanna's presence.

After dinner, we all helped clean up. Then the guys moved to the deck for a beer and turned on the heaters so it was bearable.

"What do you think about this auction business?" I asked the group in general, hoping I'd have a few allies.

Cole's lips turned up. "I think it could be fun. I hope Marley finds some single women in town I haven't met yet."

I opened my mouth to protest, but Knox smacked my arm. "He's single. He's not looking at this the same way you are."

I rubbed the sting. "What way is he looking at it?"

Knox gave me a look. "He wants to meet women, whereas you don't want anyone bidding on Hanna."

"That's not true."

Knox gestured inside to where the women were talking around the island counter. "Isn't it? You reacted strongly to it in there."

Ignoring his observation, I turned my attention to Emmett. "You don't like it."

"Lately, the women around here are doing whatever they want without our input. I mean, they listen to us, but they don't stop doing whatever it is they're going to do." There was disgust in his voice, but a mix of affection, too. He loved Ireland, and he probably wanted to indulge her. He would feel differently if she were single and being auctioned off.

There was a weird sensation in my sternum that I rubbed with my fist. "What are we going to do about it?"

Emmett shook his head. "There's nothing we can do. The women want to host this thing, and I think we're going to be helping them."

I shook my head in disgust. "Since when did you start caving to their every whim?"

Emmett lifted his beer and tipped it toward his mouth. "Since I fell in love with one of them."

"Is that what happens? You fall in love, and everything changes?"

Knox, Heath, and Emmett considered my comment and then slowly nodded their heads.

Knox tipped his head to the side like he was considering it further, and finally settled on, "It's not a bad thing."

Heath nodded. "You want your woman to be happy."

"And you'll do anything for them," Emmett added.

"I don't see what the problem is. We can bid on women, and they go on a date with us right there. There are no phone calls or talking on an app. You're attracted to a woman, you bid on her, and then you go on the date. It takes the stress out of it. You might find someone you're interested in. You don't want to be single forever, do you?" Cole asked.

I wasn't aware that Cole was interested in dating or settling down. I didn't think he was giving me a hard time, either.

Unlike my brothers, he wasn't around as often and probably didn't know anything about my history with Hanna.

Knox touched Cole's shoulder. "We think he likes Hanna as more than a friend, but he's never confirmed it."

Cole's eyes widened. "Ah. I didn't realize. Then there's only one thing to do."

"And what's that?" I asked, picking at the label on my empty beer.

"You have to be the highest bidder," Cole said simply.

That would mean declaring to everyone that I didn't want her to be with anyone else. It made me nervous. There wouldn't be any turning back after I made that move.

"That's your plan, isn't it?" Knox asked.

"I don't know." A muscle in my jaw spasmed.

"You're going to watch her go on dates with other guys?" Emmett asked, his voice level and reasonable, when I knew if it were Ireland being auctioned off, he'd lose his mind.

"Marley's throwing the hot tub in as one of the dates," I said, unable to confirm my thoughts on the matter.

"What if they don't bring a bathing suit?" Cole tipped his head back as if he were looking at the stars, but his eyes drifted shut. "This is going to be the best date ever. I'm bidding on that hot tub."

I wanted to get into the hot tub with Hanna. I wanted to spend one-on-one time with her when I wasn't worried about not crossing lines or personal boundaries. I'd always been careful to stay out of her personal life when it came to men, but no more. I didn't have a lot of time before the auction to ease her into the idea of us.

The conversation drifted toward the end of the season, how many trees we had left, and whether we'd shorten the hours when things slowed down closer to Christmas. There were always last-minute shoppers to consider. We'd never figured out a good way to slow things down because there was always someone wanting a tree or a gift that last week. It meant long hours for us the whole season. But with Cole here this year, I'd been able to cut back.

Knox touched my arm. "Seriously, you need help to come up with a plan?"

I sighed. "I think I've got it. I just need to speed things up. Hanna said she was going to start dating, and I have no idea when that will be. I figured I had until January, but now I have this auction to worry about."

Knox clasped my shoulder. "Whatever you need, we'll help you."

My mouth was dry. "Make sure she doesn't end up in the hot tub with anyone else."

Knox grabbed another beer from the cooler we kept outside when we gathered and handed it to me. "That's all you. I can't interfere with the bidding. You have to be the highest bidder."

I unscrewed the cap and tipped the bottle to my lips. The cool liquid soothed my dry throat. "What if the bidding gets out of hand, and we're talking thousands of dollars?" I had some money saved, but I'd rather use it for something else, like a vacation.

"This is supposed to be fun. I don't think the girls meant for it to be like that."

His explanation didn't make me feel any better. Shortly after, I excused myself to get the carriage from the neighbors' property. Knox took Sarah and Addy out on it when he first met her, and I figured Hanna and Ember would enjoy it, too.

I grabbed a few throw blankets from Mom's house and put them in the carriage. The air was cooler than when we arrived. Everyone had drifted to the porch to watch my progress.

"Are we going on a ride?" Addy asked Knox.

"No. I think this carriage ride is for Ember and Uncle Sebastian."

"Can I go, too?" Addy asked, holding Knox's hand, pleading with him.

I stepped in because Knox had a hard time saying no to her when she used puppy eyes. "I'm taking Hanna and Ember this time. They've never been."

"Oh. Okay," Addy said.

Her expression dropped slightly, and Knox said, "We'll watch a movie tonight instead."

Addy smiled slightly, hopefully forgetting all about the carriage ride. The rest of my family said their goodbyes and went to their trucks to go home.

I helped Ember into the carriage and then turned to find Hanna standing next to me. "Are you sure you want me to go with you? It might be nice for just you and Ember to go."

"I want you to see the farm, remember? If you're going to be living here and helping with the events, it's helpful if you know what's here."

"That makes sense," Hanna said, placing her hand in mine.

Hanna stepped into the carriage and sat next to Ember, arranging the blankets over their laps.

Mom handed me three to-go cups. "I made you some hot chocolate, too."

"Thanks." I was pleased she'd thought of it because I was too distracted by thoughts of Hanna being auctioned off to some guy.

"Have a great time." Mom patted my cheek before turning and going into the house for the night.

I settled next to the girls, my heart longing to call them mine. But I had a long way to go before that would be the case.

I flicked the reins, and the horses moved forward slowly. I planned to take the lane past Emmett's and Heath's cabins and toward the pond. It was the best place to take guests. The lights lined the pathways and reflected nicely off the water.

"Are you okay with everything that's happening?" Hanna

asked as we ambled down the lane, her body bumping into mine when we went over a rut.

"Marley isn't listening to our concerns."

Hanna wrapped her hand around my bicep. "It sounds like it could be a lot of fun. Romantic dates on the farm sound amazing, and it could be good publicity for the farm."

Her chest rubbed against my elbow, distracting me. I wanted to take her on a romantic date. It didn't have to be the hot tub. I just wanted her to see me as someone other than her best friend. Maybe my bidding on her would do the trick. She'd have to see that I was interested in her. Maybe this was the best thing that could come out of it. "You're right. The dates will be something for people to talk about, and it will be good for the farm."

"You're okay with it now?" Hanna asked carefully.

"I guess I have to be, and you're right, it sounds like a nice evening."

"Are you going to help plan the dates?" Hanna asked.

I felt her gaze on the side of my face. "I'll leave that to you and the rest of the women."

"It's going to be so much fun," Ember said.

I moved so I could see her face. "You're going to help? What do you know about romantic dates?"

"I know what girls like," Ember insisted.

"You're going to be a big helper, and you can help us decorate."

Hanna was a natural with Ember. Whenever we went anywhere together and ran into people we didn't know, they assumed she was Ember's mother. They both had lighter colored hair, dirty blonde, although Hanna's was straight, and Ember's was wavy.

We rode in silence for a few minutes, enjoying our hot chocolate and the night air.

We passed Heath's house, and I continued on the path

toward the pond. As we approached, I saw green and red lights emanating from the water.

"What is that?" Ember asked, confused.

"I have no idea. Maybe Talon put more of his light display by the pond?" The light display meant for the public was on the new lane we had created for an easy exit onto the main road.

Hanna gripped my arm tighter. "It's amazing. How did he place the lights in the water like that?"

"I have no idea." Talon kept to himself for the most part. He didn't like to be interrupted while he was working, and we respected that. He didn't make it to every family dinner or holiday event, but we were happy when he was able to.

I wondered if something was going on with him because he hadn't mentioned this development to anyone that I knew of.

"Sometimes I think he creates things to work out all the emotional stuff," Hanna said softly so only I could hear.

"What emotional stuff does Talon have?" I asked, genuinely curious about what she was thinking.

Hanna glanced at Ember, who was enthralled with this new light display, and lowered her voice further. "Your father dying and whatever happened between him and Holly."

"What do you know about that?" I figured women might confide in each other more than my brothers did.

"Holly doesn't talk about it, and I didn't want to bring it up."

We wanted to help him, but if he didn't talk about his feelings, how could we? The problem was, my father was stoic and didn't like it when we cried. We learned quickly not to express emotions. I think it was even harder for Talon because Dad didn't understand his artistic interests. "I want Talon to figure things out. I mean, three of my brothers are in love. I never thought I'd see it."

She touched her shoulder to mine. "What about you?"

I tensed. "What about me?"

"Don't you deserve to be happy?" Hanna asked.

"I have Ember. She's everything." Was I happy? Sometimes I felt a little lonely. Being a single dad separated me from the other families at her school. They looked at me differently when they realized I wasn't married, and they were surprised when they realized Ember's mother wasn't around.

"Mmm," Hanna said, and I had a feeling she wasn't convinced.

"I love spending time with my best friend. She makes me feel like I don't need anyone else." It was as close to a confession as I'd ever gotten.

Instead of Hanna smiling, though, her expression was thoughtful. "I'm wondering if we need space so we can meet the people we're supposed to be with. If we're always together, then how will we meet our person?"

My heart sank. She didn't think I was the one. Were my brothers full of it when they said she'd crushed on me since we were kids? Or if they were right, had she stopped having those feelings for me? Was I too late? I wanted to ask *what if that person is right in front of you but you can't see him?* But I couldn't because it would be giving away how I felt, and I wasn't sure she felt the same way. The idea of being that vulnerable sent my heart racing, and my palms were sweaty on the reins.

"Addy's my best friend. I want to spend all my time with her."

Ember's comment lightened the mood.

"It's a good thing you live so close now. You can see each other a lot," Hanna said.

"Uncle Knox said I could sleep over whenever I want. So, can I?"

"What's your policy on sleepovers these days?" Hanna asked.

We'd discussed parenting before, and she tended to think I was a little overprotective. She was a teacher and understood child development, but she wasn't the sole parent of a child. "I think that would be okay. We live close enough that I can come get you if you decide you want to come home."

Ember's face screwed up. "Why would I want to come home?"

"To sleep in your own bed."

"Uncle Knox said he'll build us a fort in the living room in front of the fire. It will be just like camping out." Ember's voice filled with excitement.

"That sounds like fun," Hanna said.

My heart squeezed. My little girl was growing up, and I couldn't do anything to stop it. Soon, she'd want to go to the movies and hang out with friends. Then she'd want to date. I shivered, and it had nothing to do with the cold.

We admired the red and green lights under the water.

"I'd love to know how he did this," Hanna murmured.

"Me, too. And why?" A part of me wondered if this was for Holly. I wanted to ask him, but I wasn't sure he'd be honest with me.

"Has Holly seen it yet?" Hanna asked.

"I didn't know it was here, so probably not. Maybe Talon was experimenting with something new and didn't want to tell us because he's not done with it." There were red and green lights but not a discernible pattern. Knowing Talon, he wouldn't want to show anyone until it was perfect.

"It's beautiful."

I wish I could do something like this for Hanna to show her how I felt. But I wasn't artistic like Talon or good with my hands like Heath, Knox, and Emmett. I was smart. It wasn't an exciting talent when we were talking about getting a girl.

I worked out but wasn't athletic. I was smart but didn't have a sexy job where I worked with my hands like my brothers. Did I even stand a chance with Hanna?

What if the guys bidding on her were police officers, firefighters, or contractors? All those were more interesting professions than mine. My brothers had teased me about my job for years, saying I was uptight. Women were not impressed when I told them what I did. In fact, a few said I'd be too cheap if they allowed themselves to be in a relationship with me. It was a stereotype, but, in my case, they would have been accurate. I was cautious. I believed in saving money and not taking risks, but I wouldn't say I was cheap. It was just some preconceived notion women had of me. "You asked about whether I was happy with how things are, and the truth is that it's hard to meet people when you're a single dad."

"What about at work?"

My partners at the firm were men. There were a few secretaries, but both were older and already married with children. "No single women."

"You don't meet with clients?"

"I have a rule about not dating clients. Not that it's ever been an issue." I focused on work when I was there.

Hanna pursed her lips. "You should. I worry about you."

I turned my head to see her face. "You want me to be happy."

Ember waved a hand between us. "You both said you wanted to date, so date each other."

Hanna laughed, but it sounded off.

"We're good friends," I finally managed.

"I love hanging out with you and your father. If we date, and things don't work out, it would be awkward," Hanna said in her teacher voice.

"You wouldn't hang out with me anymore?" Ember asked, hurt tinging her voice.

"That's not what I meant. I just don't want to hurt your dad or you."

"It's complicated," I added, hoping Ember would drop the subject.

Ember sighed. "You always say that."

The problem was that being an adult was tricky. There were

pitfalls that a child couldn't begin to understand. I wanted safety and stability for her. Opening my life to dating was the opposite.

But I didn't know what I'd do if Hanna met someone at the auction and fell in love with him. She was an amazing woman, and if she wanted to meet someone great, she would. I was sure she hadn't been looking that hard the last few years. Once a guy met her and realized how amazing she was, he'd lock her down.

And I'd regret it forever.

# CHAPTER 7

## HANNA

The carriage ride was magical. It was the combination of being with Sebastian and Ember, the amazing light display on the water, and then coming home *with them*. It was something that would probably be so simple for anyone else. But I loved living with them, the simple routines, and the comfort of having someone close.

Then there was the sound of their soft voices in the morning when they were worried about waking me up. The giggles that inevitably drifted up the stairs to my room. I wanted to bottle up the feelings and keep them for when I was living on my own again.

I had a few more weeks of school, where the kids would be overly excited about the holidays, and then the holiday break before I had to look for a place to live. In the meantime, I'd soak up all the holiday events at the farm.

Each day, I went to school and then met Ember at the main house afterward, where she was having a snack with Lori. The original plan was to have Lori watch Ember after school, but they were worried about her overdoing it. This way, she got some time with Ember, and then I took over after her snack time.

"How was your carriage ride?" Lori asked after school on Friday night.

Frankly, I was surprised she hadn't asked about it earlier. "It was beautiful with the lights on the pond."

"You mean the ones that line the path?" Lori asked us.

"The ones on the water," Ember said around a mouthful of cookies.

Sebastian was concerned that Lori fed Ember too many sweets, so I tried to sneak veggies and carrots into her at dinner time.

Lori frowned. "What lights on the water?"

I shrugged. "Sebastian thought Talon had done it when he was experimenting with something new."

Lori leaned on the counter. "Hmmm. That sounds like him. What was it like?"

I pulled out my phone and showed her the pictures we'd taken. I realized I hadn't taken many because I was so wrapped up in the conversation with Sebastian.

"These are amazing. Did he mean for it to be part of the light show? We could make it longer."

"I doubt Emmett and Heath would appreciate the cars going past their cabins." And if Talon was ready to share it, he'd have told someone.

"That's true. But this is too nice not to share," Lori said, handing the phone back to me.

"Do you think that everyone feels the magic of the holidays when they see it, Grandma?" Ember asked.

My heart squeezed at her comment. Marley and Ireland were forever talking about the magic of the farm and the season.

Lori nodded. "I do."

"I think my daddy needs more of it, then. He's been sad

lately."

I frowned. "What do you mean?"

"He's different lately. Not as happy."

"Maybe it's the stress of the season and the move?" I asked.

Lori's brow furrowed. "He said he was happy he finally made the move, and he'd wished he'd done it sooner."

"Do you know why he's sad?" I asked her gently, wondering if Ember's mother had tried to get in contact with him or if he was just feeling off because of the holidays. It made me lonely when I realized I was spending another season alone.

Ember shook her head.

I wondered if my moving had set something off inside him or changed our dynamic. While I enjoyed our time together, not having spent those intimate times with him before, maybe he didn't. "I'll talk to him about it," I assured her.

Ember nodded. "Good. He likes you."

"Helping each other is what friends do," I agreed.

Lori raised a brow, but I refused to think about what it meant. Ember was only seven. I wasn't sure she understood the intricacies of adult relationships and feelings. In fact, I was positive she wouldn't. So, I put it out of my mind.

"How do you like living in the cabin?" Lori asked as she grabbed a washcloth to clean up the crumbs Ember left behind.

"I love it. It's like Christmas all the time. I see the trees from my window, and it always smells like evergreen."

"Did you decorate that tree you put up?" Lori asked Ember.

She nodded. "Hanna helped us."

Lori's eyes widened. "You did?"

"I think if we left it up to Sebastian, he wouldn't have done it in time. I added some fresh garland to the mantles and windows, a wreath on the door, and candles in the windows. Now it's more inviting."

"I wish you didn't have to move," Ember said.

"I thought you'd stay at the cabin through the end of tax season to help Sebastian out?"

"We haven't really discussed an end date. I have a feeling he wants to start dating, and I don't want to cramp his style."

"Oh, I don't think that's true. He hasn't dated much since—" Lori looked pointedly at Ember, who was reaching for another cookie and not paying attention to us.

"If he's unhappy with me living there, though—"

"I'll talk to him. Maybe something's going on at work, and it has nothing to do with you. I thought he was thrilled you were coming to live with him. But he was upset after Marley mentioned the auction the other night."

I shrugged. "He wasn't happy about it at first, but I think he's come around to the idea. Or he realized that he can't fight Marley and Ireland when they have an idea."

"Hmm," Lori said. "None of the boys were excited about the auction, but I think it will be fun, especially for Talon and Sebastian. They're the last two single ones."

"You think they'll bid on someone?" I asked, not having considered that possibility before.

Lori shrugged. "Why wouldn't they? You said yourself he's looking to date. It's the perfect opportunity."

"The dates sound wonderful." I'd been part of the women's text chain where they discussed locations and decorations. But I didn't like the idea of Sebastian going on one of those dates with someone else.

"It will be so romantic and the perfect opportunity to meet someone. For you, too."

So, Lori didn't see me with Sebastian either. Everyone said she was a matchmaker. If she wanted us together, or thought there was something there, wouldn't she be pushing us together, not apart? She was his mother and knew him best.

I felt a little shaky and needed to escape from the conversation. "We should probably head home. Sebastian said he'd be home early to have dinner with us."

"Are you cooking?" Lori asked as she took Ember's plate.

I stood and helped Ember gather her things. She'd pulled out an art project she'd completed in school to show Lori. I carefully rolled it so it wouldn't get bent. "He said he was going to pick up something for us. I have no idea what."

Ember frowned. "We usually have pizza on Fridays. Just the frozen stuff from the store."

She didn't sound excited about the prospect. "Maybe he has something special planned for us."

I hope for her sake he did. My impression was that Sebastian was just surviving in their old home. He was doing his best as a single father. But now that he'd built his cabin and moved to the farm, it was the perfect time to start over and try new things. I had the same feeling when my roommate told me she was moving in with her boyfriend and not extending the lease.

It was a chance to take a different path, and I thought that meant looking for someone special for myself. Moving away from Sebastian and finally meeting someone new. But I was living in Sebastian's house and taking care of his daughter. I was more entrenched in his life than ever before.

I carried Ember's book bag and art project to the door.

Lori hugged me. "I'm so glad you're here. You're good for him." Then she lowered to Ember's level. "And I love having you close by."

"Grandma," Ember whined when Lori hugged her, but I could tell she enjoyed the attention.

She had me and Lori, but not her biological mother. I didn't want her to feel abandoned, but with the way her mother disappeared from her life, it was inevitable.

We drove the short distance to Sebastian's house, which was close to the main house but with a private feel under the cover of the woods. Since it was dusk, the lights on the porch were glowing.

"We should put a tree on the porch," Ember said as she got out.

"That would look nice." It was big enough for a tree. I could see us sitting out here on the rocking chairs.

"Do you think Daddy will cut down another one for us?"

"I bet there might be an extra one on the lot that one of your uncles would bring us."

"Are you serious?" Ember asked as I unlocked the door and sent a quick message to Knox and Heath. One of them would be happy to help. I was sure of it. They adored their niece and Addy.

"Why not? I love the idea." While we were here, I wanted to take part in all the holiday traditions. "Besides, you can never have too many trees."

"I love you, Miss Hanna."

"I love you, too," I said, ruffling her hair as she hugged me. "But you don't have to call me *Miss* anymore. I've known you my whole life, and you're not my student."

She nodded, then said, "I'm hungry. Can I have a snack?"

"Let's cut up some fruit. We don't want to spoil your dinner." Any more than it already was. Sebastian asked me to rein in his mother's snacks, but it was hard to step in when she loved providing Ember with after-school treats she'd baked fresh just for her.

"Uh. Fine."

I put grapes, cheese, and crackers on the table. "What do you think about starting the cookie dough for cut-out cookies? We'll need to refrigerate it for a few hours. So, we could put the dough in the fridge overnight and roll them out tomorrow."

"Yes, cookies!" Ember exclaimed before popping a grape into her mouth.

I'd ordered everything we needed earlier in the week, so I

gathered the ingredients and placed them on the counter, then hunted for the cookie trays until I finally found one. "I think we're going to need to invest in more cookie things. Your father only has one tray and no cooling racks."

"He never bakes cookies. Not from scratch. Just the pre-made ones from the store."

My eyes widened. "Well, that's not going to cut it."

Ember giggled.

"We need the real deal. You want to help?" I asked Ember, but she was already scooting a chair across the floor, which made a loud screeching noise. Hopefully, she wasn't scratching Sebastian's new wood floor.

I propped my phone on a holder that Sebastian kept on the kitchen counter so I could show her the recipe. Ember read the list, and then I helped her measure and pour each ingredient into the bowl.

Lori made a ton of cookies for the shop and the family, so I only made one batch. These were just for us and Santa.

When Ember was mixing the batter, and flour covered us and the counter, my phone buzzed with an incoming text.

"Is it the tree?" Ember asked, her tongue peeking out as she concentrated on her task.

I picked up the phone to see the full message.

**Knox: I can bring one by at close tonight. Does that work?**

**Hanna: That's perfect. Thank you!**

**Knox: Anything for my niece.**

Even if Ember was missing her mother, she had so many uncles who adored her. "We're getting a tree."

She squealed. "Do we have lights for it?"

"I think there was another box of lights. I'll look once the dough is in the fridge."

"We can't cook them tonight?" Ember asked, her lower lip popping out into a pout.

"It needs to sit in the fridge for a few hours so they're easier to roll out. We want to do cut-out cookies, remember?"

"My arm hurts." Ember handed me the spoon, and I took over, making sure the flour was all mixed in.

Then I rolled it into a ball, wrapped it in cellophane, and placed it on a shelf in the fridge.

"Lights?" Ember asked, jumping off the chair.

"Don't jump off chairs. That's dangerous," I said, my heart leaping in my chest.

She ran toward the basement door without listening to me.

"Hold up, Ember. We have to clean up our mess."

Ember stopped and then turned to face me; her eyes widened as she took in the state of the counter. Measuring cups, spoons, and bowls littered the surface, and everything was covered with a thin sheen of powder. "Do we have to?"

"Yes, we do."

We'd just placed all the dishes and utensils in the dishwasher when the front door opened. Sebastian walked inside, carrying a bag of groceries. He smiled and said, "Honey, I'm home."

"Daddy!" Ember exclaimed as she ran up to him. "What did you get?"

"I got dough to make pizza. I haven't done this in a while. We'll see if I remember how to do it right."

"You're making homemade pizza?" I asked him as he set the paper bag on the counter.

Sebastian winked at me. "That's right. I'll make the dough. You two need to pick your toppings."

"We just need to finish wiping the counters. We made cookie dough."

Sebastian's face softened as he addressed Ember. "You made cookies with Hanna?"

Ember nodded proudly. "I did all the measuring and pouring."

"She was a good helper," I added as I finished wiping the counter.

"Thanks for doing that. I'm not the best baker."

"You probably don't have to bake much, with your mom making so many baked goods this time of year."

His eyes widened. "Is that what she had after school?"

"Yes, but we had some grapes and cheese here." I'd put them in the fridge earlier so they wouldn't go bad.

Sebastian washed his hands, then pulled the groceries out and set them on the counter. We sat on the stool while he prepared the dough, kneaded it, and rolled it out on the counter. At some point, I hit play on a holiday music playlist on my phone.

Sebastian paused and stepped back from the counter. "You think this is good enough?"

"It's really thick." I moved around the counter and showed him how to make it even thinner.

Ember hopped down from the counter and went into the living room to play with toys. So, it was just us, and I was hyperaware of him standing behind me. "There, how's that?" I asked him.

He leaned over my shoulder to see. "It's perfect."

"Ember, come help with toppings."

Ember helped Sebastian pour pizza sauce over the dough and smooth it over every inch with a spatula, then she sprinkled cheese on top.

"Can we do pepperonis on half?" Sebastian asked her.

I had a feeling she usually said no, but this time she nodded.

She carefully placed the pepperonis on the pie, and then Sebastian put it in the oven. "Let's make salads."

Ember disappeared again.

"I want to make an effort for her to eat healthier."

I placed my hand on his arm. "You're doing a good job."

Sebastian tipped his head to the side. "Even if she doesn't eat fruits and veggies?"

"Aren't you putting them in her lunch?" I emptied her lunch box each evening, and there were a few items left, but I could see she'd been eating what he'd packed for her.

"I do that. But I'm not as good at dinner. I'm tired when I get home, and I'm scrambling to get a decent meal on the table. Sometimes I forget to add a veggie or a fruit."

"That's what you have me for, right? I gave her a healthy after-school snack, and we'll have a salad with dinner. I say you're doing a great job."

"That's just today, and because you're here." He pulled me into his arms, and my cheek landed on his chest. We hugged sometimes, but not like this. He didn't pull me into his arms to thank me for helping him. I breathed in his scent and snuggled into his body. I could get used to this.

"I'm happy to help," I said as I reluctantly pulled away. "Before I forget, Knox is bringing a tree by tonight."

He raised a brow. "I thought we had a tree."

"This one is for the porch. Don't worry, I'll pay for it."

Sebastian waved a hand at me. "We always have extra trees, so that's not an issue. But why do we need one on the porch?"

"Ember suggested it, and there's plenty of room for one. I just thought it would be nice. It's your first Christmas in your new cabin, and I want it to be special."

"I don't know what we'd do without you, Hanna. You're always there for us and thinking about us."

"You would have been fine. You have your mom and your brothers. And you forget that you're a wonderful dad."

His shoulders lowered. "It's tough because I worry about her mother not being here. How is that affecting her?"

"I don't know, but she seems to be doing okay, and that's because of how great you are with her. You don't let her feel the absence."

He closed his eyes for a second. "I'm sure she still does. When the other kids at school talk about having a mother volunteer in the classroom or for the PTA."

"She has her dad to be there for her, and that's special, too. Not everyone has a dad who can take off work to go to her concerts." Sebastian worked long hours at the firm, but he always made it to her activities.

"So, I'm not screwing everything up?"

I would have laughed, but his expression was somber, as if this was something he was genuinely worried about. "Of course not. You're a wonderful father. One day, Ember is going to thank you for being there for her."

His eyes were glossy, as if he was emotional over my words. "I hope so."

"I know it's been hard doing it yourself, but you show up for that little girl every day. And she's surrounded by people who love her." Sebastian was the best dad. It was one of the many reasons I was attracted to him.

Even if he wasn't perfect, he strived to do better. And living this close to him, witnessing him being her father in these moments, cooking dinner or getting her ready for school, was dangerous for my ovaries. Because I could see a little boy with light-colored hair running around the cabin.

# CHAPTER 8

## SEBASTIAN

The pizza crust was thin and crispy—just how we liked it. After we'd eaten and cleaned up, Knox pulled up in his truck with a tree in the back.

We bundled up in coats, boots, and hats and went onto the porch to greet him. Ember was practically jumping; she was so excited.

Sebastian helped Knox carry the tree to the porch. When they set it down, Knox asked Ember, "I had a request for a tree. You know anything about that?"

Ember clasped her hands together. "It's for me."

Knox grinned. "Where do you want it?"

It was heartwarming to see these burly men go all soft for the little girls in their lives. It made me want children of my own. I wanted to be part of this big family. But I was getting ahead of myself, especially when I'd already declared I was interested in meeting someone new.

Ember ran ahead of him and stood in the empty spot on the corner of the porch. "Right here."

Knox assessed the space. "That's a perfect spot for it. Are you going to help decorate?"

Ember nodded. "Uh-huh."

Knox turned to Sebastian and asked, "You have an extra tree stand? If not, I brought one."

"I don't." Sebastian reached into the bed of Knox's truck and grabbed the tree stand.

"We have a ton of them," Knox said.

"Perks of owning a Christmas tree farm," I said.

"There aren't many trees left. This is about it." Sebastian set the tree stand on the porch and helped Knox get the tree into it.

We helped them make sure it was straight.

When they were done, Ember said, "It's perfect. Just like I imagined."

It had me wondering what else she'd imagined. Did she want a family with a mother and a father? A brother and a sister? Maybe even a puppy?

Sebastian brushed his hands off and said, "I'll grab the lights."

"I meant to get them earlier, but you came home early."

Sebastian grinned at me and squeezed my shoulder. "No problem. I'll be right back."

Ember followed him. "I'll help, Daddy."

Sebastian shut the door behind them, leaving me and Knox alone on the porch.

"You like living here?" Knox asked as he sat in the rocking chair, pushing off with his feet.

I leaned against the railing, still admiring the tree. Ember was right; it was the perfect spot for a little something extra. "I love it."

Knox raised a brow. "Yeah?"

"It's so quiet out here. I don't hear traffic noise or people walking on the sidewalk. I don't need to worry if my roommate is bringing her boyfriend over to spend the night." I shrugged. "Not that she did that much at the end. I was mainly living alone. So, it's nice to have company."

Knox raised a brow. "You still going through with the auction?"

I laughed. "Is there an option not to? I thought when Marley and Ireland made up their mind about something, it was a done deal."

"That's the gist of it, but if Sebastian isn't happy about it—"

The front door opened, and Ember bounded out ahead of Sebastian, who was carrying a box.

I wanted to ask why it mattered. Sebastian had seemed grumpy about it at first but then came around. He hadn't brought it up since, and I guess I was careful not to.

Frankly, I was tired of worrying about it. I was going to let it play out. Maybe even leave it up to the universe. Perhaps I'd meet someone worth getting to know, or Sebastian would finally make a move.

Knox and Sebastian worked on stringing the lights while Ember gave tips on their progress.

I watched them interact, my heart feeling full. I didn't have one tree in my apartment, much less two. It was nice to fully experience the holiday this year, and I had several more weeks to soak it all in.

Knox placed the last row of lights. "We're hoping to do a family walk-through of the light display at some point."

"That sounds nice," Sebastian said.

Knox stepped back to admire the tree. "The season is busy. Sarah wanted to make sure we had time to do a few family activities."

"That's a good idea," I said, impressed Knox was heeding her advice.

"We have kids now, and they make us slow down and enjoy things," Knox said, ruffling Ember's hair.

"I don't slow things down. I speed them up," Ember said, and we laughed.

How would I go back to living alone in an apartment in town? All my friends and colleagues were paired off, and Sebastian had a family with Ember, his brothers, and his mom. My family was close, but not like the Monroes.

"Should we put a few ornaments on the tree before bed?" Sebastian asked Ember.

She nodded. "Yes."

Sebastian lifted a red and a green ornament out of the box, and Ember eagerly took them and hung them on the tree.

I watched them for a few minutes, my heart squeezing at the beautiful family they made. Knox hung a couple higher up, and Sebastian praised Ember for how the tree looked. Was I ready to walk away from these two? Or would I regret not telling Sebastian how I felt?

Feeling conflicted, I eventually went inside to make hot chocolate.

I busied myself warming the milk, pouring the cocoa, and hunting for mini marshmallows and candy canes. I had the mugs lined up on the table when all three walked in, bringing a gust of cold air.

"Hot chocolate!" Ember exclaimed when she came into the kitchen, dropping her hat and gloves on the floor.

"Ember, put your stuff away first," Sebastian reminded her.

Ember's face screwed up, but she grabbed the things she'd dropped and placed them in the basket by the front door.

When I was around them, I realized parenting was never-ending. Ember needed constant reminders about cleaning up, being nice to others, and considering how her actions affected others. It was similar to teaching but on a much bigger scale. Sebastian was responsible for this little human growing into a caring and responsible adult. I respected him for doing it alone.

"You didn't have to do this." Knox sat in the chair next to Ember and made a dramatic show of blowing air over the top.

"You can drink it. It's not hot." Ember lifted her face, revealing a chocolate-covered nose.

I sat across from them. "It shouldn't be. It's been sitting for a few minutes." Then, to Sebastian, I asked, "Is the tree done?"

"We decided to finish it up," Sebastian said with a smile in Ember's direction. He stood at the counter.

"I'll have to take a look in a bit."

"We can go back out once this one's in bed," Sebastian said with a wink.

I wished he was insinuating we'd be doing something else after Ember was in bed. But that was my overactive imagination envisioning what it wanted to see.

Knox blew bubbles in the hot chocolate, and Ember giggled.

Sebastian leaned against the counter and crossed his arms over his chest. "You're acting like a child."

Whenever I observed Sebastian with his brothers, he was the more serious one. He didn't let loose and have fun. I wondered if that was something I could help him with while I was here.

"It's supposed to snow tomorrow," Knox said.

"Will it be enough to go sledding?" Ember asked, excitement filling her voice.

Knox nodded. "They're saying four to six inches. If it's the right kind of snow, we should be good. The light and fluffy flakes aren't great for snowmen or sledding."

Ember pouted. "I want it to snow, but I want to miss school."

"We don't get everything we want," Sebastian reminded her gently.

"I'll just be happy with snow." What could be better than staying in Sebastian's cabin and getting snowed in for a day? I couldn't think of anything else I wanted to do than play in the snow with them.

Knox nodded before draining his mug. "We were lucky to get that big storm last year. Before that, it hadn't snowed much."

"If it snows, we'll sled on the hill by Mom's," Sebastian said.

"You think she's ready for the snowmobile?" Knox nodded in Ember's direction.

Sebastian's forehead wrinkled. "I don't feel comfortable with that yet."

Knox tipped his head to the side. "We did it at her age."

"It's different," Sebastian said, and my heart twisted. He wanted to protect his little girl, and it made him even more attractive.

"How about you let Ember sleep over with Addy tomorrow, and you can take Hanna out for a night ride?" Knox suggested.

"That sounds fun," I said, never having been on a snowmobile. My parents lived in town. When it snowed, we all convened at the elementary school's hill and sledded all day. It was fun, but I could see how the Monroe boys had more to do on the farm. Their hill was larger, and they had snowmobiles and an unending supply of Christmas trees to decorate.

"It's a plan, then," Sebastian said.

"Yay!" Ember said as she drank the rest of her hot cocoa.

"It's time for this one to go to bed. It's getting late."

Ember stole another marshmallow from the bag I left out. "I need to stay up if it's going to snow."

"You'll be up at the same time, no matter what time I put you to bed, and I don't want you to be too tired to enjoy playing in the snow tomorrow."

I stood and placed Ember's mug in the sink.

"Can you reheat mine? I'll drink it outside," Sebastian said to me, and my heart skipped a beat. "That sounds wonderful. I'll heat up some more milk for me, too."

Knox stood and placed his mug in the sink. "I'll leave you guys to it. I want to say goodnight to Addy before she's asleep."

"Thanks for bringing the tree," I said to him.

"Anytime. I love making this one smile." Knox grinned and squatted so Ember could hug him. She threw her arms around him and squeezed him tight. "Love you, Uncle Knox."

I met Sebastian's gaze over their heads, and my heart flip-flopped again. Their family never failed to slay me.

Knox stood and headed out the door with a wave. "Have a good night."

"That was nice of him to bring the tree," I said.

"Our porch is more festive now. Even though we're the only ones that see it."

"Sometimes I think that makes it even better. Only you know how warm and inviting your house is." The cabin was private and secluded, yet close to Lori's home and his brothers. It was the perfect combination.

"Maybe you're right," Sebastian said, then he lifted Ember over his shoulders. "Time for bed."

Ember squealed and kicked her legs as he took her up the stairs. I smiled after them before moving to make more hot chocolate. I wasn't in the mood for it when I was making it earlier, but if he wanted to sit on the porch and drink some, then I would, too.

I tried not to think about how romantic it would be to sit on the porch with Sebastian, drinking hot chocolate and admiring the tree he'd just decorated with his daughter.

I grabbed some throws and carried everything out to the front porch.

A few minutes later, he joined me. "You were supposed to wait for me."

"I just came out." I held the blankets to my chest.

They'd used all red and green decorations, and the effect was gorgeous. "It's beautiful."

"I'm glad you think so." Sebastian moved his chair closer to mine.

It felt like a friendly move, yet my heart was galloping in my chest.

Sebastian nodded toward the tree. "Thank you for getting the tree. I wouldn't have thought to do that."

"It was Ember's idea. I just asked your brother for help."

He squeezed my thigh, then quickly let go.

His touch sent sparks through my leg to my core. He seemed unaffected as he grabbed the mug of hot chocolate and settled into his chair.

"Your home is beautiful," I said to him, meaning every word. "From the stone and wood elements you added to the views and the decorations. Ember will have an amazing life here."

"You think so?" Sebastian asked softly.

"I know so. She has so many people who love her. She's a lucky girl."

"Even if she doesn't have her mother?" Sebastian let his head fall back. "All girls need a mother, don't they?"

"I'm sure it's an important relationship in any girl's life. But sometimes, men take a step back when mothers are involved. You stepped up, and you're an amazing father. Not every girl has an involved father, even if she has two parents living with her."

"I hadn't thought about it like that."

"A lot of families are going through something similar. There's a little boy in my class whose mom died suddenly of breast cancer last year. I have a little girl who has two daddies. And many more whose parents are split, and they're going back and forth. Who says what the ideal family is? As long as you provide her a loving home, that's all you can do."

Sebastian swallowed hard. "I love and support her."

"And so does your family."

He looked at me then, his gaze intent. "Plus, I have you."

"You have me," I agreed, even as the words felt a little disingenuous. In order for me to move on from this crush, I needed space. Living with him had only intensified my feelings for him, despite my intention to meet someone else.

"I appreciate you moving in here to help me."

I let out a breath, my heart thumping in my chest. "You don't have to keep thanking me. I know how you feel. I love being here with Ember."

"Do you enjoy being here with me?" Sebastian asked softly.

I opened my mouth, then closed it. I loved it. A little too much. But how do I address that with him? "I'm loving being here with you guys over the holidays."

Sebastian cleared his throat. "I don't want to hold you back or make you feel like you could be doing other things."

"You're helping me, too, remember? I couldn't find an affordable apartment."

"There's no rush for you to leave. It's convenient for you to be here if you're helping me."

"I know. But I feel like I'm taking advantage of you." It wasn't that. Not exactly. I just felt like I needed to preserve my sanity and create some distance.

"You're not," Sebastian insisted.

We fell into a comfortable silence. We were friends. This is how things would always be. I'd be helping him with Ember, enjoying his family. What would happen if he moved on and met someone? He wouldn't need me anymore.

I'd never felt so torn in my entire life. Usually, I knew what I wanted and went after it. But with Sebastian, I'd always held back for fear of losing him. It hadn't gotten me anywhere.

I gazed at the twinkling lights on the tree until they blurred. "I'm excited for snow this weekend. I wanted to bake some cookies and enjoy being stuck inside."

"We're not going to be stuck inside. We're going to go sledding, build a snowman, and go snowmobiling at night. You're going to get the full experience."

"That sounds nice, but I don't want to interrupt your time with Ember."

Sebastian set his mug to the side and leaned forward with his elbows on his knees. "You won't be. To be honest, it feels weird when you're not here, and I think it's going to get worse when you move out."

I wasn't sure how to respond. I didn't like being alone either. And it wasn't that I wanted to be with other people; it was Sebastian and Ember specifically. And I adored his family. I'd gotten to know them even better while living on the farm. I wasn't ready to give any of them up.

"When you start dating, it will seem weird that you're living with me." Sebastian's voice was strained.

My heartbeat slowed. "I can say I'm your nanny."

"I wouldn't want anyone I'm dating to be living with a single guy." His voice was stronger this time.

"That's true." If I was going to be serious about meeting and dating other people, I'd probably need to move out. "For now, I'm going to enjoy the holidays and worry about real life in January."

Sebastian shifted in his seat, straightening his legs out in front of him. "I wish everything could be like that. That we could just put it off for another time."

"I read somewhere that ninety-nine percent of the things we worry about never come to fruition," I said, remembering an article I'd just seen last week.

Sebastian shook his head. "So, we worry for nothing?"

I laughed. "Seems like it."

"That's an interesting idea. As a parent, it feels like all I do is worry about whether I'm messing things up."

"What if we let everything go and just enjoy being in the moment?" I asked.

"I like that idea." He pushed his foot off the porch and rocked his chair back. We were in the woods with the twinkling lights surrounding us. The only thing that would have made the moment better was if I were in Sebastian's arms. But there wasn't a couch out here. Just two separate chairs. There was no way to finagle that unless I was sitting in his lap. That was not something a friend would do, no matter how attractive the idea was.

"Why are you so fidgety? I thought we promised not to worry about anything?" He leaned over and rested his palm on my thigh, effectively stilling my foot that had been moving.

"It's easier said than done, I guess." I laughed, but it sounded off.

He moved his hand higher, and my breath hitched. The muscles in my thighs tensed, and my core clenched. Did he know the effect he was having on me? He couldn't, or he wouldn't be touching me.

"You're safe with me." He squeezed my leg one time, and all the air inside my body whooshed out. When his hand moved back to his space, I still felt the heat of his palm through the material of my jeans.

I'd never had this strong of a reaction to another man touching me, and the gesture was meant as friendly.

A little while later, Sebastian stood and picked up his mug. "I'd better get to bed. Ember will be up early, excited about the snow. Whether the forecasters are right or not is another story."

We both stood at the same time, and I tried to move around him but ended up leaning into his chest. His hands moved to my upper arms to steady me, and my heart raced in my chest. When our gaze met, there was heat and desire for me.

Had I been wrong about him this whole time? Was he feeling the same sparks I was?

"Wouldn't want you to fall. Not when we're going to have fun in the snow tomorrow."

"I'm looking forward to it." I smiled up at him, trying not to think about the way my breasts were pressed against his body and his thighs touched mine. But I couldn't move backward without knocking into the tree, and I couldn't get past him. He was standing tall and strong in front of me, seemingly in no hurry to move.

He brushed a strand of hair out of my face. "Why haven't we ever kissed?"

I huffed out a breath, my heart pounding at this point. "What are you talking about? Friends don't kiss." My voice was high-pitched and off-key.

His hand cupped my chin, and he gently lifted it until I was looking at him. "Have you ever thought about kissing me?"

# CHAPTER 9

## SEBASTIAN

Why had I asked if she'd ever thought about kissing me? There was something about this moment, drinking hot chocolate on my new porch while admiring my newly decorated tree, that had me forgetting about all the reasons I hadn't asked this question before.

The moment was intimate, as if nothing could touch us. But all bubbles eventually burst. The walls stretch thin before they inevitably pop with a noise loud enough to make everyone startle.

That was what my ill-timed question was—the proverbial popping of the bubble. Hanna was looking up at me as if she couldn't believe what I'd asked. I couldn't either. I'd broken the one rule that was supposed to preserve our friendship. Never reveal how I felt about Hanna. Not my real feelings. The ones I only thought about when I was alone in bed at night or in the shower.

Backtracking as fast as I could, I stepped back, the cool air doing little to put out the flames touching her had set off. I waved a hand at the tree as if it was the atmosphere and not me. "There was something about the tree and you living here that made me wonder what it would be like to be with someone."

I'd make it sound like I was in love with the idea of being in love, not attracted to my best friend.

Hanna flinched. "No worries. I'd imagine we've never kissed because that's not what friends do. That neither one of us ever felt the need to cross that line."

There was something about her statement that felt like a challenge. There was a right answer to these questions; I just wasn't sure what it was. I'd never admitted that I'd thought about kissing her for the first time years ago, when she'd come over for a holiday bonfire with my family, and we'd found ourselves away from the group. She'd shivered from the cold, and I'd offered her my jacket. There was something in her eyes when I settled it over her shoulders that called out to me, making me think she wanted me to kiss her.

I wasn't experienced with girls at the time, so I told myself I'd misinterpreted the whole experience. But over the years, when my brothers said she'd crushed on me, I'd wondered if I'd screwed up.

"Right," I said, still at a loss for what to say.

"So, there's your answer," Hanna said in a snippy tone I almost never heard from her, and she moved around me and into the house. I wanted to go after her and tell her she had it all wrong, that I'd liked her for far longer than she thought.

But I couldn't. I had to think about Ember and my family and what it would mean to tell her the truth, especially if she didn't feel the same way. She hadn't admitted to wanting me to kiss her. At best, she'd deflected. But without concrete evidence, I wasn't sure I was willing to risk what we had.

I lowered myself into the rocking chair and dropped my head into my hands. She'd auction herself off to some great guy who'd know exactly what he had in Hanna. That thought made it hard to draw in a breath.

This time next year, she'd be living with some lucky guy, with his ring on her finger and babies on her mind.

What happened to my plan? The one where I was going to show her what she loved about me and Ember? I was so scared to mess up our friendship, but I was screwing everything up anyway.

My only option was the auction. I needed to plan the perfect date for her and make sure I won her. She was the prize.

I called Knox, and when he answered, I said, "I need your help to show Hanna how I feel about her."

Knox was quiet for a few seconds.

I checked the phone to make sure he was still on the line, and sure enough, the seconds were still ticking.

When I pressed the screen against my ear, he asked, "Are you serious?"

I closed my eyes and remembered how Hanna had felt in my arms just a few minutes ago in front of the tree. The expression on her face, the look in her eyes. I wanted her to look at me as if I were the only man for her. And if she felt the same tingle I got whenever I touched her, I couldn't let her meet someone else. "I can't let her move on with someone else when she doesn't know how I feel. How I've felt all these years."

"It's about time."

I let out a breath. "I just hope I'm not too late."

"I saw the flyers Marley and Ireland posted around town. The auction's all anyone is talking about."

I ran a hand through my hair. "That's what I'm worried about. You know she's a catch. She's sweet, caring, and great with kids."

"I'm happy to help with whatever you need. But make sure you're doing this for the right reasons. Are you pursuing her because we've teased you all these years about her liking you, or because a relationship with her makes sense? She's already your friend, and you're living together—"

"I've never felt this way about anyone else. What if she's the one, and I've ignored it because I was worried about what it would mean for our friendship? I can't sit back and watch her date someone else. Not when she doesn't know how I feel. I need this chance."

"Okay. Okay. I believe you. I'll do whatever you need me to do. What did you have in mind?"

I sighed. "This is a big ask. I'm not even sure it's possible." I sighed, then relayed my idea. Marley and Ireland already had other dates planned, but this one would be mine. I didn't want anyone else's input except possibly Knox's.

"I'll look into it and do whatever I can to make it happen."

"You don't think it's too much?"

"I think it's romantic as fuck. Are you sure you want to take this step? She won't have any doubt after you bid on her, win, then show her the date you planned."

"That's the idea." I thought about using one of Marley's dates, and they were nice, but I wanted something that was all me. "You think Talon could help, too? I saw what he did with the pond."

"You can ask. He's busy with a commissioned piece, but he might have time for this."

"I hope so. I need all the help I can get."

"I'm proud of you. You're finally going after what you want."

"It feels right." Instead of feeling scared, I was hopeful. I was finally doing something about this crazy attraction to Hanna. I planned to go all out and leave nothing on the table.

"What if you don't win?" Knox asked.

"I was hoping you could help with that. You have any pull with Marley? You think she can help a bit?"

Knox chuckled. "I think she wants it to look real. If she altered the results, how would that look? I think you have to come prepared to spend some money."

"I'll do whatever it takes to get her. No matter what it costs."

"The other guys won't stand a chance, especially since I suspect she likes you, too."

I ran a hand through my hair. "Hanna said she wants to start dating again. She's ready to get married and start a family." The panic flowed through me, making me feel sick.

Knox chuckled. "I think she's tired of waiting for you to make a move."

I stood and paced the porch. "I'm going to tell her how I feel. How I've always felt. I just hope she feels the same way and hasn't moved on from whatever feelings she's had for me." If she ever had any at all.

~

I woke to a bouncing bed and high-pitched squeals. "Daddy, Daddy, it snowed. It snowed. You have to come see."

I opened my eyes, blinded by the white shining through the curtains.

Ember jumped off the bed, and I was too tired to remind her not to jump on or off beds. Then she opened the curtains, and I used my arm to block the glare. "See? It's snowing."

"I can see that," I said, my voice hoarse. The clock read seven. I could have used a few more minutes of sleep, but Ember's excitement was easy to get caught up in. "Do you think we should eat some pancakes and then go outside?"

"Snow, snow, snow," she cheered, ignoring my questions as she ran down the hallway to her room, presumably to get dressed.

I swung my foot over the side of the bed and sighed. Sometimes I wished I had someone to share parenthood with, but I wouldn't want to be with Ember's mother. I still had a chance with Hanna, though.

I got up, washed my face, brushed my teeth, and threw on long johns under my jeans and hoodie.

When I was ready, Ember came skidding down the hallway. "Let's go!"

I held up my hands, hoping she'd listen to reason. "Let's eat first. We need energy to build a snowman."

Ember sighed. "All right."

"What do you think about pumpkin pancakes?" I asked as I followed her down the hall.

Ember shot me a disgusted look over her shoulder. "Ew, Daddy. Gross."

"Maybe Hanna likes them," I mused.

"No one likes those," she mumbled as she made her way down the steps.

The door to Hanna's room opened, and she leaned out the door. "What's going on?"

"I'm sorry. We didn't mean to wake you," I said as I took her in, one cheek red with a crease, her hair sticking up, and her nipples clearly visible through the white, silky top.

"It snowed." Ember reversed course and ran up the stairs to tug on her hand. "We're going to play after we eat."

"Let Hanna get ready for the day. She probably wants to get dressed." She needed to get dressed or I wouldn't survive breakfast.

Hanna shot me a grateful grin. "I'd love to join you. Just give me a few minutes to make myself presentable."

She was dressed appropriately for what I wanted to do to her. But my daughter was present, and I needed to get my dick under control. It wasn't the time or place for him to be at attention.

Hanna's door shut softly behind her, and we continued downstairs. I grabbed the pancake mix, eggs, milk, and a bowl before going through my usual Sunday routine on a Saturday.

The TV in the living room clicked on. Ember was allowed to watch cartoons in the morning if she wasn't helping me cook.

Since it was a snow day and I needed time to calm down after our encounter with Hanna in the hallway, I didn't insist she help me this morning. Instead, I pushed play on a holiday music playlist and used the time to think about anything other than Hanna's nipples.

Her breasts were full underneath that shirt, and I wanted to palm them, run a thumb over one hard nub, and suck on the other.

I shook my head, forcing myself to think about the bachelorette auction and the other men who'd be bidding on her. It worked to get my mind off her naked body.

When she padded down the stairs a few minutes later, I felt less distracted and was able to smile at her without feeling any guilt about my wayward thoughts. "Morning."

"Morning."

"Sorry about waking you up. We don't get snow every day, and she was excited."

Hanna waved a hand in my direction. "You already apologized, and there's no need."

"I bet you'll be happy to move into your own place and have peace and quiet."

Hanna slid onto a stool at the island, watching me crack the egg on the side of the bowl. "I kind of like it here."

"You like being awakened every morning by a seven-year-old?" I asked, amusement tinging my voice. I found that hard to believe. It's why I'd been so reluctant to date over the years. I was busy with Ember, but I also knew having kids was a lot of work, and it was too much to ask of someone who wasn't already a parent.

"This place feels like a home. I enjoy waking up to the sound of your voices and laughter."

Her comment warmed my chest. "Then you're never going to want to leave."

She laughed, but the sound was off. I wasn't sure exactly what that meant. Would she be happy to move on from us? The thought left me feeling chilled.

I mixed the batter and poured it into the pan. I was so used to doing this, it had become routine, and I didn't have to think about what I was doing. Instead, I was hyperaware of the woman sitting at my counter.

I was going to miss her when it went back to being just me and Ember. I enjoyed her company as much as she enjoyed ours.

"Are you ready for the bachelorette auction?" I asked, even as my heart picked up at the thought.

"Ireland and Marley are handling most of the details. We'll help decorate."

The guys were in charge of my idea, with strict instructions to keep the women away from the area and not to give away any details. "What's the plan for the event and the dates?"

"We'll hold the auction itself in the barn, the one you usually reserve for family events. Five women will be auctioned, including me and Holly. One of the dates will be the hot tub, a second will be the gazebo, the third will be a carriage ride and picnic meal at the pond, the fourth will be in the middle of one of the Christmas tree fields, and the fifth we haven't figured out yet."

"Did anyone sign up for the auction itself?" I would be surprised if anyone did.

"We had a ton of applicants. We had to limit it to those over the age of twenty-two to eliminate college students. Marley was worried if college kids came, they wouldn't take it seriously. It would be an opportunity for them to have fun and party. Not find a significant other."

I stilled as I watched the pancakes cook. "You think that one of these women could find a man they'd want to be with?"

"Absolutely. Why? You don't?"

I turned to look at her. "I'm not sure. I guess you could find someone who was serious about a relationship, but you could get a lot of guys looking for a good time. One night with a beautiful woman."

"Hmm. I just want to meet someone nice who has the potential of being something more."

My heart pounded in my chest because I met that criteria. I felt the potential of something more like a fire simmering just beneath the surface of my skin. All she had to do was light the match to set me free.

I flipped the pancakes so she wouldn't see my expression. I was positive that my emotions were written clearly on my face. I just had to get through this week, and then I could put my plan into action.

"You honestly think you'll meet the one?" I asked, my voice shaking. I hoped she didn't notice.

Hanna shrugged. "Sure. Why not?"

I didn't have a response for that. "I'm just not sure what kind of guy would respond to a call for a bachelorette auction."

"I think it would be someone who was serious about finding someone special. Not someone looking for a good time. He has to pay money to take me on the date. And that's before we've had a chance to meet and talk. It's a risk."

That's what I was afraid of. These guys would be serious about a relationship. Someone playing the field wouldn't want to spend a lot of money or take the time to woo a woman. I just hoped none of them were as determined to be with Hanna as I was.

It was going to be a long week, and I wasn't sure I'd survive it.

# CHAPTER 10

## SEBASTIAN

We ate breakfast at the table, then bundled up to go outside. From what I could see, flakes had been coming down at an angle. I was excited in a way I hadn't been in a long time. When was the last time I got excited by the prospect of snow?

When we opened the door, we were hit with a gust of wind.

"They said there'd be drifting. It will make clearing the lane difficult."

Hanna touched my arm through the thick layer of my jacket. "I wouldn't worry about it too much. The storm will end, and you'll have time to do whatever you need to do."

I rubbed my hands together. "What should we do first? A snowman or sledding?"

"A snowman!" Ember exclaimed, so I tested the snow in my hands, packed a snowball, and then threw one in Hanna's direction. I was careful to aim lower so it wouldn't explode in her face.

"Hey!" Hanna yelled as she reached for the snow and packed her own snowball. "Come on, Ember. Let's get him."

Ember giggled. "Snowball fight."

I ducked behind a tree and quickly built a small arsenal of balls. I just hoped my brothers didn't show up. They took snowball fights too seriously, and someone usually ended up getting hit in the face multiple times. I peeked out from behind the tree to see the girls building a fort.

I lobbed a snowball over it to see if they were ready to engage. They ducked down, and I heard giggling. I smiled, my chest full. I couldn't think of a better way to spend the morning.

I let a second one fly, but this time, they reared up and let a ton of snowballs fly in quick succession. I bit off a curse as I dove back behind the tree. I waited for the deluge to slow, then threw a few balls back at them.

Each time, there were giggles. It made my heart feel light, as if anything were possible. There was no way a stranger could walk into Hanna's life and claim her heart. Not when I'd had my stake in it since we were teens.

Hanna was mine. I just had to show her.

Lost in my thoughts, I didn't realize they were sneaking up on me until it was too late. They were a few feet away when they let their balls fly. I covered my face and tried to move away from them. But they followed.

I reached for them with one hand shielding my face. They were laughing so hard they were stumbling in the snow. I was able to easily hook Hanna's shoulders and pull her into my body. I reached for Ember, but she darted away.

Then I was falling to my side, taking the brunt of the fall as Hanna landed on top of me. I quickly moved so that she was underneath me and I was straddling her. I'd pulled her wrists together over her head and anchored them there.

Her chest was heaving and her cheeks rosy as I gazed down at her. I'd never seen anyone more beautiful. The blue jacket brought out the hue of her eyes, and this close, I saw flecks of yellow.

"What are you going to do to me?" Hanna asked.

It might have been an innocent question, but my dick had taken it in an entirely different direction. With the object of my desire underneath me, it had one objective in mind, plowing into her and not the snow.

I moved to let go of her hands when I was struck with a snowball on the side of my face.

"Let her go."

I released my hold on Hanna and stood, needing to get to my arsenal of snowballs, but Ember was standing over them, throwing them at us.

Hanna raised a hand to protect her face. "Hey! You're supposed to be on my team."

I reached for her, and she placed her hand in mine while we ran away from Ember, rounding the house and hiding behind the side of the deck. I pulled her into my arms.

Hanna's eyes were wide. "Do you think she'll find us?"

I chuckled. "Oh, yeah. This is her favorite hiding spot when we're playing hide-and-seek."

Hanna shot me an incredulous look. "Then why are we here?"

In that moment, I couldn't register anything but the redness of her lips, that the lower one was fuller than the top, and how I wanted to nibble on it.

Hanna's gaze searched my face. "Seb. What are you doing?"

Seb. Only my brothers called me that. I could count on my hand the number of times that Hanna had. It came out soft and pleading, and my dick was standing at attention, ready to do her bidding.

"Found you!" Ember declared, and we stiffened.

But Ember wasn't holding anything. "Are you ready to make that snowman? I'm cold."

Hanna stood first and pulled her hair out of her hood, brushing the ice off her neck. I felt like a bad parent for not considering that snowball fights were cold and messy.

"That was fun," Ember said with a smile for both of us.

Hanna smiled. "It sure was."

When Hanna was done cleaning her off, Ember said, "It's more fun when Hanna's here."

That sent a pang to my heart. I wanted Ember to like Hanna, but what if Hanna liked someone else? What if she made her own family and left us? I wouldn't be able to withstand the pain. I brushed away the melancholy thoughts and grinned. "I think so, too."

"You two are good for my ego," Hanna said as she brushed off her butt and led the way around the house to the front.

"Because we selfishly love having you live with us?" I teased her, bumping her shoulder with mine.

Hanna laughed, and the sound was a balm to my soul. If Hanna was happy, I was, too. I wondered if I would be if she found another man that she could love. I'd like to say I would support her, but I wasn't sure I was capable of that.

I packed the snow carefully before rolling it. With Ember's and Hanna's encouragement, we got the size just right and then placed it in front of the porch, where anyone driving up could see it.

This time, Ember helped me with the second one, and I told her how to get the snow packed just right. Then I helped her place the smaller ball on top of the base. Then the head.

"We need a hat, a scarf, and a nose." Ember ran inside, leaving us alone.

"This is fun," Hanna said.

"I can't remember a better morning." Waking up to Hanna, pancakes, the snowball fight, and now this.

Hanna raised her face so that the breeze caught the ends of her hair and lifted it. "Being on the farm is magical. I can let all the worries about my job go when I'm here. There's no noise or other people. It's just us."

"And my large family."

"Yeah, but they don't intrude. Does your mom ever show up at your house because she lives so close?"

"Not since I've lived here, but she's always promised she'd give us privacy if we built a cabin here. We can go to the main house if we want to visit. Of course, she makes that enticing with the food she always has on hand. I just wish my dad were still here to enjoy us all living together again."

"Your family is special. Not many would all move home to take care of their mother."

I laughed, feeling a little uncomfortable. "I wouldn't say that."

"Your father built this place, and you're ensuring it will be a viable business for future generations. You're holding a bachelorette auction when I know you hate the idea."

I chuckled. "I wouldn't say I hate it."

She gave me a shrewd look. "You're not a fan."

I couldn't lie to her. "You could say that."

"But you're willing to do whatever it takes for the farm to be successful," she said, as if she were working something out in her head.

"And for my mom to be supported. Mom always said the farm was her retirement. It meant safety and security. The bottom dropped out when my dad died. We didn't expect it. We thought we'd have more time before we needed to step up." I lifted my hand, gesturing at the blanket of snow and the trees. "But this is our family's legacy. We'd do anything to protect and nurture it."

"It's commendable that you're concerned about your mother enough to all live on the land, raise your families, and make the business work."

"I'm more the numbers guy. I don't have anything to do with the trees, other than ensuring they're profitable. That's why I've taken a step back on Marley's ideas. If it brings in more money, then it's worth it. Besides, Mom's excited about it. She's hoping it pulls Talon out of his funk and forces him to talk to Holly and fix whatever the issue is between them so he can move on and find someone.

"They were hot and heavy in high school. It's almost as if something happened. Like someone cheated. I don't have any proof, but it was a quick cooling-off period. And there was no information about what happened. There was speculation, but nothing that rang true.

"Talon wouldn't have cheated on her. At least I don't think so." I sighed. "I guess he could have. Teenagers don't always make the best decisions. I hope they're able to clear their history so both can move on."

"You don't think that they'd get back together, do you?"

"They refuse to talk to each other, so probably not. I think they could forgive each other and let go of whatever it was. But I don't see them getting back together."

Ember burst through the door, forgetting, then going back to shut it. "I got everything we need."

She threw everything on the ground between us. "A scarf and a hat."

"That's one of Hanna's scarves. You can't take things without asking."

"Can I use your scarf? I only have one." Ember pleaded, with her hands clasped in front of her face.

"I don't mind. Our snowman has to be dressed properly."

"Right?" Ember said, taking a knit hat and trying to fit it around the head. She finally discarded it, picking up the plastic fireman's hat that must have been a dress-up toy. Then Ember put the small carrot in the center of his face.

Hanna helped her wrap the scarf around the neck. Then we hunted for rocks for the eyes, mouth, and buttons.

When we were done placing the items, Hanna said, "It's perfect. Can we take a picture?"

Ember posed in front of the snowman, and we took a few of her in different positions.

"Get in there with her." Hanna gestured toward me.

I wrapped an arm around Ember, and Hanna smiled as she snapped a few pictures.

Was it too much to ask if Hanna could be ours this Christmas?

I snatched the phone from Hanna's hand and hauled her to my side. "We have to take a selfie."

I held up the phone and snapped several pictures of all three of us snuggling close. Hanna looked happy, her cheeks red from the cold and her eyes bright.

"Thanks for a great morning. If I was snowed in at my apartment, I would have spent the day watching TV and maybe baking cookies. But I would have been alone. This was so much better," Hanna said as we scrolled through the images.

"You're always welcome here with us," was all I could manage because my throat was tight. I cleared my throat, then asked, "What do you say? Is it time for sledding?"

"Yes!" Ember cried, running toward the garage.

"I'll lock up, grab the sleds, and then we can walk to the main house. You're coming with us?"

"Of course. I wouldn't miss it. I haven't been sledding since I was a little girl."

"Be right back." I walked with long strides to the porch, going through the house to open the garage door. I grabbed a few plastic sleds before heading back outside and handing the girls the strings. "We can just pull these."

Ember didn't waste any time taking the string and running down the lane. We followed more slowly. "You can ride with me. I only have two. But the rest of my family might show up."

"Is Addy coming?" Ember yelled over her shoulder.

"I texted Uncle Knox and told him to meet us there."

She whooped and ran harder down the hill.

"I love seeing her so happy," I said, my mouth moving without a filter. I was caught up in the joy of the day. The snow coming down was already blanketing the ground and trees. It was a winter wonderland.

Hanna looked at me with something akin to affection in her expression. She let her head fall back and opened her mouth to catch the flakes on her tongue.

I laughed. "I haven't tried to catch snowflakes since I was a kid. My brothers probably made fun of me."

Hanna smiled. "Sometimes it's nice to just let go."

I grabbed her hand and smiled. "I think we made a promise about letting go of everything until after the holidays."

We were both wearing gloves, so I couldn't feel the heat of her palm, but I felt the connection in my heart. "That's still my plan," she said.

We were quiet for a few seconds, content to walk through the snow. There were probably a few inches on the ground and a few more to come.

I squeezed her hand and grinned. "I can't believe I waited so long to build the cabin."

"You thought living in town was best for Ember."

"This is what's best for her. Here, she's surrounded by family who loves her, and she has you."

Hanna shrugged. "I'm just a friend."

"You're so much more than that. Don't sell yourself short. You've been there for us from the beginning. I can't tell you how much I appreciate it. Without you, I couldn't have done it."

"I know for a fact that you have your mom's and your brothers' help.

I draped an arm over her shoulder. "I'm so lucky to have all of you."

"Come on. Addy's already here," Ember called to us.

We hadn't been paying attention because the main house was already in sight. Knox and Sarah were at the bottom of the hill as Addy glided down. They shouted and encouraged her.

Their puppy, who was about a year old now, bounded around in the snow, the white stuff covering his nose.

"Comet loves the snow," I said.

I cherished the few minutes we had just to ourselves. I could almost imagine us dating. That this was just another snow day we spent together as a family. This was our life. Evenings on the porch, pancakes for breakfast, and days spent playing together, baking cookies, and having fun.

Sarah and Knox walked up the hill, towing Addy on the sled.

"You survived the storm?" Knox asked when he reached us.

I rested the sled at the top of the hill and waited while Ember climbed onto it. "It's not a big one. Just enough to have some fun. But I bet it will be gone in a few days."

"Enjoy it while you can." Knox set Addy's sled next to Ember's.

"Are you ready for a push?" I asked as I moved behind the girls.

"We're ready," they both cried as they gripped the sides, and Knox and I pushed them.

They screamed all the way down, making us smile.

"There's nothing like living life through a kid's eyes. Before Addy, I'd be annoyed that I had to clear the lane, and a day off was missed profit," Knox mused.

"And now?" I asked.

"It's one more day I can spend with my family."

Sarah hugged Knox, and he kissed the top of her head.

My heart squeezed at their connection. I wanted what they had. I wanted Hanna to look at me the way Sarah looked at Knox.

Was it possible for us, or were we doomed to be friends forever?

# CHAPTER 11

## SEBASTIAN

The girls flew down the hill, screaming and then laughing when they came to a stop at the bottom. They immediately jumped up to do it again.

"It's your turn," I said to Hanna, placing the larger sled at the top of the hill. I sat first, then gestured for her to climb in.

Hanna shot me a dubious look before she glanced over at the girls, who were pulling their sleds up the hill, and finally nodded. "Let's do this."

I carefully avoided looking at Sarah or Knox while she settled in front of me. Even between our thick layers of clothes, I was hyperaware of her body pressed to mine.

I placed a hand on her stomach and eased her back slightly so that her back was pressed to my front.

Then I turned to Knox, who was watching us with an amused expression. "Can you give me a push? A *light* push?" I quickly corrected. Back in the day, my brothers were known to go overboard.

Thankfully, he only ran a few feet with his hands on my back before letting go. It was the perfect amount of momentum to send us down the hill at a decent clip, and not at breakneck speed. I didn't want to scare Hanna. I wanted to show her a good time.

I wrapped my arms firmly around her while her hands gripped my thighs on either side of her body. It felt good to have her so close, even though the ride was over almost as quickly as it started. When we came to a stop, Hanna popped up and said with a smile, "That was fun. Let's do it again."

Pleased, I got up a little slower and grabbed the sled's string. At the top of the hill, the girls were lining up for another ride. "Let's watch the girls come down."

Hanna moved closer, but I didn't reach out to touch her. I was aware that Knox and Sarah had been watching us closely. Knox knew how I felt, but I wasn't ready to broadcast it to everyone else. Not before I spoke to Hanna at the bachelorette auction.

The girls came flying down the mountain, their smiles wide and their cheeks pink as they came to a gliding stop next to us.

"That was so much fun, Daddy!" Ember exclaimed as she hopped off and waited for Addy to do the same.

I couldn't remember a time that I'd been happier. I had Ember, my family, and now Hanna here. I couldn't see how the day could get any better, but I was practically light-headed with anticipation.

I helped Addy when she tripped getting up, and we all walked up the hill together. The girls talked about how they could go faster down the hill, and I was content to just take it all in. At the top, Sarah and Knox had gotten onto their sled and were waiting for me to give them a push.

"Let's push them," Addy yelled to Ember, as they dropped the strings to their sleds and raced toward Knox. They both put their hands on his back and moved their feet, but it barely budged.

"I think we're too big," Knox finally said.

"Let me get in there," I said so the girls would think they were helping, too. With all three of us, they got off to a great start, and we could hear Sarah's screams all the way down.

"Let's go again," Addy said as they lined their sleds up, and I pushed.

"You want to go again?" I asked Hanna when we were alone.

Hanna smiled wide. "I'd love to."

We sledded down and climbed up the hill for an hour before Ireland and Emmett and then Marley and Heath showed up. No matter how grumpy we got over the holiday season and Christmas tree sales, we all loved a good snow day. Sure, there was stress about money and profit, but we could let go for a few hours and just have fun.

Eventually, Mom told us she had hot chocolate and cookies, and we took a break in the house.

"You have plans for the rest of the day?" Lori asked Hanna.

"I need to bake some cookies," Hanna said, and Ember nodded eagerly. "Then I heard something about a nighttime snowmobile run."

"After the kids are in bed," Heath said.

Knox and Sarah would stay with Addy and Ember so I could have some time alone with Hanna. I wasn't sure if Knox had told Sarah of my plan, but I was grateful he was taking Ember for the night.

When we went home, Hanna rolled the dough out on the counter, and Ember stood on a chair next to her, eager to help.

I excused myself to hang the extra lights on the deck. I had a feeling these would be a year-round decoration once the girls saw them. I chose white like the lights that hung on the paths around the property.

The lights had been a signature look for the farm over the years, giving it a year-round cozy quality. Everyone enjoyed them, even though Heath and Emmett originally hung them for my mom after my dad died.

I finished before the girls, since they were making multiple batches of cut-out cookies. By that time, Ember was ready for a break, so we set up in the living room with the TV to play a holiday movie. I enjoyed the lights on the deck, the decorated tree, the smell of baking cookies, and Hanna in my kitchen. It was the perfect day.

"This was the best day ever," Ember said to me as she snuggled against my shoulder.

"I think so, too." Then I called out to Hanna, "What should we do for dinner?"

"Lori offered to host dinner. Would you want to join them, or should we do our own thing?" Hanna asked from the kitchen.

"Own thing," Ember said sleepily.

"Let's stay in. We already had a busy day." I wanted nothing more than to snuggle with my girls on the couch, but I'd promised Hanna a snowmobile ride, and I couldn't wait to see her reaction.

I texted Mom our plans, and she wished us a relaxing night.

Together, we whipped up a quick chicken stir-fry and ate at the table. Afterward, we watched TV until it was time for Ember to go to Knox's house. I packed her a bag, and she perked up at the prospect of a sleepover.

When I returned, Hanna was ready in a snowsuit and winter gear.

"We don't have to go out." Although, the snow had stopped at six inches, and the wind had subsided. It was the perfect amount of snow for a ride.

Hanna was grinning widely, her eyes bright with anticipation. "I want to. I can't believe I've never been."

"I haven't been in a while, since we'd been living in town."

"Are you happy to be here now?" Hanna asked me as I pulled on my gear.

"Everything I've ever wanted is here." The truth filled every crevice of my heart.

If Hanna realized I was including her in my comment, she didn't let on. She waited patiently for me to get dressed, and then we headed outside to the snowmobiles. The guys had helped me get them off the trailer in the garage earlier in the day. I was ecstatic to finally get to use them.

"When we were teens, we had so much fun on these. Mom worried about us, but Dad knew we'd get into trouble whether they condoned the outing or not. He gave us the freedom to be us." Even if I was more subdued than my brothers, I always had a good time. Dad usually said something to me about keeping my brothers in line. I wasn't always successful, but I liked to think I had a calming effect on them.

"We're just taking out one?" Hanna asked when I got one ready.

"Yeah, you can drive next time." It was a selfish move on my part. I wanted her on the back of my snowmobile with her legs wrapped around me. It was also partly for safety. She needed to learn how to drive it before I'd let her go out on her own.

"That makes sense."

I got on first and motioned for her to climb on behind me. Her hands rested tentatively on my waist until I pulled them tighter around my middle. That brought her front flush to my back.

Her legs tightened around me.

"Are you nervous?" I asked over my shoulder, the wind whipping my voice away.

She nodded against my back where her head rested. "A little."

"Just hold on tight. I've got you."

"That's what I'm hoping."

I revved the engine, and we took off. We were meeting Heath, Marley, Emmett, and Ireland on the trails by Heath's house. We didn't stop when we saw them. They just fell in line beside us, and we rode to the illuminated pond and around the perimeter.

The night air was cool, and the snow blanketing the ground gave the farm a hushed quality. No one spoke or called out. Not like when we were kids and would scream and holler to one another. On the way back, Heath and Marley peeled off at their house, then we dropped off Emmett and Ireland.

"I have a feeling they have other plans for the evening," Hanna whispered in my ear when we stopped briefly to wave goodbye.

"I bet," I said, even though my throat was dry at the prospect of spending time alone with Hanna. We had the evening to ourselves, since Ember was at Addy's. But I wasn't ready to bare my soul to her. Not yet. That was what the bachelorette auction was for, but I could lay the groundwork for what I wanted tonight.

We headed home and parked the snowmobile in the garage.

When we removed our helmets, I asked, "Did you have a good time?"

"The best." Hanna grinned at me, and the happiness in her eyes was contagious. Her cheeks were red, and her hair was wild and frizzy down her back.

"You ready to warm up?" I held my hand out to her.

She rested her hand in mine as we walked inside. We removed our clothing and settled on the couch. The fire was on, and the overhead lights were off, so we could enjoy the lights on the tree and the deck. "Your home looks great."

"It exceeded my expectations, but that was all Heath. This was his first solo project as a contractor, and he wanted to do a good job."

"He did, but you made it a home with the holiday decorations and the warm and inviting furniture."

"It wouldn't be the same without you here." She was what made my home inviting.

Hanna looked at me curiously but didn't ask any follow-up questions about what I meant by my comment.

Instead, she rested her head on my shoulder. A move she'd done dozens of times over the years. But this time, I lifted my arm and let her head roll to my chest. Her palm rested over my pounding heart.

Instead of revealing my feelings, I clicked on the TV and navigated to a holiday movie I knew we'd both enjoy. The best part about being in love with my best friend was that I knew everything about her wants and desires. Her favorite movies, the flowers she preferred, and even her hopes and dreams. The only thing I wasn't sure of was her feelings for me.

I pushed aside the anxiety and enjoyed being in the moment with her. Her hair tickled my chin, and the warmth of her palm seared my skin through the thin cotton of my shirt. When her breath evened out, I let myself enjoy every inch of her that was touching me.

Eventually, I must have drifted off, too, because when I jerked awake, it was still dark out, but we were lying on our sides, Hanna's back to my front. My hand was draped over her waist.

I breathed her in, reveling in the warmth of her body and the closeness. I quickly fell back asleep, content.

~

When I woke up the next morning, I was alone on the couch. Hanna must have slipped away at some point. Hearing a noise in the kitchen, I swung my legs over the side of the couch, stretching the muscles in my neck that were sore from sleeping in a cramped position all night.

I stood and moved toward the kitchen counter.

"You're awake," Hanna observed.

"We must have fallen asleep on the couch," I said, unsure how she would react.

Hanna smiled. "Yeah, when I realized it, I moved to my bed."

The words, *You didn't have to, and I enjoyed sleeping with you in my arms,* got stuck in my throat. I couldn't admit any of that out loud yet. I had a plan, and I needed to stick with it.

I didn't have an impulsive bone in my body, which drove my brothers crazy over the years. But it had served me well. Patience was key to this plan, and I had that in spades. I'd waited this long to tell her how I felt; I could wait a few more days.

"I cooked eggs." Hanna transferred the fried eggs from the pan to two plates that were garnished with cut-up strawberries and avocados.

"I wasn't expecting this," I said as I sat down, grabbing a fork and digging in. "It's nice to have someone other than my mother cook for me."

Hanna laughed and pointed between us. "Don't get used to it. This is temporary."

I could have said there was no rush for her to leave, but I'd said it before. I could only hope telling her how I felt would change everything. If it was too late, I'd have to deal with that, too. Hopefully, our friendship would survive.

Hanna sat next to me, and we ate in relative silence. Music played softly from her phone. "I love the holiday season."

"I'll be happy when it's over. Then I only have to worry about my regular job." It was something I'd said a million times during the months of November and December, but I wasn't sure it was true anymore.

"Do you think the events you held this year will add to the bottom line for the farm?" Hanna asked.

She wasn't privy to the family meetings about finances, but I'd filled her in over the years. "I hope so. I've already seen an increase in customers buying trees. One can assume it came from Marley's efforts to increase marketing online and through newsletters. Then there was the movie night we held."

A slow smile spread over Hanna's face. "You've definitely increased your brand awareness, as Marley would say."

I nodded. "She's good at that stuff."

"Is she still running her online business?" Hanna cut into her eggs and popped them into her mouth.

"As far as I know. She has mentioned a few times that she already built the courses, and she'll place them on sale throughout the year to promote them. I have a feeling she built her business, and she can coast through the year."

"What about her house in California?"

"She's keeping it so they can use it for vacations. She loves the beach. I think they're planning on going in January after the season is over."

Hanna's eyes clouded over. "I don't get to go on vacations at all. What's the point when you'd go on them by yourself?"

I took care of my dish and moved to the carafe to pour a cup of coffee. "I didn't know you wanted to travel."

Hanna shrugged. "Everyone enjoys a week at the beach. When we were kids, we traveled with my family, but only to the beaches within driving distance. I'd love to go to the Caribbean, maybe try a cruise, or even go to Europe."

I never thought much about traveling. I had enough to keep myself busy here, but the idea didn't sound terrible. Not if I was spending that time with Hanna and Ember. "I should plan a beach trip with Ember. I get so caught up in work that I forget that most families go on vacations in the summer."

Hanna shook her head, her eyes pinched with regret. "I didn't mention it to make you feel bad. There are no rules about how to parent. You can do whatever feels right."

"But it's a good reminder about what else I could be doing. I'm sure Ember would love to go to the beach."

Hanna braced a hand on the counter. "You could make it a family trip. Do any of your brothers go on vacation?"

I chuckled. "No one has time. Our lives are full, between our jobs and the farm."

"You're busy guys, but you have to take the time to rest and recuperate. Maybe that's why you're so run-down by December. You work hard and don't take any time to play." Hanna grinned, and I couldn't help but think about what she meant by the word *play*. I resisted the urge to cross the room and kiss her.

My heart was thumping wildly in my chest, and I couldn't get the image out of my head. I wanted Hanna, and I couldn't see my life feeling complete without her in it. I wanted to wake up and come home to her every day. I wanted to go on vacations with her. Build a life with her. I wouldn't be the same without her.

I had a feeling that Hanna was the woman for me. I hadn't met anyone, not because I'd been busy as a single father, but because she was the one.

My phone buzzed with a text from Knox.

**Knox: We're on our way over. The girls had fun last night. They stayed up until ten, watching movies. Then they fell asleep in the fort in the living room.**

**Sebastian: Thanks for watching Ember for me.**

**Knox: I hope you took advantage of the situation.**

I shook my head, even though he couldn't see me.

**Sebastian: I'm sticking to the plan.**

**Knox: Why am I not surprised? One day, that's going to bite you in the ass.**

I hoped it wasn't this week or the bachelorette auction. I needed to make Hanna see how I felt about her, and making an impulsive move on her because Ember wasn't home wasn't enough. She would think it was a onetime thing, and that was not the impression I wanted to make.

I lifted my head from the screen. "Knox is on his way over with Ember."

"I want Ember to help me decorate the rest of the cookies."

Most of the cookies were in tins, but there was a batch that was on the counter, without any icing. "Thank you for doing that with Ember. I'm not a baker, and I don't want to leave her at my mom's all the time."

"I'm happy to help any time. You know that."

The thing was, I didn't want her help. I wanted her love. Now I just had to earn it.

# CHAPTER 12

## HANNA

Between work, watching Ember, and planning the bachelorette auction with Marley and Ireland, it had been a busy week. By Saturday, I was drained.

I should have been looking forward to fulfilling my New Year's resolution to date. I was going to put myself out there, but I felt off.

Sebastian had been acting weird all week. He was even busier than usual at work, and we didn't see him until after Ember's bedtime. He was home in the morning for a few minutes, then rushed out the door to get to work.

It wasn't tax season yet, so I wasn't sure what his deal was. Unless he was avoiding me. Maybe our living situation wasn't working out for him. That hurt because I loved living here with them.

It felt warm and cozy, almost like we were a real family. Ember had mentioned several times how she enjoyed it, too. But maybe Sebastian didn't like having me in his space.

It was better to know that now than after I revealed my feelings for him. The thought that this crush I had on Sebastian wasn't reciprocated, hurt. But it made me more determined to make a good effort to talk to whomever won a date with me at the auction.

In the morning, I left Ember with Sebastian so I could help Marley, Ireland, and Sarah finish decorating the barn.

When I arrived, Harrison, who worked with Ireland at Happily Ever Afters, the wedding planning service, was carrying in the planks for the stage. Since it was winter, the entire event would be inside, at least until everyone paired off to experience the dates.

The response from the community had been great. People loved the idea of having the date so soon after the auction. It alleviated the stress of calling the person or them changing their mind.

Marley had even used this for marketing. *Do you need a date for the holidays? Don't want to be alone when the ball drops? We've got you covered. Ladies, auction yourself off for one amazing date, and guys, bid on a lovely woman.*

The interior of the barn was covered in white, pink, and red flowers, which Sophie supplied from her shop in town, Petals.

We decided not to go with a holiday theme in the barn, but rather a romantic one. For the dates, it was red, green, and white. We figured we needed to use the Christmas tree farm to our benefit. It was a beautiful backdrop.

When the barn was finished, we ate lunch at the main house, and then Marley hired makeup artists and hairstylists to style the bachelorettes. There were five of us, including Holly, Daphne, Rhiannon, and Stacey. We used the bedrooms upstairs to get ready. The guys were running the farm, and Lori was in charge of the shop for the day.

"Do you think any guys will actually show up?" I asked, voicing my nerves out loud.

Marley's mouth dropped open. "Hush. Don't even breathe that possibility into the universe. We've had an amazing response. I've gotten so many questions from guys about the event and the dates themselves. We even had some individual requests."

"What do you mean?" I asked as the makeup artist lifted my chin to examine her work on my cheeks.

"Some of the guys offered to pay more to add their own spin to the date. If they win, of course."

I closed my eyes as the artist applied the eye makeup. "I can't believe so many guys are willing to meet a woman this way."

"Here's what I figured out from the emails and comments on social media. Guys are tired of online dating apps, and they feel like they can't talk to a woman in a coffee shop or on the street because everyone has earbuds in. You can't just strike up a conversation in the grocery store anymore," Marley said as the stylist blew out her hair.

"I hadn't thought of it like that. But I don't wear earbuds."

"Your heart has been taken for a long time. You haven't been open to the idea of finding someone until now," Holly said gently.

I frowned. "What are you talking about?"

"Sebastian. We all thought you'd end up with him." Before I could protest, she continued. "This is the first time you've made an effort to meet someone."

"I've dated." I chewed my lip nervously. If it was obvious to the girls, wouldn't Sebastian already know? It was telling he hadn't made any kind of move.

"Not seriously. Can you be honest with yourself? How many of those guys did you give a fair chance to?"

I thought back to the last few dates. I'd gone on them because my friends bugged me to go. I'd looked for things that I could label as a red flag. One had just broken up with a girlfriend. He was just getting out of a serious relationship. He wasn't a good bet. Another one jumped from one job to another. Instead of thinking he wanted to find something that fulfilled him, I assumed it meant he couldn't commit. "You might be right."

I could say I wasn't ready to meet the right guy. But the truth was more like I had already found someone I felt potential with. The only problem was—he didn't want me.

Holly reached over to squeeze my hand. "I'm proud of you for putting yourself out there."

"I could say the same about you." I opened my eyes as the makeup artist stepped away.

"I'm nervous about this. I'd like to meet someone, but I'm not sure I'm ready to be with anyone seriously," Holly said.

"This is for fun. A test run, if you will. Maybe you'll meet someone. Maybe you won't. No pressure," Marley said.

"That's easy for you to say. You're not being auctioned off to the highest bidder," I said to her, but my tone was light.

"True, but it's all in good fun." Marley's hair was curled at the bottom, and her lips were red and pouty.

Talk turned to the farm and the holidays, but all I could think about was whether I was making the right decision. Should I have told Sebastian how I felt?

When my hair and makeup were done, I stood with shaking legs and changed into the dress I'd picked for the evening. Marley had assured us we'd be standing on the stage while the guys bid on us, but it would be classy.

Admission for the event went to the farm, but the money from the auction went to a local animal rescue.

We drove over to the barn where the event was being held. When it was ready to start, Marley stood at the podium and thanked everyone for coming. "We want to have a fun night, and I hope you enjoy the farm this evening. Even if you don't win a date, you're free to walk through the light display. You can buy a tree this evening, too."

I was pleased that tonight wasn't solely focused on the

auction, but it was the main event. Nerves crept up again as Sebastian approached me. "Are you sure you want to do this?"

I laughed shakily. "I'm rethinking this whole thing."

He nudged me with his arm. "You wanted to date. This is the perfect opportunity."

"I keep telling myself that." But something had been bothering me all week. I couldn't shake the feeling that this wasn't a good idea. That I should have talked to Sebastian about how I felt instead of ignoring it and hoping it would go away.

The first woman went onto the stage, and the bidding began. Daphne smiled the entire time and seemed a little uncertain about men bidding on her.

Cole approached us to ask, "Who is that?"

"Her name's Daphne. I think Marley said she's the baker from that nearby farm you were talking about one day. Everyone loves her pies."

A shadow passed over Cole's face. "She works at Pine Valley Farms."

"Is that a bad thing?" I asked him.

"It's our competition. They're a smaller operation but closer to town, so they get more traffic than we do."

"I didn't realize."

"Obviously, Marley didn't either," Cole said as he strode closer to the stage.

"Do you think he's going to say something to Marley?" I asked Sebastian, but his eyes were on Cole, who'd lifted his hand to bid on Daphne.

"Do you think he likes her?" I asked Sebastian.

"I don't know Daphne, but in general, we don't associate with her family. They are our competition. We don't have anything to discuss with them that wouldn't be revealing our business strategies."

"Then why is he bidding on her?" I asked him.

"I have no idea."

I pursed my lips as someone else started bidding against Cole. "This is a little weird."

"It's all for a good cause," Sebastian reminded me.

"What if I don't like the guy that wins me? Then I'll have to spend hours with him on a romantic date." I hadn't thought this through. I'd assumed anyone I'd meet with would be a potential boyfriend for me. But if he wasn't right for me, then it would be an awkward evening. "If he's paid for me, I'd feel obligated to show him a good time."

Sebastian raised his brow.

"Not like that. But I'll have to stay for the entire date, whether I'm having a good time or not."

Sebastian's gaze locked on mine. "I think you're going to enjoy it."

I frowned. "How can you be so sure?"

Sebastian shrugged but didn't offer any more information. He looked relaxed, as if he didn't have a care in the world. He obviously wasn't concerned about other men bidding on me.

It shouldn't have bothered me, but it did. I was the one who wanted to go through with this. I wanted to move on from this crush, but I wasn't so sure I had. And it was becoming clearer by the moment that Sebastian wasn't phased by this at all.

A winner was declared, but I barely processed that it was Cole who walked on stage. After speaking with him, Marley announced that Cole had requested the hot tub date. There were cheers and a few boos from the men close to the stage.

I was relieved that I wouldn't have to get in a hot tub with a stranger but couldn't process anything else because I was next. I wiped my sweaty hands on the skirt of my dress when Marley called my name.

I'd asked to go early in the evening so I could get it over with. Maybe I could be done with the date in time for some TV with Sebastian.

I mentally shook my head. I was supposed to be looking

forward to meeting someone new, not ending the night with Sebastian. As I stood on the stage and looked out over the crowd, I wondered what I was thinking. Why was I so hung up on Sebastian?

I sought him out in the crowd, and when I found him, he winked at me. *He winked.* He was my friend. He wanted me to be happy. If I wanted to date, then that's what he wanted, too. He wasn't jealous of me seeing someone else.

I rolled my shoulders back. I was doing the right thing. Marley read through my short bio, the list of things I liked to do, my occupation as a teacher, and my love for kids. A few guys stepped forward, their gazes assessing.

When Marley opened the floor for bidding, there was a rapid-fire yelling of numbers. I felt dizzy and light-headed under the strong spotlights. I couldn't even focus on the voices or who was raising their numbers. Suddenly, I felt hot. Too hot.

I was going to pass out on the stage. I couldn't remember when I'd eaten last. But I was sure it was breakfast. There had been trays of food around all day, but I hadn't been able to eat. My stomach had been twisted up.

Just when it seemed like the calling out had slowed, Sebastian raised his arm.

*What is he doing?*

My skin felt hot and flushed, and I swayed slightly.

His bid, which was significantly higher than the others, sparked more bidding. That's when things got a little hazy. There were black spots in my vision; I swayed and couldn't right myself, falling backward. I didn't remember hitting the floor or blacking out.

There was a soft brush of fingers on my face. "Hanna, wake up."

It was Sebastian's voice. My eyes fluttered open, and it was his face that filled my vision. "What happened?"

"You fainted." His tone was filled with concern.

"It was so hot."

"Hanna," Sebastian chided, as I tried to sit up.

"Is it over?" My heart was racing, and I wanted nothing more than to escape from this room, the press of people around us, and the heavy weight of concern I felt.

"The auction? You were only the second person to go."

"Am I done?" I asked him, the panic rising in my chest.

"Let's get you out of here and get you something to eat." Sebastian took my hand and pulled me gently to my feet.

"Are you okay?" Marley asked, her face filled with concern.

"I'm okay. I just need fresh air."

"If she's up to it, you know where the date is," Marley said with a grin.

"What is she talking about?" I asked as Sebastian guided me through the crowd, grabbing my jacket from someone, and arranging it over my shoulders before opening the door.

I gratefully stepped into the night air, pulling my coat tighter around me. The crisp air helped, but I was still hungry and thirsty.

"Here, drink this." Sebastian handed me a bottled water.

I unscrewed the cap and let the water cool my throat. He led me over to a bench on the porch and guided me to sit. The music from inside was filtering through the windows, and Marley announced the next bachelorette.

"What happened in there?"

"I didn't feel good. I was so hot. Then I realized I hadn't eaten lunch or dinner."

Sebastian texted someone and then tucked his phone away. "Heath will bring you a few crackers."

"Thank you. But you don't have to stay with me. You can go back inside and enjoy the evening."

"I'm here for you."

I wanted to ask what he meant, but the door opened, and

Heath strode out with a sleeve of crackers. "Here you go. Are you feeling better?"

I took the offered crackers. "I think I'm just hungry."

Heath squeezed Sebastian's shoulder. "You think she's up for it?"

I didn't register what he meant by that.

"We'll see," Sebastian said.

Then Heath nodded at him and said, "Take care of her."

"I'll be fine. I think I'm going to head home. You can enjoy your evening." I knew he didn't get many nights without Ember, and Lori was watching the girls tonight.

"I won a date," Sebastian said as he relaxed, with his hand over the back of the bench.

I tensed. Had I been out longer than I thought? "You won a date with someone?"

"With the most beautiful woman in the room."

Cole had won Daphne, and I was the second woman to be auctioned off. What was he talking about?

Thinking I'd missed something important, and not wanting to see him on a date with another woman, I moved to stand.

Sebastian grabbed my wrist, and when my gaze met his, he said, "You're my date."

I rested back on the bench. "What are you talking about?" Then I remembered he'd bid on me. "Did you bid on me, or was I out of it and imagining things?"

Was this all a dream? I'd wake up, and this whole thing wouldn't have been real. I'd still be living with Sebastian and hiding my feelings for him.

A slow smile spread over his face. "I was the highest bidder. Or at least Marley declared it when you went down."

"The bidding wasn't finished when I fainted?" I was so confused. Why had Sebastian bid on me? Why would he want to?

"Marley had just said I was the winner when you started falling backward."

I touched my head. "Nothing hurts. Did I hit my head?"

"Heath caught you. He was standing just off to the side and saw you go down. I just wish I'd been standing closer."

"I'll have to thank him." If he wasn't there, I would have gotten a goose egg on my head, and probably a headache.

"If he hadn't caught you, I wouldn't be able to take you on our date. There's food there. If you can eat a few crackers, will you feel well enough to ride the golf cart over?"

"Oh, you don't have to take me out. I can ask Marley to award the date to someone else."

Sebastian frowned. "Why would you do that?"

"You didn't mean to win me, did you? You were just bidding so I wouldn't feel like I wasn't desirable." Why else would a friend bid on me? The other possibility was too crazy to even mention out loud. I didn't want him to laugh.

Sebastian shook his head. "I bid on you because I want to take you on a date. In fact, I planned something special for you."

I wasn't processing anything he was saying. "I planned the dates. Which one is it?"

Sebastian grinned as if he was pleased with himself. "I planned the entire thing from start to finish."

"Marley mentioned something about add-ons to the dates, but not a bachelor planning one himself."

"We kept it a secret from her. Heath just told her when I led you outside."

"What is it?" I asked, instead of asking the more important question: *Why did you bid on your best friend?*

His dimple popped. "It's a surprise."

I'd already eaten a few crackers and drank the water. I was feeling better, but I was still unclear about how Sebastian had won the date with me and planned something special.

"You feel okay for the ride?" Sebastian asked.

"I think so." My head felt better, and I wasn't sore from the fall.

He held my hand as we stood, and he led me over to the golf cart, helping me inside. Then he rounded the hood and climbed in next to me. He started the engine, and we made our way down the lane. It was more romantic to travel the paths in the open golf cart. The cool air still felt good to me, and the lights were twinkling around us. Everyone was still in the barn, so it felt like we were alone.

"You're really not going to tell me what you have planned?" I asked him.

His lips twitched. "Nope."

I chewed my lower lip.

He interlaced his fingers with mine on top of my lap, and my heart flip-flopped in my chest. I could wave it off as a friendly gesture, but it wasn't. This wasn't friends holding hands. He'd interlaced his fingers with mine. It was intimate.

Did he feel protective of me for fainting? That couldn't be the entire story because he'd planned this date personally. I felt like I'd missed something huge.

"Wait." I pulled my hand from his as he came to a stop in front of some trees. "Did you plan this date for someone else?"

"What? No," Sebastian said as I climbed out of the golf cart. I could probably walk to Sebastian's house from here. Then I could climb into bed and pretend this night never happened. That I hadn't fainted at the auction in front of my friends and random strangers. That I wasn't humiliating myself in front of my friend on a pity date.

Sebastian caught my wrist and pulled me into his body. He brushed a strand of hair out of my face, and his expression was so tender I sucked in a sharp breath. "I planned this date for you."

My forehead wrinkled as I tried to figure out why Sebastian

would plan a date and take me on it. “But why? Were you worried that no one would bid on me?”

Sebastian shook his head and smiled softly. “I bid on you because I wanted to take *you* on a date.”

His words were not lining up in my head. “You wanted to take *me* on a date? But why?”

“Let me show you something.” His hand drifted down my arm and interlaced with my fingers as he guided me through the row of trees.

I wasn’t sure what to expect. I was curious about the date but more interested in what Sebastian had to say about us. I felt like I was missing something vital.

# CHAPTER 13

## SEBASTIAN

"Did you do this?" Hanna asked as she took in the small ice rink that we'd installed earlier today. The lights we'd strung over the rink gave it a romantic vibe.

It was difficult bringing the trucks in without the girls noticing. But it helped that they were at the main house most of the day, getting ready for the auction.

"I had some help." Knox and Talon helped me build the ice rink. To keep Marley in the dark, I had to explain to Heath what was going on, too. It wasn't as bad as I thought it would be. They didn't give me a hard time. They were excited and relieved I'd finally admitted my feelings to them and had a plan to win Hanna. I still worried that it was too late or that Hanna never felt anything more than friendship for me.

"I can't believe you went to all of this trouble," Hanna said, her tone full of awe.

"You're worth it. I wanted to show you how much you mean to me."

Hanna frowned as she turned to face me. "Why?"

"I've always wondered what would happen if we crossed that

line from friends to something more. But I was more worried about how that would affect our friendship. I was scared to take that step for too long. At first, I was busy raising Ember, but I waited too long to explore this thing between us."

Hanna placed her hand on her chest as if she could still the racing of her heart. "What are you saying?"

I took her hand and placed it over my heart, which was racing in my chest. "I like you. As more than a friend."

"You feel it, too?" Hanna asked, her voice tentative. "I thought it was one-sided. That's why I was resolved to meet someone in the new year. I couldn't wait any longer to see if we could have something."

I wanted to know why she hadn't said anything, but I already knew. She was just as scared as I was. "I feel something between us. Something I've never felt with anyone else, and maybe it's because we've been friends for so long. But I'd like to explore the possibility of us."

"I'd like that, too."

I wanted to kiss her, but I wanted to do this right. We'd waited this long. I could feed her before she fainted again and then give her the date she deserved.

"Can I feed you? And then if you're up to it, we could skate." I led her over to the seating area, where we'd placed large pillows and a picnic basket of food. I had everything I needed for the evening, so there wouldn't be any interruptions.

I helped Hanna sit on the blankets and pulled out the food from the basket. It was a shrimp cocktail, cool from being on ice, and fruits. I handed her a fork and a water. There was wine, but I didn't think that was a good idea since she'd just fainted.

We ate in silence while we stared at the ice rink. "I can't believe you did all of this."

"I wanted something special. The other dates were great, but I wanted to surprise you."

Hanna shook her head. "You did. I think I'm still in shock."

I reached over to touch her. Now that I'd revealed my feelings, I didn't want to hold back. I wanted to act on them.

We ate quickly, and then I put away our trash. "Are you ready to skate? We don't have to if you're not feeling up to it."

The ice rink was only temporary, but we'd investigated the possibility of keeping it for the season.

I helped her put on the skates and tied them. Then we stepped onto the ice. I held her hand as we took the first few tentative steps. I'd skated many times before, and I knew she had, too. But it had been a while.

I was so busy with the business of being a parent and the responsibility of the farm, it was rare to let loose. Growing up, I was the studious Monroe brother. I didn't get into fights with my brothers or kids at school.

Sometimes, it felt like I had the weight of my family on my chest. As we glided across the ice, gaining confidence with each lap, I felt it melting away.

Hanna laughed, and the sound carried over the ice. "This is so cool."

I smiled so hard I thought my cheeks would crack. I held tight to her hand, maybe under the guise of helping if she slipped, but really, it was because I wasn't ready to let her go. Now that we'd given ourselves permission to explore a relationship beyond friendship, I couldn't stop touching her.

My chest was overflowing with emotions: hope, love, and anticipation. I had no expectations for the evening other than her giving me a chance. But now that she had, I couldn't stop my wayward thoughts of jumping to all the possibilities.

I wouldn't rush her, but at the same time, I was eager to take the next step with her. Remembering we'd set up speakers, I stopped skating to turn on the music. Holiday tunes played around us.

"This couldn't be any more perfect." We stood in the center

of the ice, staring at each other. Then I grinned and pointed above us. "The guys hung mistletoe with the lights."

Hanna's eyes widened as she followed the trajectory of my finger. "Were they hoping we'd kiss?"

I stepped closer and cupped her cheek. "I don't know about them, but I was."

She tilted her chin up in silent invitation, and I slowly lowered my lips, savoring this moment I'd thought about for far longer than I wanted to admit. The first press of my lips to hers was cold. Her lips immediately softened under mine, and she parted them so I could explore her mouth.

I deepened the kiss and stepped even closer so that we were touching from chest to thigh. Even through our layers of clothes, I could feel every inch of her.

I forced myself to slow down, giving her small presses of my lips before pulling back slightly. Her eyes were slightly glossy, as if she'd been just as lost in that kiss as I'd been.

Then I interlaced my fingers with hers and took off again. We skated for a while. The music played, the lights twinkled, and I couldn't get enough of being with Hanna. It felt good to declare my feelings.

I couldn't believe she'd agreed to this. That she felt the same way I had. That her vow to date was to put me out of her mind.

The evening was a beautiful mix of revelations and new beginnings.

"We should bring the girls here tomorrow."

I came to a stop, and she followed suit. "I love that you thought of them."

"Ember's a part of you, and Addy's family."

Her words were so simple, but they hit me square in the chest. This is why I felt this way about her. She was sweet and kind and everything I'd ever wanted. "How did I get so lucky to meet you?"

"I don't know." Her eyes searched mine as if she were looking for something. "But I feel the same way about you."

I think those feelings were the reason why we were both so scared to make the first move. It was her agreeing to do the bachelorette auction and her New Year's resolution to date that was the catalyst for me making a move, and I couldn't regret the outcome. "I don't think I've ever felt so happy. Maybe the day when Ember was born. But then you were there that day, too. You've been there for all my important moments."

"And I hope to be here for many more."

We came together, this time in a rush. There wasn't a slow seduction or any whispered words. We'd barely steadied ourselves on the blades as we pulled each other closer and kissed in a tangle of teeth and lips.

I couldn't get enough of her. I wanted more. But my legs were tired from skating.

When I finally pulled back, Hanna said, "As much as I loved this date, I kind of want to go home and relax. Or did you have something else planned?"

"I didn't plan anything beyond food and the rink. I have dessert, but we can enjoy that in front of the tree."

"I'd love that." Hanna smiled, and it filled my chest with something more—love.

I could easily love this woman. I probably already did. But I could see it becoming deeper and more meaningful as we got to know each other in a different way. We didn't have to hold back or worry about crossing lines. It was like the wall between us had been knocked over, and there wasn't anyone stopping us from being our true selves.

"Do we need to clean anything up?" Hanna asked as I grabbed the basket with our dessert and headed toward the golf cart.

"Heath and Knox said they'd come by when we were done

and turn off the lights." I'd never been more grateful for their help.

We got in, and I turned on the engine.

Hanna waved a hand at the rink. "I'm impressed you kept all of this a secret."

"It wasn't easy. We had to get Heath involved so he could distract Marley from this part of the property. Most of the dates were on the other side of the farm."

"I wonder why Cole requested the hot tub date with Daphne?" Hanna asked, with amusement sounding in her voice.

"I have no idea. After you fainted, you were all I could think about."

Hanna snuggled close with her hand wrapped around my arm as if she couldn't be apart from me either.

At my house, I parked the car next to my truck, and we hurried to the door. "As nice as that was, I'm cold."

"Let's get you warmed up." I turned the key in the lock and opened the door.

Hanna took off her outerwear while I got the fire started. Then I arranged the chocolates on the table with the dessert wine Marley provided all the couples for the evening. We'd worked with a local winery to pair the wines with everyone's dinners.

We snuggled together on the couch, and I held one truffle to Hanna's lips. She opened her mouth and bit into it delicately, closing her eyes and moaning. The sound had my dick stirring in my pants.

She ate the rest of the candy, and I offered her a sip of the wine. "This is amazing. You have to try it." She chose one of the candies and held it to my lips. I opened my mouth to accept the morsel, making sure to touch her finger with my lips.

Her eyes darkened with desire, and once I chewed and sipped the wine, which was decadent together, I leaned close and kissed her. My hands were in her hair, and her hands were on my arms. The combination of chocolate and wine went right to my head.

The kiss quickly turned from sweet to more, and I pressed her back onto the couch until I was hovering over her. It had taken us so long to get to this point, I didn't want to stop. I didn't want to think about the what-ifs or the potential consequences. I just wanted to feel her curves under my body and her hands all over me.

I wanted to eliminate the layers of clothes between us, the hidden truths, and the walls we'd erected to protect us from being hurt. I wanted to lose myself in her. It was like everything I'd ever wanted was right in front of me, and I wanted to show her how I felt in every way imaginable.

I never wanted her to question where I stood again. I didn't want her to decide someone else might be a better fit. No regrets. No looking back. The present was the only moment that mattered.

Her legs widened, and I settled between them, still kissing, my hand hovering at the edge of her sweater.

I shifted my hand underneath, seeking the heat of her skin. Her muscles flexed in anticipation. But I forced myself to pull away and rest my forehead against hers.

"I don't want to stop, but I will. I'm just going with what feels good, and I know it's too soon. We should slow down and date for a while. But I'm tired of denying myself what I want."

Then I lifted my head so I could see her face. Her eyes were glimmering with unshed tears. "I don't want to wait either. I don't care what the right timeline is or what the rules are in this situation." Her fingers tangled in my hair. "It's just you and me and what we want. We don't have to answer to anyone but ourselves." Then she bit her lip. "Unless you're worried about Ember."

I appreciated that she'd mentioned her, but there was no way Ember wasn't on board with us dating. "Ember loves you. She already thinks of you as another mother. One who's present in her life."

"I don't have anyone dependent on me who's affected by our actions."

"I'm okay with this if you are."

She smiled and gripped my neck, pulling me down to her. "Then kiss me. Touch me. Make me yours."

All my blood surged to my dick. It was hard and aching against my zipper. I kissed her, covering her lace-covered breast with my hand. My teenage brain couldn't comprehend that the object of every one of my fantasies was lying underneath me, kissing me, and urging me for more.

It was too much for me to handle, so I let go of any thoughts or expectations and did what felt right. I pulled the cup of her bra down and palmed her bare breast.

She arched into my hand, and I knew she wanted more. I shifted her sweater higher so that I could access her breast. "You're so beautiful," I murmured right before I sucked her nipple into my mouth.

Her hands were everywhere at once, lifting my shirt and gliding over my bare skin. "You're so hard everywhere."

I pressed between her legs, letting her feel how hard I was, and she gasped.

"Too many clothes." She pushed my shirt up until I got the hint and surged up, pulling the shirt over my head and tossing it behind me while she unbuttoned her jeans, shoving them over her hips.

I helped her with getting them off and removing her socks while she took care of her sweater. Her bra disappeared, and she was naked on the couch, the fire illuminating her skin.

"You're so beautiful." More beautiful than words. I couldn't believe the object of my desire was here.

"I need you, Sebastian."

My name on her lips, while she was naked, had me shucking

the rest of my clothes and grabbing a condom from my wallet. I threw it onto the couch before easing her legs farther apart and settling between them. I blew over her swollen clit.

"Sebastian," she moaned as her fingers tangled in my hair and applied pressure so that I'd give her what she wanted.

I devoured her, sucking and licking until she was writhing on the couch, begging for more. By the time I used my fingers to enter her wet heat, she was biting her lower lip, every muscle trembling with want.

Her gaze met mine as I lowered my mouth to her clit and sucked hard, my fingers making a come-hither motion over that cluster of nerves that drove her wild.

She cried out as her body arched, and then her muscles spasmed from the tremors of the aftershocks. I was so hard; I wasn't sure I'd last long inside her.

"Are you sure this is what you want?" I asked, even as I smoothed the condom over my dick and lined up with her glistening pussy.

"I've only ever wanted you."

"Fuck, yes," I said as I eased the tip inside her. She was tight. Her heat enveloped me like she was welcoming an old lover.

I hoped this was the first of many times I'd be inside her. We'd have a lot of time to get to know each other's bodies and find out what made each other crazy.

When I was fully seated inside her, I took a moment to look at the spot where my cock entered her. I was inside my best friend, and it didn't feel weird or awkward. It felt right. The best thing I'd ever experienced.

Her hips lifted, urging me to move. "Please."

"I got you, babe," I said as I pulled back and thrust inside. Each thrust was a rush to my system, a building of something so powerful, I never thought I'd recover. She was wrecking me in the best way possible.

I lowered my head and sucked her nipple into my mouth,

hoping to get her closer because I was ready to explode inside her. Just the thought of us getting to the point of no condoms between us had me barreling toward a release I couldn't stop.

I circled her clit until she was bucking beneath me, and I followed her over. Against my better judgment, I collapsed on top of her. My body was spent.

Every moment in my life led to this one. It exceeded any expectations and blew the doubt out of my head.

Hanna was meant for me.

I finally eased off her to take care of the condom. After throwing it into the trash, I returned to the couch, where she was resting with her hand over her forehead. I gathered her to me and asked, "Do you have any regrets?"

She chuckled, her body moving against mine. "No. You?"

"Absolutely not."

Her lips curved into a smile. "Was it better than ice skating?"

I kissed her softly. "There's no comparison."

She was quiet for a few seconds, then she asked tentatively, "You don't think it was too soon?"

I kissed her shoulder. "We've been around each other most of our lives. We were inevitable."

Hanna smiled. "I'm wondering why we didn't do this sooner."

I tightened my arms around her, tucking her face against my chest. "It was the perfect timing."

# CHAPTER 14

## HANNA

I woke up earlier than usual to a quiet house. The only sound was Sebastian's breathing. I missed the sound of Sebastian making Ember breakfast in the morning, but watching him sleep was everything.

Last night, we fell asleep on the couch, and at some point, Sebastian woke me up so that we could go to bed. As soon as we settled into bed, we reached for each other. No talking was necessary. We knew what we wanted. We had one night without Ember, and we were going to make the most out of it. It was slow and sweet. We held hands while he made love to me.

I was falling for him. There was something about our connection that was deeper than anything else I'd ever felt, and it had everything to do with our underlying friendship.

Sebastian's even breathing faltered, and he said, "You're watching me."

My lips curled into a smile. "How do you know? Your eyes are closed."

"I can feel you."

The sensation in my chest warmed further at his words. "I like watching you sleep. I don't get this opportunity."

Sebastian opened his eyes and stretched. "Enjoy it while you can. Ember is the first up, and there's no sleeping when she's awake."

I laughed. "I'm aware. The house is too quiet without her here. I miss her."

Sebastian surged up and over me. My legs widened, welcoming him into the apex of my thighs. We never bothered getting dressed last night, so his hard cock was at my entrance. "Do we need a condom?"

My entire body flushed with need. "I'm clean and on birth control."

"I'm clean, too," he murmured as he leaned down to kiss me, the tip already pressing inside me. Every time we came together, it was a natural meeting of our bodies. It wasn't awkward because we were new lovers; it was like our bodies knew exactly what to do.

It was as natural as our breathing. We didn't have to think about it or question anything. I wasn't self-conscious about my body because Sebastian was effusive with his admiration. I'd never felt more beautiful or desired.

"I'm never going to get enough of you," Sebastian said, his voice still rough with sleep.

"I love waking up to this," I said.

"Hmm. I'd like to say *get used to it,* but that's not possible with a seven-year-old."

I ran my hands down his back, his muscles flexing underneath my palms. "I'll take whatever I can get."

"We'll have to get creative," he said as he moved over me.

"And make the most of our time." I let out a gasp as he filled me completely.

Then he intensified his efforts, stealing the breath from my lungs. He was quickly building me up and throwing me over the edge. I was in a free fall, and I hoped he'd be there to catch me.

After waiting all our lives for this moment, I hoped nothing could tear us apart.

Even though Ember initially suggested we date, I wasn't positive she'd be okay with the reality of her father dating someone. I'd never do anything to upset that little girl. She was as important to me as Sebastian.

Sebastian pulled out abruptly, and I cried out in protest. But he quickly flipped me so that I was on all fours in front of him. He didn't waste any time re-entering me, going deeper this time. He bottomed out on each thrust, making it impossible for me to think about anything other than the rising storm in my body.

He lowered his body so that his front pressed to my back, and he circled my clit with his fingers. I tried to hold off, but I couldn't stop the inevitable. My orgasm crashed over me in huge waves. I bit my lip as I rode out the high.

A few seconds later, Sebastian thrust deep and emptied inside me. When he carefully pulled out, I felt the sticky release on my thighs.

"Give me a sec. I'll clean you up."

I rolled onto my back, wondering what he was doing.

In a few seconds, he was back with a warm washcloth, cleaning me before throwing it into the nearby hamper. "Now, where were we? I think you were admiring my hot body."

"Your hot dad bod?" I teased as I ran my hand over his well-defined abs. For being a self-proclaimed math nerd, his body was a road map of muscles.

He rolled onto his back, folding his arm behind his head. "I take care of myself, exercise, and eat healthy."

"I can see that."

"My brothers are more athletic than me, and I always wanted the same admiration they got. I built muscles easily, especially when I focused on my diet. It became a bit of an obsession with me."

I rested my chin on his chest. "What else are you obsessed with?"

He smiled down at me and cupped my head. "You."

"Has that always been the case, or just recently?" My heart pounded in my chest as I waited for his answer.

"I wouldn't say always because we were kids when we met. But when I was a teenager and first started noticing girls, I was aware of you. But our friendship was important to me. I had my brothers, but you were the only female friend I had. It was a different kind of relationship, and I liked it."

It was probably for the best because how many teenage relationships make it? Holly and Talon's hadn't. We would have been too immature, and it could have ruined everything. "Why didn't you ever say anything?"

"Same reason as you, I suspect. We didn't want to do anything to hurt our relationship. It was too important."

"But you're not worried about damaging our friendship now?" I asked, needing to know the answer.

He sighed. "I wouldn't say that. But I couldn't see you date someone else. Not when I hadn't told you how I felt. I had to make a move."

I wasn't sure how I felt about that. He'd only made a move because of the bachelorette auction and my vow to date in the new year. Was it a case of he didn't want me, but didn't want anyone else to have me?

I didn't want to think the worst when I'd felt so happy a few minutes ago. But I couldn't help but think about it.

"Wherever your mind is going, please don't. Trust that I want to be with you. I'm exactly where I want to be. I don't have any regrets."

I smiled, ignoring the concerns and worries. He was what I wanted, too, and who cares why he finally made that first move? It only matters that one of us finally did.

"Let's take a shower and eat before Ember comes home. I

have more plans for you." Sebastian got out of bed and pulled me to stand next to him. "Never doubt that I want you here. I've always wanted to get to this place."

The words washed over me like a cozy blanket. "Me, too."

"It doesn't matter how we got here, or when, just that we did."

He was right, and I was being overly cautious. "You're right."

He smiled at my admission and kissed me softly on the mouth before leading the way to the bathroom.

He turned on the water and kissed me some more while we waited for the water to heat up. By the time he tugged me under the stream, I was hot and bothered. He used the soap to clean me, while at the same time, making me want more.

"I'll never get enough of you," he murmured against my skin.

His words only ignited my libido. I wanted him.

He slipped his finger inside me and used his mouth on my nipples to build me up. Then he lifted me into his arms so that my back was against the cool tiles and surged inside me. There was nothing sweet about it. I could feel his muscles flexing and how much he wanted me.

If I ever had concerns that we wouldn't have chemistry, he'd proven me wrong. There were sparks between us, and they didn't seem to burn out, no matter how many times we had sex.

He'd said numerous times that he couldn't get enough of me, and I felt the same. He was burrowing into my heart, and I wouldn't be able to let go or see a future without him in it. I gave myself over to the knowledge that Sebastian was it for me.

I wrapped my arms around his neck and held on while the orgasm shot through my body. It only seemed to urge him on, and when he finally thrust deep, he bit my shoulder lightly, then soothed it with a swipe of his tongue.

We stayed like that, his cock softening inside of me, my body slumped around his, until he slowly lowered my feet to the floor. We washed quickly, cognizant that Ember might be home soon, and we didn't want her to find us naked in the shower together.

Then we hurried to dry off and get dressed. Even though Ember was coming home soon, the mood was light.

In the kitchen, I sat on the stool while Sebastian fried up some eggs and cut up avocado on the side. While he waited for the eggs to cook, he rounded the counter and stood between my legs. "I love having you here."

I tipped my head to the side with a smile. "I've been here for a few weeks."

"But not like this. Not as my lover and my friend. This is new for me," he said with wonder in his tone while he brushed my hair out of my face.

"For me, too," I said softly.

"I don't know how to navigate this thing with Ember."

"Are you okay with her knowing we're dating?" I asked gently.

He frowned. "I'm not sure how she'll react."

I suspected she'd be okay with it, but I wasn't her parent. I'd defer to Sebastian's feelings on it.

"Let me feel her out."

"Of course. You're her father. How we move forward is up to you." I'd never come between him and Ember or push myself on him in a way he wasn't comfortable with. But at some point, she'd need to know. I'd hate to only have just gotten him and then have to hide our relationship.

We'd ignored our feelings our entire lives. I didn't want to deny myself much longer.

He kissed me softly before moving the eggs from the pan to the plates. He slid mine across the counter.

He settled beside me. "What are your plans for the holidays?"

"I'll spend it with my family. My sister is coming home this year. She's not dating anyone." Sometimes she missed the holidays when she went to a boyfriend's family's house, but not this year.

"You must be excited to see her."

"Definitely." Except this year, I wanted to spend it with the Monroe family, too, but I'd wait for an invitation. "You'll spend it with your family?"

"Yeah, our traditions have changed a bit since the girls moved here. A couple of my brothers are planning to be here on Christmas morning to watch Ember open her presents. There's nothing more magical than watching kids opening presents."

My heart contracted in my chest. "I didn't realize they did that."

"Last year, they couldn't because we didn't live here, and I think Ireland and Emmett went to Addy's."

"Are you going to get a puppy now that you're living on the farm?" I asked, thinking of how Heath and Knox already had one.

"I don't think so. I'll be too busy at work."

"Oh, right." With Sebastian, work was his priority, whether it was the farm or his accounting firm. I wondered if I'd fit in there somewhere.

He cleaned his plate and put it in the dishwasher.

In the past, I'd admired that he was set in his ways. That stubbornness made sense with a child, but now I was wondering if it would be a problem when it came to a relationship. Would he not want to try new things?

I was looking forward to a future that was different than the one I had yesterday, but maybe nothing had changed for Sebastian. I'd still be living here, taking care of Ember while he worked. There was nothing wrong with that, but it wasn't exactly what I was looking for. I wanted more. I wanted a family. I wanted the marriage, the kids, everything.

What if he didn't want that because he already had the kid? I wasn't getting any younger. All my coworkers were married, and a few had already started families of their own.

The thing was, we'd only expressed our feelings last night. My heart was galloping ahead. We had plenty of time to figure out the details. I shouldn't be worrying about our relationship on day two.

Sebastian's phone buzzed. "Knox is bringing Ember over."

"Oh, good. I missed her." Although it was nice to have Sebastian to myself, I wondered how often that would be the case. If Sebastian didn't want Ember to know about us, would we only spend time together after she went to sleep?

I should have asked more questions, but I didn't want to seem clingy or desperate.

"Do you have plans for the day?" Sebastian asked me as he washed the frying pan.

"I have a few things I need to do for school." I wanted to plan a new holiday craft for the winter stations scheduled for the end of the week.

Sebastian nodded. "I almost forgot. It's Sunday Funday, and we got dressed in real clothes."

"Should we have stayed in pajamas?"

"I guess we'll find out how Ember feels about that soon," Sebastian said with a shake of his head.

A few minutes later, Knox knocked on the door and then stepped inside. The guys didn't seem to lock their doors, which made sense on the farm. The gate was closed when the farm wasn't open.

Ember flew into Sebastian's arms. My heart fluttered to see him crouch to her level and pick her up. "I missed you."

She wrapped her arms around his neck. "I missed you, too."

"Did you sleep?" he asked, setting her down.

Knox chuckled. "At some point, they fell asleep. But I think we were out before them. There was a lot of giggling. But don't worry, I slept on the couch so I could keep track of them."

Sebastian's brow furrowed. "You kept track of them while you were asleep?"

"They were good. They stayed in the fort and played."

"You look tired," Sebastian said to Ember.

Ember rolled her eyes. "It was a sleepover. You're supposed to stay up all night."

"Not at your age. Now you'll be tired and cranky all day." Sebastian sounded like the father he was.

"No. I won't," Ember insisted as she stomped into the living room.

Knox held up his hands, palms facing us. "They had fun, and they did sleep. Just not as much as they would have had they been in their own beds."

Sebastian shook his head. "I'm not mad at you. I get it. Thanks for taking her."

"How did everything go last night?" Knox asked, looking at both of us.

A slow smile spread over Sebastian's face. "It was great. Thanks for your help in getting the ice rink in place."

"It was an amazing date, and I bet it was no small feat keeping it a secret," I added.

Knox's gaze bounced from Sebastian to me. "So, you're together now?"

Sebastian lowered his voice. "I don't want Ember to know just yet."

Knox's brow furrowed. "You waited all this time to peruse Hanna, only to keep it a secret?"

It felt good to hear Knox acknowledge that Sebastian had liked me for a while.

Sebastian's shoulders tensed. "Not exactly. You know. Heath and Emmett know about us. I'm sure Mom does, too. I just want to take it slow with Ember."

Knox's concerned gaze landed on me.

I had reservations about this plan, but I was willing to give him some time. "It's up to Sebastian. He's Ember's father. I'll do whatever makes him comfortable."

Knox's forehead wrinkled. "We never hid anything from Addy. She was happy when we started dating. I think she was starved for a father figure in her life since hers was absent. But when I came into the picture, it prompted him to do more. Our relationship lifted up everyone around us. I can't see how it would be different for you and Ember."

I'd heard that Addy's father, Gary, moved to Maryland to be closer to Addy and exercise his visitation.

"My situation is different than Gary and Sarah's. Brandy isn't around, but she could show up at any time."

The thought of Ember's mother sent a chill through my body. She'd been around only a handful of times, and each time, she expected to be the most important person in Sebastian's and Ember's lives. I'd kept quiet about the effect on Ember because it wasn't my place, but I wasn't sure if I could, going forward. If anything, I was even closer to Ember now, and I didn't want her mother hurting her.

"What does that have to do with your relationship with Hanna?" Knox asked.

I felt a little out of place with them discussing me while I was here. But I was curious to know what Sebastian's thoughts were on the situation.

"Everything. I just don't know what the future holds, and I don't want to confuse Ember." Brandy was a force when she showed up, and we couldn't predict when she would.

"Why would it be confusing for Ember? Hanna's been around her whole life, and Ember loves her like another mother."

"But she's not her mother. Ember has one who is not present in her life. She could show up at any time."

I barely refrained from flinching. I wasn't Ember's mother, and I wouldn't take Brandy's place, but I could be someone important in her life. "I thought we were keeping things quiet because of Ember, but are you saying it's Brandy?"

Sebastian hung his head. "Yes. No. I don't know. This is new. Just give me some time to figure things out."

Knox held up his hands. "I'm around to talk whenever you want. I just wanted to say I'm happy for you guys, and I hope you both realize what you have. Don't take it for granted."

I appreciated his concern and levity. I hoped Sebastian would go to his brothers about this situation because I thought he was being overly cautious when it came to Ember. But then he always was.

"I appreciate your concern," Sebastian finally said, but I wasn't so sure he did.

I plastered a smile onto my face. "Thank you for planning last night's date. It was amazing."

"Good. I'm glad." Knox smiled, but it didn't quite reach his eyes. He was concerned for us, and that made the pit in my stomach grow.

I couldn't ignore the warning signs that Sebastian wasn't all in with me. There was still a chance for me to get hurt in this situation. I couldn't forget that.

# CHAPTER 15

## SEBASTIAN

My time with Hanna was amazing. But now that Ember was home, I was having a hard time reconciling my old relationship with Hanna with the new one we forged last night.

Knox felt like nothing had to change. That I should tell Ember about this new development, and we'd all be one big, happy family, but I couldn't shake a sense of foreboding.

I wanted to keep Ember's life as stable as possible. Brandy showed up at random times and rocked our schedule. As a result, I felt extra pressure to keep things stable.

Wasn't introducing a live-in girlfriend too much at one time? If I'd started dating while Hanna lived somewhere else, we'd have had a slower progression. I could've introduced the idea to Ember over time. It would have been easier.

Instead, we'd jumped into the deep end last night without thinking about the consequences. And now, every worst-case scenario was running through my head.

I made pancakes for Ember while they played board games in the living room. Despite Ember's protests, she was tired. I'd enjoyed my time alone with Hanna but wasn't looking forward to a cranky kid.

"Can we take Ember ice skating at the rink? Is it still set up?" Hanna asked.

"Yeah, they were going to leave it here through Christmas. I thought the family could take advantage of it." It was an expensive endeavor, but it was worth it.

Hanna came into the kitchen. "Can we invite Addy, too?"

I nodded toward my phone. "Go ahead and send an invitation over the group chat. It would be fun for the family."

When Hanna was done sending the message, she lowered her voice. "Are we pretending that nothing changed after last night?"

My jaw tightened. "Just in front of Ember."

"If someone asks about the date, what do I say?"

Irritation surged through me. Why was everyone pressuring me about this? "I'll let them know we're keeping it under wraps for now."

Hanna chewed her bottom lip. I had a feeling she wasn't happy about the situation. But I had to protect Ember. It was literally my main job in life. I needed to make sure she was safe and happy. It was a tall order, and I was the only one in her life that could deliver on that promise.

I sent a quick text to everyone and shut off my phone. I didn't want to see the messages of *Congratulations!* And *Are you sure? But Ember loves Hann*a. I knew without looking what everyone would say. Knox already gave me a preview this morning. I just hoped everyone kept their opinions to themselves.

Worried about Hanna, I moved close to her. "It's just until I can get my head on straight and figure a few things out."

The wrinkles in her forehead smoothed out, and her shoulders relaxed. "I understand."

But I wasn't so sure she did. Hanna was a nice person, and it took a lot for her to confront someone. I just hoped that I figured things out before she gave me an ultimatum or, worse, decided I wasn't worth the effort.

"I want to have a fun family day," I said, and she smiled.

"I want that, too."

Love for her filled my chest. It was like the feelings we had for each other over the years intensified and expanded in less than twenty-four hours. I couldn't lose Hanna when I'd only just gotten her.

I needed to temper my cautious nature and ensure I was meeting her expectations. Hanna was an amazing woman, and she'd waited for me, but I couldn't expect her to do that forever.

I glanced into the living room where Ember was reading a book, her back to us, and lowered my lips to Hanna's, needing that reassurance from her that we were okay. "I'm sorry about this morning."

Hanna pulled away from me with a smile. "You're a great father. You have nothing to be sorry about."

Her smile didn't quite reach her eyes, but I took her words at face value. Hanna understood me. She'd be patient. I just couldn't let too much time go by without me coming to a decision on Ember. Hanna deserved everything, and if I couldn't give it to her, I had to let her go. No matter how much it would hurt.

"You want to go ice skating, Ember?" I called into the living room.

Her head popped up immediately, the book falling from her hands. "Ice skating? Where?"

I grinned. "Here on the farm. We had ice brought in."

Her eyes widened. "You're kidding."

"Nope. We went ice skating last night," I said, going into the living room and sitting on the couch next to her.

Her gaze went to Hanna, who stood near the fireplace. "You went ice skating without me?"

"There was an adult event last night, remember?"

"That's right. Did you go on a date?"

It would have been the perfect opportunity to tell her the truth, but the words got stuck in my throat.

"I fainted last night, and your father was kind enough to feed me, and when I was feeling better, he showed me the ice-skating rink."

"We have an indoor rink?" she asked, completely forgetting about the date aspect of the conversation.

I chuckled. "It's outdoors. It's small, so let's get there before the rest of the family shows up. Maybe we'll have a few minutes to ourselves."

Ember cheered and ran to the bench by the door to grab her boots and jacket.

"I think she forgot she was tired," Hanna said to me.

"She'll crash tonight. I just hope she doesn't have a tantrum or two before then. If so, I'll have to rethink sleepovers."

"She had fun, and she doesn't have school until tomorrow," Hanna said softly.

"You might not be a mother, but you've been a support to me and Ember over the years." She knew kids because she was an elementary school teacher, and she was good with them.

"Come on. I want to get there before everyone else," Ember said, already pulling open the door to leave.

"Wait for us," I said, as I hurried to get ready, grabbing gloves, my hat, and boots. I had the forethought to grab snacks, too. A tired and hungry kid wouldn't be any fun in the cold.

When Hanna saw the snacks, she said, "Lori texted to say she's bringing sandwiches for the kids."

"Perfect."

I handed the snacks to Hanna and grabbed the skates from the garage. I'd purchased them when I got the idea for the rink. We walked, and Ember ran ahead of us. The snow from the storm had mostly melted, except for a few spots.

When we stepped through the trees that surrounded the ice, it was empty. The pillows and blankets from our date last night were still there. I hoped Ember didn't ask any more questions about it. I wasn't prepared to answer them yet.

We put on our skates and took a turn on the ice before everyone showed up. I didn't need to worry about food because everyone had brought something. I held hands with Ember until Addy showed up, and then the two of them took off on their own.

I saw the women descend on Hanna, so I gave them space. We hadn't discussed what we'd share with everyone else other than Ember, and I wasn't sure how I felt about her disclosing the intimate details of our relationship.

Hanna was private, so I suspected she wouldn't reveal much, if anything. I saw Hanna smile a few times and drop her head back to laugh at something. Otherwise, I couldn't even tell if she was talking about us.

We stopped for lunch, letting the girls eat on the blankets while the guys stood off to the side.

I received concerned looks, but thankfully, no one confronted me about my request. Knox and Cole were in charge of the farm for the day, so I didn't have to worry about him saying anything.

"You want to do a family walk-through of the lights and then a bonfire back at the main house?" Heath asked.

Now that most of my brothers had paired off, they were more willing to do family events. It started with Ember and then expanded as more people were added to the fold.

"Ember would love it. But we might have to head out early. She and Addy had a sleepover last night."

"How'd that go?" Heath asked with a glint in his eye.

I knew what he was asking, but I avoided answering him directly. "Knox said the girls were up late but must have fallen asleep at some point. But then, he was asleep, so I'm not sure he's the best source of information."

"Stand down, Daddy," Heath chided. "Knox is great with the girls. I'm sure they were fine."

I just shook my head, even though I knew he was right. I trusted Knox and the rest of my brothers with Ember.

"But I was asking about your date with—" and then he mouthed the word, "Hanna," while he pointed his hot chocolate in her direction.

My jaw tightened. "I told you I didn't want to talk about it."

Heath snorted. "You don't get to get out of it that easily. We helped you build this rink with the sole purpose—"

I shot him a look.

He smirked but lowered his voice. "Of wooing your girl."

Emmett's lips stretched into a rare smile. "You owe it to us."

He loved it when he wasn't the center of attention.

"It was nice." I remembered back over the evening, her fainting, and me taking care of her. Her surprise when she saw the ice rink hidden behind the trees. How the evening had progressed from kissing to so much more. How we'd gone from friends to lovers in a matter of a few hours. It was fast. Too fast.

I'd pumped the brakes when Ember came home this morning. I wasn't sure what it meant, but I knew I was making the right decision when it came to my daughter.

Emmett winced, and Heath smacked my shoulder hard enough to sting. "Nice?"

"I thought your text said—" Heath pulled out his phone and scanned through the messages.

"We're together but not telling Ember about it yet," I interjected.

"But nice? If you guys are better off as friends—" Emmett began.

I flinched. "That's not it. I'm just worried about how it will affect Ember. I have to think of her first."

"She'll be ecstatic, like Addy was with Knox. At some point, Knox pulled back, thinking his family came before his relationship with Sarah and Addy, until he realized it was a huge mistake," Heath reminded me.

"Don't do the same thing he did," Emmett said, his voice gruff.

I was surprised that my brothers were so invested in my relationship with Hanna that they wanted it to work out. "You know how I like to think about things before I jump in."

"It seems to me that you've had years to consider the consequences, and once you made your move last night, you should have made peace with it," Emmett said, sounding mature.

"That's not how I am." I thought about every other important decision I'd made in my life; it required thinking, and lots of it. I needed to analyze every angle, and I wasn't done in this case. I had a long way to go.

Emmett let his head fall back. "You're fucking this up."

Irritation shot through me. "I'm doing the right thing."

Heath leaned in close. "Your *right* thing is going to push away the *best* thing to ever happen to you."

"I don't—" The disgruntled looks on Emmett's and Heath's faces had me pausing mid-sentence.

"Keep telling yourself that, and you're going to live a nice, long life alone. Even your daughter is going to feel sorry for you," Emmett said, his tone full of disgust.

Was I being too cautious? This was who I was, and if Hanna couldn't understand it, then she wasn't the woman for me.

Heath touched my shoulder, blocking Emmett from view. "Don't be so careful that you lose the one person who's always been by your side."

The thought of Hanna leaving me, moving out, and dating someone else sent a slice of pain through my heart. "That's not going to happen."

"Hanna's a nice girl, understanding and sweet, but even she

has her limits. I wouldn't blame her if she walked away at some point."

"She said she'd give me time."

Heath shook his head. "Just don't take too much. She was close to walking away with the auction and her New Year's resolution."

He walked away and Emmett followed him. I rubbed the ache over my heart.

The girls were back on the ice, laughing and giggling like they didn't have a care in the world. And why would they? They had a few more days until the holiday break, and then it would be Christmas. The only thing they had to worry about was whether they'd get what they wanted under the tree on Christmas morning.

They weren't worried about bringing a new person into their kids' lives that could change everything. A part of me was hopeful about the future, but the logical side was worried about Brandy and how she'd react if I was dating someone when she visited. How would Ember feel about me moving another person into our family?

Would she grow to resent Hanna? Would she feel like I was replacing her? I needed to talk to her, but every time I thought about it, the knot in my stomach grew tighter.

I sipped my hot chocolate, trying not to act like the world was spinning around me.

Hanna looked over, her gaze catching mine. When her brow furrowed with concern, she stood and made her way toward me. I wanted to reach for her and pull her into my arms. I wanted to kiss her. But we'd agreed to keep things hands-off in front of my daughter.

Hanna respected my wishes and stood a foot away from me. "Is everything okay?"

I nodded, my throat tight with emotion.

"Do you want me to leave?"

I reached a hand out to her; the urge to reassure her was strong. I realized too late what I was doing, and my hand fell back to my side. "Of course not."

The words came out harsher than I intended.

"I understand that you need some time, but I don't know if this is the right situation for me. Maybe I should find my own place."

That was the last thing I wanted. "Don't go. I want you here."

"I said I'd give you time, but I don't feel good about this." Her gaze drifted over my family.

My heart raced in my chest. "I'll figure it out. I promise."

Hanna nodded, then walked over to Marley, Ireland, and my mom. Heath and Emmett were on the ice, engaging with Addy and Ember. They were joking around, pretending to fall, and asking one of the girls to pull them up. It was comical and sweet, but I couldn't think past the roaring in my ears.

You had to date for a while and see if it was a good fit. That didn't happen overnight, did it? Last night, being with Hanna felt natural. How could something that felt so right be wrong?

I rubbed at the renewed pain in my chest. What if I was making a mistake?

I could show Hanna how I really felt. When we were alone, it felt natural and right. It was when I factored in the rest of my life that I faltered.

I just needed to spend some time with her, and then everything else would fall into place.

# CHAPTER 16

## HANNA

It was a beautiful day spent with this family. When Talon appeared with Holly it raised everyone's brows. I think everyone was so relieved that they'd gone on a date last night and were hanging out today, that no one wanted to ask him or her what was going on.

When Ember got tired, we went home. Sebastian insisted she take an early bath before we ate dinner and then settled in front of the TV to watch a movie.

Within minutes, Ember was asleep. I waited while Sebastian took her upstairs, got her dressed, and tucked her into bed.

My heart rate picked up slightly. I wasn't sure what to expect after the conversation with Knox earlier. Had Sebastian decided that pursuing something with me was a mistake?

When he returned to the living room, his eyes were intense. He stalked across the room, braced his hands on either side of me on the couch, and kissed me thoroughly. He gently maneuvered me until I was resting on my back, and he was on top.

I wanted to ask if he was sure if this was a good idea, but his hands were everywhere at once, pushing my shirt up and palming my breast, his mouth warm and insistent on mine. I couldn't stop the onslaught if I wanted to, and I didn't.

I wanted to experience Sebastian like this. I want to get lost in his desire for me. He unbuckled my jeans and slid his fingers inside me, alternating between thrusting and curling them against that bundle of nerves that sent the orgasm crashing through me faster than I wanted.

"Upstairs," was all Sebastian said as he scooped me up and carried me up the stairs, past Ember's closed door and into his room. He set me down, pausing only to lock the door, and then he was on me again, kissing me and pulling my clothes off.

My hands tugged at his jeans, and he moved to help me. Soon enough, my breasts were pressed against his chest, his hands on my ass pulling me tighter to him. Everything in me was liquid hot.

I wanted this. I wanted him. I wanted to feel him wild with desire for me. When we were alone in the dark, everything else fell away, his worries and my insecurities.

This was right. He couldn't argue that we weren't meant to be. That we didn't have chemistry.

He lifted me until my legs wound around his waist, and then we were falling to the soft bed, his cock nestled at my entrance. I was already wet, and the tip easily slipped inside.

Sebastian groaned before he took a nipple into his mouth and rocked inside me. It was so good with him. I didn't have to worry about anything because the movements and steps felt natural.

He rolled us so that I was on top, his hands palming my breasts as I rose over him.

I bit my lip, the sensation of his cock filling me at this angle almost too much. His hands moved to my hips as he helped me. "You're so beautiful."

I let his words and the love I saw for me in his eyes send me over the edge. I was lost in him, in us, and in the promise of what we could be. If only Sebastian would let go and allow himself to feel this. I grabbed a hold of his wrist and held on as he pressed into me from the bottom and let go.

I lifted off him, moving to the bathroom to clean up. But Sebastian caught my wrist. "You're coming back?"

His voice was low and vulnerable.

"I just need to clean up." It was messier without a condom, and I'd never experienced that with anyone else. I trusted Sebastian sexually; I just wished I could fully trust him with my heart. A part of me worried that his tendency to overanalyze every situation would be our downfall.

I'd made a vow that I wouldn't let Sebastian pull away. He was either all in or he couldn't have me. I was done being someone he kept close but didn't make his.

I deserved so much more. I wanted to be the woman in his life. The one he could count on and come home to at the end of the day. But I couldn't be that if he didn't let me in.

Sebastian nodded, his gaze scanning over my naked body appreciatively.

"Be right back."

"Hurry." His voice followed me as I made my way to his bathroom. I peed, washed my hands, and cleaned up the stickiness from my thighs. Then I grabbed a towel in case he needed one.

When I got back to the bed, he grabbed my wrist and pulled me until I tumbled over him. I lay sprawled over his body, his hand wrapped around my back, and the other in my hair. "I like having you here."

"I like being here," I said as I placed a kiss on his chest.

When we were alone, warm in bed with nothing separating us, I could pretend that everything would be fine.

I listened as his breathing evened out, and his fingers went slack. Then I rolled off him but not away. I slung a leg over his and kept my hand over his heart, listening to the steady beat.

I wanted Sebastian and Ember to be mine. I just wasn't sure if it was possible or if I was making a wish that could never come true.

I struggled to fall asleep, and when it felt like I'd only been sleeping minutes instead of hours, I was shaken awake.

It was Sebastian. He leaned over me, his voice insistent. "You should go back to your own bed. Ember will be up soon."

I nodded, afraid of what I might say if I spoke. It wasn't an unreasonable request, but combined with everything else, I was on edge. I gathered my clothes and got dressed before heading for the door.

Before my hand could turn the knob, Sebastian whispered, "Thank you for doing this."

I turned to face him, straightening to my full height. "I won't be your dirty secret forever."

Before he could respond, I slipped out, my heart pounding in my chest. I'd never said anything like that to a guy before. But then again, I'd never felt so much for someone who was denying his desires.

In my room, I slid under the covers, knowing I wouldn't be getting any more sleep tonight. The clock read four a.m.

I knew Sebastian wanted the same things I did, but he was sabotaging everything because of his need for perfection. Would he ever let himself go and be with me fully, no secrets and no pretense? Just unconditional love?

I tossed and turned the rest of the morning, finally giving up around five. I got up and pulled out worksheets to grade.

When I was done, I researched craft ideas. I liked to have one old thing that the students' older siblings might have done so they could share it with them and one new thing to keep it exciting.

A soft knock sounded on the door at six-thirty. I opened the door, wondering if it was Sebastian wanting to apologize for last night.

Instead, it was Ember. "Do you want to come down for breakfast?"

"I need to shower quickly, and then I'll be down." We had school today, and I needed to stop feeling sorry for myself.

Ember headed downstairs, and I raced to get ready for the day. I had a job and responsibilities. I couldn't lay in bed, lamenting the way Sebastian treated me.

In the shower, I rationalized his behavior as him just being an overprotective dad. I loved him for being one, so why was I getting hurt when he didn't want Ember to find me in his bed? It was a perfectly reasonable request. It wasn't his fault that I hadn't gotten any sleep last night.

Or maybe it was a little his fault. Instead of enjoying our new relationship, it felt weird. As if he didn't want one. He was just enjoying his time with me, stolen moments after Ember was asleep.

I shook off the melancholy, needing to be the happy teacher my students had come to expect. Downstairs, Sebastian was moving slower than usual. He was still in his sweats, pouring orange juice for Ember.

"I made eggs." He gestured at the plate on the table.

"You didn't have to do that," I said as I sat and lifted the fork, my stomach already rumbling in anticipation.

He carried the carafe of coffee and a mug to the table, pouring it before setting it in front of me. The creamer was already on the table, so I poured a dash into it.

"Did you sleep well last night?" Sebastian asked, as if he didn't already know.

I shrugged. "I had trouble falling asleep."

He winced, but I didn't add more.

"I had a dream last night that Santa came and brought me everything I asked for," Ember proclaimed.

I smiled, unable to stay upset when she was so excited.

"Remember, Santa doesn't always bring everything you want."

"But it was on my list," Ember insisted.

I let Sebastian handle it because he'd made it clear he was the father, and he handled all things Ember. I ate quickly, gathering my things before heading to the door.

Sebastian raised a brow. "Are you leaving early?"

"We have a staff meeting this morning."

"I'll walk Ember to the bus stop," Sebastian said, as if he hadn't relied on me to do that since I moved in. It would have been easier if Ember attended my school, but she didn't.

"Have a great day, Ember."

"We're doing holiday stuff all week," she declared.

"That'll be fun," I said with a wave as I walked out. It was a wasted week when it came to learning, but the kids were in high spirits, and I enjoyed this time with them.

On the drive to the school, I pushed my worries about Sebastian and our new status out of my head. I had other things to tackle. I shouldn't put pressure on our new relationship.

So, I'd keep it light and easy, and if he didn't make a change in the new year, then I'd have to make a decision. But until then, I'd enjoy this new connection. And try not to worry.

~

The rest of the week, I slipped into Sebastian's bed at the end of the night. Our passion was just as hot as that first night. Being with him was a guilty pleasure, but that was only because I had to slip out before Ember woke.

If I were stronger, I'd leave after we were intimate, but I loved cuddling with him afterward. He always held me close, with a hand in my hair and one on my hip or back. I'd gotten quickly used to his touch.

Being with him was addictive. But when the sun rose, I felt

guilty for not demanding more for both of us. How amazing would it be to wake up to him in his bed, to greet Ember, prepare breakfast, and get ready for school and work together?

But I wouldn't push him before the new year. It was a busy time for everyone, especially the Monroes with the farm.

"We are going to walk around Annapolis today to do some shopping. Do you want to come with us?" Sebastian asked on Saturday as I was mixing the batter for a cake.

"Why don't you go with Ember and spend time with her? I wanted to bake this morning."

Sebastian nodded toward the bowl. "Is that for your family?"

"I'm making one for you and Ember and one for my family."

Sebastian nodded, but it looked like he wanted to say something else. But he couldn't argue with my desire for him to spend time alone with his daughter, and I'd already started baking. I couldn't stop in the middle.

"We'll see you later?" he asked hesitantly.

"I'm going out with a work friend for dinner and drinks."

"Oh." But he didn't say anything more, and what could he say in front of Ember? *I hoped to spend more time with you*? We hadn't crossed that line because he was holding us back. That was his doing, and I wouldn't make this easier for him.

"I might be late. Don't worry if I'm not back before bed," I said as I poured the batter into the loaf pan.

"Sounds good," Sebastian said as he ushered Ember out the door. But it didn't sound like he was okay with my plans. If he wanted to spend the day together, he should have asked. I finished baking to the sounds of holiday tunes and tried not to think about the situation with Sebastian.

Our bodies knew just what to do when we were together, but my feelings were getting deeper each day.

When the cakes were cooling, I showered and got ready for dinner. I decided to head out early. I needed some space and perspective.

I did some shopping at the mall to avoid running into Sebastian and Ember in town. Then I met my friend, Amelia, at Max's Bar and Grill by the harbor.

As soon as I saw her at the hostess stand, she hugged me. We'd worked together when we first became teachers. She'd since married her high school sweetheart and moved to a school district further out. But we made it a point to get together a few times a year.

"How are you?" Amelia asked as she pulled away, and we followed the hostess to our table.

"Good. How about you?" I asked when we sat, and I accepted the menus from the waitress.

A smile spread over her face. "We're thinking of having a baby this year."

"Amelia, that's great news. I'm so happy for you." I knew she wanted kids sooner rather than later.

"Thanks! I am so happy." Then she lifted her gaze from the menu. "How are you? Are you seeing anyone?"

I bit my lip. "Kind of."

Her brow furrowed. "What does that mean?"

"You know I'm living with Sebastian and watching his little girl, Ember?"

Amelia grinned. "You're the hot nanny. Wait, did you hook up with Sebastian?"

My face flushed.

She nodded in approval. "It's about time."

"Not so loud. He doesn't want anyone to know."

Her mouth dropped open. "Are you serious?"

"He wants to wait to tell Ember. He's not sure if she'll be okay with it."

"Her mother isn't in the picture, right? And you've been helping him since she was a little girl?"

I nodded. "That's right."

"Why would she have a problem with it? From what you've

said over the years, Ember adores you. She'd probably love to have you in her life in that role."

I let out a breath as the waitress stopped by our table to introduce herself and get our drink orders. When she walked away, I said, "You know how Sebastian is; he likes to overanalyze every decision in his life."

"He's waited this long to make a move on you."

"That's the thing. I told him I wanted to start dating in the new year, and then Marley, Sebastian's brother Heath's girlfriend, planned this bachelorette auction on the farm."

Amelia leaned in.

I took a deep breath. "Sebastian bid on me, and I was so stressed out by the whole thing, I fainted."

Amelia sucked in a breath.

I held up a hand. "Heath caught me before I hit the floor, and afterward, Sebastian took care of me, making sure I had something to eat and drink. When I was feeling better, he said he'd won me for the date. He'd gone there with the hopes of being the highest bidder. He brought in an ice rink and decorated the area with lights. It was magical."

"That's so romantic," Amelia said, pressing a palm to her chest.

"The whole night was surreal. We ate, kissed, and skated. Then we went home, where we couldn't keep our hands off each other." I smiled at the memory of the best night of my life.

"Well, yeah, you both have been denying yourselves your whole lives."

"It was amazing, but the next morning when his brother, Knox, came by with Ember, Sebastian said he wanted to keep us a secret. It makes sense because he's worried about Ember and how she'll feel. But it's bothering me. I can't ignore how it makes me feel to be in his bed every night and have to sneak out before Ember wakes."

Amelia's face scrunched. "If it doesn't feel right to you, then—"

"I don't want to say anything about it until after the holidays. He asked for time, and I promised I'd give him that."

"Yeah, but aren't you falling for him?" Amelia asked, concern etched across her face.

I sighed. "I think I'm already gone for him."

Amelia reached across the table to squeeze my hand. "Well, of course, you are. You've been half in love with him your entire life. You were friends first, and it sounds like there's physical chemistry, too. You didn't stand a chance."

"You should see him with Ember. He's the best dad. I admire that he's trying to protect her, but I just don't know how long he intends to keep us quiet."

"What's he protecting her from? Other than worrying she won't want her dad dating someone."

"Her mother. She's not been much of a factor in their lives, but she comes around occasionally."

"What does Ember's mother have to do with your relationship?"

I shrugged. "My impression is that the stress of Brandy showing up keeps his life feeling out of balance. He likes his routine."

"And what, this relationship with you is throwing him off balance?"

"I think so." Not that he'd said that in so many words.

"He can sleep with you, but he can't call you his girlfriend? I don't like it."

"I told him I wouldn't be his dirty secret. I think I need a timeline. Once we've dated a few weeks or months, then we'll need to discuss it with Ember. But I'm worried he'll never be ready."

"I don't blame you. It's taken him this long to make a move

on you, and he didn't until he had no choice. You were clearly moving on, and that was what sparked this whole thing."

I didn't like the sound of that. Had Sebastian only made his move when it seemed like I was moving on? Now I was living with him and sleeping with him every night. What motivation would he have to take the next step? I groaned. "What should I do?"

Amelia waved a hand in my direction. "Nothing yet. Get through the holidays, and if it still doesn't feel right, I'd move out."

I nodded, eager to have a plan of action.

"That way, he won't be enticing you into his bedroom every night. It won't be so easy for him. He'll have to ask you out, which means getting a babysitter and explaining to his daughter that he's dating."

"I'll tell him that's what I'm going to do. If he's not comfortable seeing me, then I shouldn't be living with him."

"The only thing is—he might break things off with you."

"I want to be the one he wants. I don't want these excuses to get in the way."

"You want him to choose you."

That was it. Sebastian had bid on me at the auction, but was that because he felt like he had no other choice? That he would lose me as a friend if he didn't stake his claim? If he didn't want a relationship, meaning a future with me—marriage, kids, the whole thing—then I wasn't the girl for him.

# CHAPTER 17

## SEBASTIAN

I should have felt on top of the world. I'd won a date with my best friend, and it had been everything I wanted it to be. In fact, it went much further that night than I originally intended. But I didn't have any regrets.

Hanna falling into bed with me each night felt good. I was happy with how things were going, but I was worried that she wasn't.

I hated that she had to leave before Ember woke, but that was the way it was when a child was involved.

We spent time together, at breakfast and at dinner, and as soon as Ember was asleep, we couldn't keep our hands off each other. Which also meant that we hadn't talked about the arrangement since Sunday.

When Hanna hadn't wanted to spend the day with us, I felt weird about it. On one hand, it made sense that she wanted me to spend alone time with my daughter. But I'd gotten used to being with Hanna since she moved in.

I wondered if there was something else behind it. Was she avoiding us? Or did she need time with her friends to talk about us? I wanted to know what she shared about our relationship.

"Everything okay?" Knox asked.

After dinner, my brothers and I usually ended up on the deck to share a drink. Tonight, I'd gone out early to sift through my thoughts. "Of course."

Knox braced his hands on the railing. "Why's Hanna with a friend and not here?"

"She's allowed to have friends," I said, even though I didn't feel great about the situation. It seemed like a red flag for our relationship. Not that she couldn't hang out with friends, but it seemed like she was creating distance between us because she was afraid of getting hurt. I hated that she felt that way.

"But you two just got together. Shouldn't you want to spend all your time with each other?"

My jaw tightened. "Maybe it's because I told her we couldn't really be together in front of Ember."

"I know you want to do right by Ember, but sneaking around with Hanna isn't the answer. Wouldn't it be better to tell Ember the truth?" Knox's tone was light, but I felt the steel behind his words.

I hadn't thought about Ember being hurt or confused that we'd kept our relationship a secret. I always thought I was protecting her. "My therapist said to take things slow when I started to date."

"This isn't just anyone, though. It's Hanna. Your best friend. She's been in Ember's life from the beginning."

"I don't know what to do. Kids don't come with a manual. There isn't a chapter on what to do when a parent starts dating again."

"What feels right to you?" Knox asked quietly.

I knew we only had a few minutes before the rest of my brothers joined us. I wanted to make the most of our time. "Not this." I hated being apart from her. Even Ember sensed something wasn't right. "She's pulling away. I don't like it. At the same time, I'm not ready to tell Ember."

Telling Ember made it real. This past week, I could pretend that nothing had changed. At least until Hanna slipped into my bed each night, and I lost myself in her. By morning, she was gone, and my routine was the same.

I took care of Ember with Hanna's help. It was scary to think what could happen if I was all in with Hanna. She could walk away; the relationship might not work out. What then? The thought of starting over, of not being friends with Hanna anymore, sent piercing pain through my chest.

"It's not fair to Ember or Hanna to continue like this. You're not being honest with either of them," Knox said, sounding reasonable.

My family was used to seeing Hanna around. Her absence was already arousing their suspicions that something was wrong. I needed to make a change. The question was, to what extent?

"Be honest with Ember. Tell her you don't want her to be upset or hurt but that you've had feelings for Hanna for years. You want to start dating again. You want to be happy."

"That's all true," I said, even as trepidation crept up my spine.

"Then why can't you say it to her?"

"I'm scared of screwing everything up—my relationship with Ember and my relationship with Hanna. It's just easier to keep things the way they are."

Knox shook his head. "You can't get what you want if you don't make changes. You're stuck."

My routine had always been my safe place. I knew what to expect each morning. There was always the possibility that Brandy could show up and upend everything. So, I kept things as predictable as possible. I thought I was helping Ember, but now I wasn't so sure. Had I played things too safely over the years?

Knox gripped my shoulder. "I know you're scared to make a

change, but sometimes it's the best thing we can do. Stop letting Brandy control your life."

"I'm not," I insisted immediately, even though I knew he was right. I was dictated by the fear of her popping in and out of my life, and Ember's.

"Talk to her."

Heath and Emmett opened the slider and joined us. The mood was lighter, and if they sensed that we were talking about something heavy, they didn't mention it. I was grateful for the reprieve. They talked about Christmas with their families while I wondered if I could talk to Hanna tonight.

Would she come to my bedroom? Or would she create even more space by staying away? I hated that she felt the need to protect herself by creating distance. It was the last thing I wanted.

I needed to show her how much I cared about her, and if telling Ember was what needed to be done, then I'd do it. I'd do anything for Hanna. I just needed to show her that.

As soon as I could, I pulled Ember away from my family and headed home. My hopes were crushed when I didn't see Hanna's car parked in front of my cabin. Would she meet someone while she was out who didn't have the same baggage I did?

"I miss Hanna," Ember said as I was tucking her in.

"I do, too," I admitted, knowing honesty was the best policy at this point. "Would you be okay if I started dating? If I met someone and took her out on dates?"

My heart was pounding in my chest. Usually, I'd research the best way to broach the subject with my daughter, maybe even consult with the therapist I'd talked to in the past, and then ruminate over it some more. But I sensed I didn't have much time before everything blew up in my face.

Ember was quiet for a few seconds. "I want Hanna to be my mom."

I let out the breath I'd been holding. "Are you serious?"

"I love Hanna."

My heart contracted in my chest. "I love Hanna, too. Would you be okay if I dated Hanna?"

Ember's eyes widened slightly. "Everyone loves Hanna. She lives with us, and she takes care of me. It makes sense."

Ember was appealing to my practical side, and I knew she saw things differently as a child. I knew Hanna was the one for me. "That makes me feel better because she's the one I want to be with."

"Are you serious?" Ember asked me, the sleepiness gone from her voice.

The muscles tensed in my shoulders. "I wasn't sure how you'd react to me dating."

Ember frowned. "Hanna was meant to be part of our family."

Goose bumps erupted over my skin, and a tingle shot down my spine. "I think you're right."

"Night, Daddy," Ember said when I fell silent.

I leaned down and kissed her on the forehead one more time. "Good night."

I slipped out of her room, leaving her door ajar. When I stepped into the hallway, Hanna stood there. Instead of talking and risking the chance of waking Ember, I threaded my fingers with hers and pulled her down the hallway to my room. I closed the door behind us. "Did you hear our conversation?"

Her eyes were suspiciously bright. "Just the last part."

I stepped close to her, pleased she'd heard my declaration to Ember because it felt right. "I want you, and I'm willing to tell everyone about us. But I'm not sure if you feel the same way. If you want to go back to how things were"—I swallowed hard —"I'll have to be okay with that."

"Is that what you want?" Hanna asked, her brow furrowed.

"Fuck no. I want you, and I want everyone to know you're

mine." I'd been holding back, but I didn't want to anymore. I wanted Hanna in my life.

"I want you, too."

It was like an invisible cord was drawing us closer. I couldn't resist the pull. My mouth slammed into hers, and her lips parted on a gasp. It was like everything I'd ever felt was rushing through me at the same time.

I wanted her, and I didn't have to hold back. I didn't have to wonder about the what-ifs. For once in my life, I wasn't going to analyze the potential side effects. I would do what felt right. And being with her like this was the most real thing I'd ever experienced.

Her hands were ripping at my clothes as I stepped into her, forcing her backward toward my bed. As we moved, I pulled off my shirt and shoved down my pants. I wanted nothing between us. Not my reservations or her walls. It was just the two of us bared to each other.

"I want to see you," I said when I was naked, and she was still dressed.

I forced myself to move slowly, and my hands shook as I lifted her sweater over her head. "You're so beautiful."

My heart ached with the intensity of my feelings for her. If I thought our relationship would be tame or safe or predictable, I was wrong. It was wild and crazy and free.

She reached around to unhook her bra, letting the straps fall down her shoulders while I unbuckled her jeans and pushed them over her hips.

Her nipples were hard points, her chest heaving, as I slid to my knees, hooked my fingers around the lace straps of her panties, and tugged them down with me.

Everything inside of me ignited. I wanted her with an intensity I hadn't felt before. There was a storm raging in my chest. One side said to claim her now, to sink my cock into her, but the other side wanted to slow down, to experience every beautiful second of our coming together.

"Lie down on the bed," I insisted through gritted teeth.

She didn't waste any time getting into position, with her feet dangling off the bed. I knelt, using my shoulders to widen her legs as I parted her folds, her sweet scent drifting to my nostrils. "You're beautiful. I can't ever get enough of you."

When I licked her softly, she sighed, as if she'd been waiting for this connection all day. I hoped she felt the touch, not only in her clit, but in her heart. Every touch, every lick of my tongue, solidified something inside of me. That I was doing the right thing.

I reveled in every sigh and whimper, determined to drive her over the edge.

Her fingers gripped my hair, tugging and pulling. The sting in my scalp was a welcome sensation as I redoubled my efforts to make her come. I used one finger, then two, to slide into her wet heat.

Her thighs trembled around me as her hips arched off the bed, and her pussy spasmed around my fingers. I sucked hard on her clit, wanting to draw her orgasm out as long as I could.

Too soon, she was pulling me onto the bed. "I need you, Sebastian."

I needed her more. I needed to feel her walls surrounding me, convulsing, sucking me in. I lined my cock with her entrance and, with one thrust, was deep inside her, the woman I'd loved for most of my life.

How had I not seen any of this earlier? That coming together would be combustible? That Hanna was way more than a friend. She was the love of my life. If only I'd seen it sooner, if I hadn't resisted.

I moved over her, wrapping an arm around her waist to shift her higher up the bed so that my body was covering her, and I felt every inch of her skin.

With every flick of my hips, I felt her slide deeper into my soul. She gazed up at me with so much wonder in her eyes. I wanted to reassure her that everything would be okay. That nothing would change. That we'd be friends and lovers forever.

But I couldn't make those promises. I knew things could change on a dime. Ember's mother could return at any time, or a parent could drop dead. There were no guarantees in life, no matter how much I wanted one.

All we had was this moment, and I wouldn't waste any more time. *Hanna is mine.* The words repeated as an affirmation in my head. With each press inside her, the tingle in my spine intensified.

Hanna was the one for me, and I was done hiding or pretending it wasn't the truth. "You are mine," I said as everything broke inside me, and I split into a million fragments.

I was pressed deep inside her, and I didn't want to move. I lowered my head to her shoulder, wishing we didn't have to leave this bed. That the outside world couldn't penetrate. But as I rolled to my side, bringing her with me, I knew I couldn't avoid reality. Not forever.

Her body was soft and pliant against mine, her thighs slick with my release. I eased away from her and walked into the bathroom, wetting a washcloth with warm water before returning to bed and cleaning her.

Hanna grabbed my wrist as I moved to discard the washcloth. "Can you hold me?"

I tossed the washcloth to the side and gathered her to me. I kissed her temple, smoothing her hair away from her face.

"Something changed tonight," Hanna said.

"I talked to Ember about us."

"And she was really okay with it?" Her voice was soft, tentative.

"More than. She said she loves you, and she wanted to know if you'd be her mother." I hadn't addressed that comment because Ember was sleepy, and I was caught up in her approval of us being together.

"She has a mother," Hanna said softly.

"Not one that deserves the title. A mother is someone who shows up with love and support, every second of every day." Not that a parent had to be present twenty-four seven, but a child should feel that love.

Hanna smiled softly. "Are you sure about this? We can't go back and change it once we tell her we're together."

"I don't want to go back to the way things were. I'm all in with you—with us. I want this to work." I didn't like Hanna pulling away, shielding herself from me. "I want to kiss you in the morning when you come down those stairs. I want to hug you before you leave for work. I want all your small moments and your big moments."

Her eyes searched mine. "You're usually so cautious."

"I know it's hard to believe, but this time, I'm not stopping to analyze every angle. I'm not saying I haven't done that already, but I'm not doing it anymore. I want to ride this wave with you, and I can't do that if I'm questioning everything."

"I know letting go is hard for you. I won't let you regret it." From the uncertain expression on her face, she didn't believe me. Not entirely. She expected me to fall into my old way of thinking. It would take her a while to trust in us, but I was patient.

"I could never regret you." Being with Hanna wasn't a mistake. Tonight, and all the moments we'd shared before, felt right. I knew that deep in my bones. Hanna was it for me. We'd weather any storm, and if Brandy showed up, we would handle that, too.

My mind tripped over that a bit, but I had time to get used to this new way of being. By the time Brandy showed up again, we'd be steady in our relationship. There wouldn't be any doubts about my love for Hanna.

She'd know deep in her soul that nothing could come between us, especially not Ember's mother.

# CHAPTER 18

## HANNA

Things between me and Sebastian had changed in the last few days. He'd talked to Ember several times about us, that we were dating, and we'd kiss and hug from time to time. But we didn't want to make her uncomfortable.

But Ember had merely rolled her eyes at him and said, "That's what people do when they date. I'm not a little kid."

It had been funny, but her words had amplified how scared we'd been to make a move. It was more Sebastian than me, since he was her father. But I could see that we were both afraid to do anything to jeopardize our friendship and relationship with Ember.

Each morning, Sebastian's face lit up when I joined them in the kitchen. He drew me to him and kissed me softly on the lips. Ember griped about it, but it was in a way that made us feel like she liked the displays of affection. They made her realize that what we had was real.

He took every chance he could to touch me, whether it was a brush of our fingertips when I handed him a coffee mug or a touch of his hands on my hip when we ran into each other in the kitchen.

We spent most nights together, too. I did lesson plans and graded worksheets while he watched TV or ran numbers with his brothers on the phone.

It sounded like the income on the farm had increased with the recent additions, the light display, the bachelorette auction, and the movie nights. They'd gotten many inquiries about what people could expect going into the new year, and Marley was hard at work on plans.

One night, when we were watching TV and Ember had already gone to bed, I looked up from a text from Marley. "I'm supposed to start that blog for Marley. I'd forgotten all about it."

"You should write about the bachelorette auction and the ice rink."

"Are you planning on opening the rink to everyone?" I asked, contemplating what I should write about.

"I'd need to talk to the rest of the family about that and research insurance issues."

"Marley wanted me to do a little write-up on each brother, and everyone agreed that I should start with you. You can talk about the cabin and what it's like living on the property with family."

"That should be easy enough."

"You're not dreading it? It didn't seem like any of your brothers were excited about the prospect."

"We're private. We don't like to talk about our father and the reasons we all live on the farm. At least not publicly. People ask about our dad all the time, and that's hard enough."

"I can understand that."

"We used to hang out in the woods when we were kids. It was the one place where our parents didn't interfere. We could build forts and wrestle without them telling us to stop or be careful. We could be free. When we were hanging out in the woods one day, and Emmett was about to graduate, he made us promise that we'd come back here one day. That we'd take care of our parents, maybe even live on the property. We'd agreed, not really thinking too much about it.

"Then Knox went away to college and got a job near his school. Then we started jobs outside of the farm. The reality is that the farm can't sustain five families."

"That's understandable. You grew up. Had different wants and needs. You were kids when you made that promise, yet you're all here."

"That took my dad dying. Knox moved back out of what we later found out was guilt. He felt awful that he wasn't here when Dad died. He thought he could have prevented it."

I'd heard varying versions of their history over the years, but not this specific story about their vow to live on the farm when they grew up. It was heartwarming to see that it had come true. That the boys wanted to live here.

"Do you want me to write about the vow?" I asked him.

"I'd rather you talk about that than my dad dying."

"If you think your brothers would be okay with it." I was conscious that not everyone had the same comfort level, especially Emmett.

"I'll talk to them."

"I can also discuss the cabin, why you moved from town to here, and how it's working out." It was a simple story. Not too revealing. Although I had a feeling the brothers talking about their vow to move back home and take care of their parents would draw more people in.

"That doesn't sound too bad."

"I'll need to talk to Talon next. He said he was willing to do it."

"He's used to magazines doing write-ups about his work. But I have a feeling he's not honest with them. He's surface level."

How deep did Marley want me to get with the blog? "I think

Marley wants some tidbit to draw people in, to personalize your family. But nothing too private."

"You don't know Marley. She believes that she's been successful in her online business because she's honest with her customers. She did a live video when she talked about her relationship with Heath. I don't know that I could be that vulnerable."

"You have been with me and Ember lately. You were honest with us about your fears and your feelings. Your wants and desires."

"That's not the same as telling random strangers online. Anyone can search for that article and read more about my life."

"I don't think people outside the community would be interested, but I suppose that's true. I'll let you look at it before we hit publish. Is that okay?"

"I'd appreciate that," Sebastian said as his shoulders lowered.

He was worried about what people would think. He was analyzing the possible ramifications. I couldn't blame him, but I had a feeling this blog would be helpful for the farm. "I should say something about the puppies. Marley mentioned that they've become quite popular and that people ask about them."

"Marley insists they have red bows on their collars when the farm is open. She calls it their uniform."

"It's adorable. Have you thought about getting a puppy for Ember?" I snuggled into his side.

"No. How would we take care of it? I work long hours, and she's too young to handle feeding him."

"I think you underestimate her. It would be good for her to feed a dog and make sure he or she has water. Besides, I'm here to help."

Sebastian let out a breath, and I wondered if he was still worried about us. That something could come between us and fracture what we were building. I didn't think it was possible, but it would take time for Sebastian to possess the same confidence.

"We've had a lot of changes, what with the new cabin, you moving in, and now us dating."

"I can understand that." But Ember would love a puppy. She deserved to have everything.

I opened a new document on my computer and wrote down everything Sebastian told me. I wasn't sure how I'd make it into a final article. I hadn't written anything like this in years.

I'd worked as a reporter in college and high school. I never intended to become a journalist, but I could frame a simple blog post. I just needed to think about what the theme should be. *Single dad making it on his own?* Sebastian wouldn't like that. *Brothers vowing to take care of family? Coming back to where it all began?* I brainstormed ideas until my head hurt.

"Are you ready for bed?" Sebastian asked a little while later, a glint in his eye.

I set my laptop aside and took his hand. "I could be persuaded."

"I have plans for you," Sebastian said as he led the way up the stairs and into his bedroom.

We ended up in his bed every night, and I'd stopped sneaking out at four a.m. Ember didn't come into Sebastian's room during the night or even early in the morning. I usually met them in the kitchen after I'd showered and gotten ready for work. Other than the public displays of affection, nothing had changed.

But my heart was soaring throughout the day. I loved that I was free to touch or kiss him whenever the mood struck me, and I adored that he was texting more throughout the day, discussing what we wanted to eat for dinner, what was going on at work, and what our plans were for the evening.

It felt like a real relationship, but Christmas was rapidly

approaching. Would we spend the holidays with his family, or would we split up? Our relationship was so new.

I wanted to be with him and Ember, but I wanted to see my family, too. I just hoped I could make it work.

A few nights before Christmas, we finally walked through the light display on the farm. The family had talked about holding a private showing, but it kept getting delayed. We were too tired the day we skated at the ice rink, and then we had other obligations. Ember and Addy had concerts and activities at school, and the farm was busier than usual.

All good things, but it meant that it was harder to find time for the Monroe family to spend together. I was starting to see why family was so important to them. Time together was at a premium.

We walked hand-in-hand down the lane, the lights on either side of us. I'd heard that visitors were impressed with the display and that Talon had more planned for next year. Being here was research for our interview about his story for the blog. I had a feeling there was a history behind his creations, and I wanted to share that with everyone.

Talon was a mystery to his brothers. For the most part, he kept to himself, worked long hours in his shop, and rarely attended family events. But there was more to him than that. There was his history with his ex, Holly, an ornament designer, and his incredible success with his art.

I'd spent time poring over any article I could find about his work. His light fixtures had made their way into several reputable design and architectural magazines. I noticed that none of the reporters had dug into his personal life. Not that I wanted to do that; I just suspected there was more to him than work.

There was something that motivated him, and I wanted to know what it was. The reporter long buried inside of me was emerging. I'd published the blog post about Sebastian, and it had gotten some attention from our visitors.

Now that we'd taken the leap and were officially dating, I wanted Talon and Holly to find closure so they could be happy, too. Whether that was together or with someone else. When I helped out in the shop, I'd become friends with Holly, Ireland, Marley, and Sarah.

It was nice to talk to them about the farm, the business, and the Monroe brothers. They had insight that I didn't. All of them either had dated or were dating a brother. The men were stubborn and slow to make any changes, so it was nice to compare notes with someone else in the same situation.

Sebastian squeezed my hand. "Are you having a good time?"

"The best," I said, smiling at him. There was nothing better than a relaxing evening with him and Ember, unless you added in his family.

Marley fell into step with me. "I'm borrowing the neighbor's carriage on Christmas Eve. We'll be offering several hours of carriage rides."

Sebastian frowned. "We only have one carriage."

Marley grinned. "Actually, the neighbors bought a second."

Sebastian tensed. "How did you manage to convince them to give us both carriages?"

Marley's lips twitched. "I think we owe them a lifetime supply of Christmas trees."

"That's a good deal," I said.

"You cleared that with Mom or Emmett?" Sebastian asked.

Marley rolled her eyes. "Of course, I did. Lori loved the idea. She said she wanted all her boys to take advantage of the carriage rides."

"If we're going to use it to make money that evening, why do you want the family filling them?"

"It's not exactly to make money. It's to increase brand awareness and to enjoy the evening. The farm will be closing for the season soon, and we should enjoy it."

This was the second year that the farm would be open during the holiday week so that visitors could see the holiday lights. The addition of the carriage rides on Christmas Eve was genius.

Marley touched my shoulder. "I hope you're free on Christmas Eve. It's going to be magical. Have you talked to Talon about the lights at the pond yet?"

"Not yet. I'm trying to schedule a time to talk to him, but it's been difficult."

Marley rolled her eyes. "Good luck with that."

"I'll get the article done. Don't worry."

"You're the best," Marley said before winking at Sebastian. "You've got a good one. Don't let her go."

"I don't intend to." Sebastian's voice rumbled around in my chest, dislodging any doubt about us that remained. Sebastian had said he was all in with me, and he hadn't been afraid to hold my hand or kiss me around his family.

Any remaining worries had dissipated. I was looking forward to spending the holidays with him and Ember, even if we hadn't discussed the exact details yet.

Was he ready to see my parents as my boyfriend and not a friend? Was he worried about what my parents would think?

When Marley wandered away, Sebastian leaned close and kissed me softly. "Thank you for coming."

"Where else would I be?" I asked him, my heart feeling light as we smiled at each other, and then Ember's squeal of delight stole our attention.

There was a new display, one with two yellow puppies with red ribbons around their necks. We paused in front of it.

"It's Comet and Dash," Addy said, pointing out each one.

"It's lovely," Lori said.

"The dogs are becoming a fixture at the farm. Customers are always asking about them," Sebastian said.

"That's a good thing, right?" I asked him, reveling in how good it felt to be here with him like this, his fingers interlaced with mine, and the knowledge that he was claiming me in front of his family.

"Marley said they're a symbol for the farm."

"Are you thinking about getting a puppy?" I asked, even though I knew his answer. He worked too much and didn't want the responsibility. Ember could play with Comet and Dash whenever she wanted, so she wasn't missing out on the experience. Unless she wanted one for herself, and she hadn't said anything yet.

Sebastian shook his head. "Not anytime soon."

I shook our joined hands. "That's not a no. I'd say that's progress."

"Don't give up on me just yet. I am a work in progress. I want to be everything you want. I don't want to disappoint you." Sebastian had pulled me slightly away from the others.

"You couldn't disappoint me." Not unless he'd asked me to keep us a secret again, and it was too late for that. His brothers wouldn't let him put up walls again. We were in this, for better or worse.

Sebastian looked at something over my head. "Are you sure about that?"

"You're loving and kind and an amazing father. Of course, I am."

His gaze drifted to mine, and a slow smile spread over his face. "You're too good to me."

"There's no such thing." Every once in a while, Sebastian made a comment that he was undeserving of me, and I wasn't sure where that was coming from.

He tugged me behind one of the displays. "We only have a few seconds before Ember comes looking for us."

"Better make the most of it, then."

Before I could finish my sentence, his lips were on mine, soft and insistent. I parted mine, and his tongue invaded my mouth, dipping and sucking and making me want him. "I can't wait until you're in my bed."

"Me either." I could see the next few days stretched out in front of me. I'd enjoy the business of the farm with Ember by my side, and when Sebastian came home from work, we'd make dinner, help Ember with any homework, and get ready for bed.

We'd fallen into a routine with Ember at bedtime, where I read her the *'Twas the Night Before Christmas*. It was satisfying in a way I never thought about before. I wanted to enjoy the holiday with her and feel the joy of the season.

"I'm falling for you," Sebastian said, his forehead resting on mine.

I swallowed down my words that I'd already fallen for him. Sebastian was slower to let himself go, and I was okay with that. I was satisfied with our progress. He'd get to the same place I was; it would just take some time.

Sebastian lifted his head and tugged me onto the road. "Let's go before someone asks where we are."

I grinned wide, feeling giddy inside that we'd kissed behind one of the displays like teenagers hiding from their parents. My love for him made my chest swell. I couldn't imagine being with anyone else. This was where I belonged.

When we reached the end of the display, we said goodnight and made our way back to our cabin. Ember ran ahead of us, singing about Santa coming to town. It was sweet and innocent. She made me long for another child with dirty blonde hair and blue eyes.

Sebastian tugged me to a stop when Ember stepped onto his porch. "I wanted to thank you for being so understanding and patient with me."

"Of course." He had a child. I knew this wasn't easy for him. He was navigating a new relationship for the first time.

"Mommy!" Ember exclaimed, and my heart dropped.

I squeezed my eyes shut, not wanting to see who was standing on the porch.

"Brandy's here." Sebastian's tone had a certainty to it and a hardness I didn't like. Then he dropped my hand and moved closer to Ember, placing an arm over her shoulders. "What are you doing here?"

I tried not to let that bother me. He needed to protect his daughter, but a small part of me wondered why he couldn't extend it to both of us. When would his instincts include me? I knew Ember came first, so I tried to shake those feelings off.

I hadn't seen Brandy in several years. I tried to stay away whenever she was in town. She never liked my relationship with Sebastian. I wondered if someone had forgotten to close and lock the gate, unwittingly letting her in.

Her hair was darker than Ember's, with a purple streak in it. Her face was lined with heavy makeup. She wore black combat-style boots, black jeans, and a jacket. "I came to see my daughter. It's Christmas."

She acted like it was no big deal, as if her presence was expected this time of year. But it wasn't. Her visits weren't predictable. Sebastian had a theory that she showed up in between boyfriends when she was bored.

Ember stood in front of Sebastian. Her expression was hesitant, as if she wasn't sure what to make of her mother's presence. My heart ached for her. I wanted to protect her from whatever this was, but none of us could.

Brandy had a right to see her daughter.

"What is she doing here?" Brandy asked, her voice filled with disgust as she gestured in my direction.

"She's been helping with Ember. You know I work long hours."

Sebastian's words were like a knife to the chest. He hadn't claimed me in front of Brandy. Why? What was the purpose of pretending we weren't seeing each other?

"What are your plans?" Sebastian's voice was carefully controlled.

"I want to spend a few days with Ember. I can stay in your new guest room. Surely, this place has one." Her tone was cutting.

Then it hit me. Marley had published my blog post a few days ago, complete with pictures of the brothers in front of Sebastian's cabin the day he moved in. The article focused on the move and his bond with his brothers. Had Brandy seen it and wanted something from him? Had I led her right to him?

Sebastian stepped onto the porch. "It does."

I was staying in the guest room; a horrifying thought came over me. I needed to leave. Brandy wanted alone time with Ember, and Sebastian wouldn't need me to watch her after school. I was also staying in the sole guest room. Or, at least, my things were. I couldn't stay in Sebastian's bedroom, not with Brandy here.

# CHAPTER 19

## SEBASTIAN

I felt like I was in a fog. I couldn't believe Brandy was standing on my porch. Hanna was fumbling to put her key in the lock.

"Here, let me," I said, stepping closer to assist her, but she doubled down on her efforts, and the door finally swung open.

"This is a cute place," Brandy said as she stepped inside. Ember stood next to me, her face riddled with uncertainty.

Hanna had disappeared upstairs, presumably to move her things. I hoped she was moving them into my bedroom. It would be awkward, but Brandy always stayed with me when she visited. Since she usually didn't have any money or a home here, it made the most sense. She'd told me she wanted to spend every minute with Ember that she could. So, I allowed it.

"Are you staying with us for Christmas?" Ember asked, while my heart thumped hard in my chest.

"Oh, I don't know what my plans are yet. But I have a little bit of time to spend with you."

Brandy acted like it was this big thing that she showed up and spent a day or two with her daughter, but it wasn't enough. It only served to leave pain and confusion in her wake. I'd need to pick up the pieces and soothe hurt feelings, but this time, she'd shown up a few days before Christmas. Then there was Hanna. How was this going to work?

Hanna returned with a bag over her shoulder. "I'm going to spend a few days with my family. I wanted to spend time with them."

Hanna hugged Ember tight. "I love you."

"You're leaving?" Ember asked when Hanna pulled away.

"I'm visiting my family for a few days so you can have time with your mom." Hanna's smile was forced.

"I don't want you to leave," Ember said.

Brandy laughed. "She can't stay, silly. You, me, and your father are a family. Hanna has to go spend time with her family."

I wanted to protest, but I was so shocked that Brandy was standing in my kitchen that I couldn't remember the advice of my therapist. Was I supposed to take control of this situation and insist Brandy get a hotel? Tell her to call and we'd arrange something, or was it best to let Ember see her for as long as she was here? I usually gave in to her demands to stay at the cabin. Why would this time be different?

That had always worked in the past, but then I didn't have a girlfriend living with me, and I wasn't sure I'd introduced her as such. What had I said when Brandy asked why Hanna was here?

Hanna hugged me, and she whispered, "Good luck," before she whirled away, turned the knob, and was gone.

What had just happened? My heart was pounding, my palms were sweating, and my mouth was horribly dry. I couldn't escape the feeling that I'd just royally fucked up everything. I hadn't done what I was supposed to do, but everything had gone down in what felt like five seconds. One minute, I was holding hands with Hanna, feeling like the happiest guy in the world, and the next, Ember was calling out to her mother.

"Do you have anything to eat? I'm starved," Brandy said as

she led Ember into the living room. "Do you have any new toys? I want to see them."

I went through the motions of making an omelet, remembering the time that I'd made Hanna eggs after we'd made love for the first, second, and maybe third time. I was filled with hope that she was my future, but I worried about what it would mean when Brandy showed up.

Now my worst-case scenario was playing itself out in my cabin, and Hanna left. Needing help, I texted Knox.

**Sebastian: Brandy's here.**

His response was immediate.

**Knox: You can't be serious.**

**Sebastian: She was standing on my porch when we got back.**

My phone buzzed. When I hit accept and lifted it to my ear, Knox barked, "Tell me this is a fucking joke."

I heard Ember's sweet voice mixed with Brandy's nasally one, and I said, "I wish it was."

"Are you alone?"

"Hold on," I said as I turned off the stove and moved outside onto the porch. Hanna's car was gone. Only my truck was parked in the driveway. Had Brandy gotten a ride here, and if so, from whom? Was there a boyfriend I needed to be worried about? "Okay."

"I can't believe she showed up a few days before Christmas."

"Do you think it has something to do with that article?" Hanna and Marley had posted that write-up on me and the cabin. I'd approved it because it had been innocent enough. She'd talked about my close relationship with my brothers, my mom, and the move.

Knox bit off a curse. "It could have been."

"When she comes, she usually asks for money and gives me some sob story about wanting a place to start over so she can spend time with Ember."

"Then she disappears. Don't give that woman any more money." Knox's tone was filled with disgust.

"What if I want her to disappear?" I asked, my heart thumping painfully in my chest.

"You can't keep doing that. What does Hanna think?"

I ran a hand through my hair. "I have no idea. She left."

"What do you mean, *she left*?" Knox was barking rapid-fire questions into my ear, but it felt like I was moving through honey. I sat in the rocking chair next to the tree we decorated just a couple of weeks earlier. Back when Brandy showing up was an idea and not a reality.

I hung my head and closed my eyes. "Brandy said something about staying in the guest room, and Hanna's things were in there. Hanna said she'd get her stuff, and I thought she would move them to my bedroom. But then she came down with a bag, saying she was staying with her parents for a few days."

"Was that her plan for the holiday?"

"We hadn't talked about it, but I assumed she'd stay with us, and maybe we'd spend a few hours with her parents. She never mentioned staying overnight." I racked my brain, trying to remember if she'd done that in the past, and I couldn't think of a time when she had. She lived close enough to her parents, so there was never a need to stay overnight with them.

"She doesn't have a place. It's gone, right?"

"Yeah, her lease is up. That's why she was staying with me." That sent a pang through my heart. Was she still planning on moving out after the new year?

"I don't like the sound of this. Hanna left because Brandy is staying in your guest room. Are you sure it's a good idea to let her stay with you for a few days?"

"You obviously don't think so."

Knox chuckled without any humor. "You moved in your ex, and your current love was so uncomfortable she left. Why didn't you stop her?"

"It all happened so fast. I couldn't process that Brandy was back, much less what that means for the next few days or the sleeping arrangements."

"Hanna didn't want to be in the same house as Brandy."

I sighed. "Brandy never liked her. She was always jealous of our friendship."

"What are you going to do?"

I stood. "I'm going to go inside and make sure Ember's okay."

"And what about Hanna? Are you going to let Brandy stay with you?"

My stomach churned with indecision. "She's already assumed she can, and I always have in the past."

"Things are different now. You're in love with Hanna. You're building a future with her."

"Am I?" My head still felt like it was filled with hot lava, and I couldn't navigate around it to make sense of anything.

"You don't know?" Knox's tone was incredulous.

I tried to think back to how I felt when I'd pulled her behind that sign to kiss her. "I want her in my life. I told her tonight I was falling for her."

"Tell me how you felt when she walked out that door."

"Like my entire world was crashing down around me, and I couldn't do anything to stop it." The words tumbled out without any conscious thought. Hanna was my world. My life. My past, present, and future. She was everything, and I'd let her walk away. I was an idiot. "What can I do about it, though? I can't leave Brandy alone with Ember."

I didn't know Brandy, not really. She wasn't great with kids. She didn't have much experience with them, and I never knew what toxic thing she would say to Ember next. Panic surged through me. "I have to go."

I clicked off without saying goodbye, knowing Knox would understand.

Inside, Ember was playing with the dollhouse we kept in the living room.

"What do you think about going with me for a while?" Brandy asked.

Ember frowned, confusion in her gaze. "I live here with Daddy and Hanna."

"Hanna? She lives with you now?" Brandy asked carefully.

Ember nodded. "Yeah, she was helping out my dad, and now they're dating."

My heart skipped a beat when I stepped into the room, and Brandy's shocked gaze met mine. "You're sleeping with her?"

I held up my hands. "First of all, it's none of your business, and watch what you're saying in front of Ember."

Her eyes narrowed. "I knew Hanna liked you as more than a friend."

"I like her right back."

Brandy pouted. "I always thought we'd end up back together. We share a daughter, after all."

"This isn't the right time and place to discuss this." We'd had a surface-level relationship. I'd been dazzled that a pretty girl liked me. One that was a little wild. But then she got pregnant, and I realized that she wasn't mother material. She wanted to smoke and drink while she was pregnant. I stuck close by so I could discourage that behavior. Then, when she had the baby, I thought it was best for the mother to be around.

But when I saw how destructive Brandy could be, how volatile, I wished she'd leave, and she eventually did. She decided being a mother wasn't for her. But she stopped by every once in a while to get her "Ember fix," as she called it.

I allowed it because I thought Ember should spend time with her mother, but this didn't feel right.

Ember looked uncomfortable. "I like Hanna."

Brandy's lip curled. "She's just using your daddy to get his family's money."

"That's enough." I remembered Brandy insinuating that the family must have money, but we didn't. We struggled just like any other business. I was careful. I saved and invested, so I was okay. But I wouldn't be if I kept giving it to Brandy.

Brandy's eyes widened. "I'm just telling the truth."

"That's not true, and you know it. If you're going to stay here, you need to watch your mouth."

Brandy rolled her eyes. "Fine."

I knew it wouldn't be the last time she went off about Hanna. She couldn't seem to stop herself. But I needed time to figure out what I was going to do.

My phone buzzed with a text from Knox.

**Knox: What are you going to do?**

**Sebastian: I don't know.**

**Knox: I'm here if you need me. We could evict her for you.**

**Sebastian: I'll handle it.**

I just wasn't sure how. I'd told her she could stay, which meant living in my guest room for the foreseeable future. The only saving grace was that she usually didn't stay long.

But where would I be with Hanna when it was over? I wanted to spend the next few days with Ember and Hanna, as a couple during the holidays. I wanted to take that carriage ride with Hanna and Ember on Christmas Eve. I wanted to wake up with Hanna in my bed and make love to her.

I wanted to sit on the couch and drink coffee while Ember ripped open the wrapping paper and squealed over her gifts. I wanted to kiss her at midnight and plan our future on New Year's Eve.

I wasn't sure how anything would work out now. When it was time for bed, I took Ember upstairs.

When she was tucked in, I read her the book, but she said, "Hanna reads it better."

My heart sank. "I bet she does."

Ember's hand curled around my arm. "Why did she leave?"

I glanced down at my daughter. "She wanted to visit her family."

"Aren't we her family?"

My heart pinged at her question, my chest filling with longing. "I want us to be."

Ember sat up. "What can we do to let her know that she's our family now?"

My mind started moving, processing the possibilities. "I'm not sure. I'm trying to figure that out."

"Can we write her a letter for Christmas, inviting her to be with us?" Ember asked, her excitement about her new idea growing.

"That's not a bad idea." I was scared to make any move. What if Hanna had had enough of my baggage? What if she was upset about the way I handled Brandy showing up? I wouldn't blame her. I'd messed up royally. "What do you think about your mom visiting?"

Ember's nose scrunched up. "She doesn't feel like a mom. She doesn't make me breakfast or bake cookies or come to school events like the other mothers."

I sighed. "We've talked about her being different."

Ember's lips pursed. "Hanna's here, though. She helps me get ready for school, makes me dinner, and helps me with my homework."

"You're right. She does all those things."

"Hanna is more of a mother to me than—"

I knew what she was saying: Hanna was more of a mother to her than that woman currently hanging out in our living room. So why was I treating Brandy with more respect than Hanna? Why had I let Hanna walk out of my house just because Brandy wanted to visit?

Brandy only showed up when it suited her, without a care

for how it affected the rest of us. "Everything you said is correct, and you're entitled to your feelings."

"I want Hanna back."

"I do, too." I just wasn't sure the best way to go about it. I couldn't just take off; I had Ember and now Brandy here. "Let me worry about the details."

"Did you hear my suggestion to invite her to Christmas dinner?"

"It was a good one. But I'm not sure I want to wait that long to see her again."

A grin spread over Ember's face. "Should we invite her on a carriage ride?"

"You have a lot of good ideas," I said, kissing her forehead. "But it's time for you to go to bed." I'd stayed longer than I usually would because I was worried about Ember, and I wanted to avoid Brandy.

I kissed Ember one more time. Once she was tucked under the covers, I turned out the light. I left the door ajar like I always had, my heart rate picking up because I usually spent this time with Hanna. This time, dread filled my chest. I needed to deal with Brandy. I couldn't avoid her anymore.

In the living room, Brandy had her legs kicked up on the ottoman, as if she was planning to stay awhile. She didn't look right there. This wasn't where she belonged.

Hanna should have been here. Instead, she was at her parents', probably thinking I was a jerk. And she'd be right.

"We need to talk." I sat on the edge of the cushion a few feet away from her.

"What the hell is Hanna doing living here? I warned you that she's liked you all these years. She's after your money and this house. She wants to be *Mrs. Sebastian Monroe*." She sneered.

I chuckled at her suggestion that Hanna wanted something from me, even as my body liked the idea of her being Mrs. Sebastian Monroe. It had a nice ring to it. "What money?"

Brandy blinked. "You have a good job, then the farm. It's a gold mine."

My jaw tightened. I earned a comfortable living, but not enough to keep funding Brandy's mistakes. "Is that why you're here? You want me to give you money so you can go wherever you do?"

"Do you want the mother of your child living on the streets? Carl kicked me out, and I have nowhere to go." Brandy's voice raised, and I worried she'd wake Ember.

I held up a hand in an effort to tell her to be quieter. "I'm sorry to hear about your situation, but I'm not responsible for your living expenses. I'm the one raising our daughter without any help from you."

When Brandy opened her mouth and merely closed it, I added, "And it's not a good idea for you to stay here. Let's be honest, you haven't been a real mother to Ember. She doesn't miss you like she should. She misses the idea of having a mother. She wants what the other kids in her class have, but she doesn't miss you."

Brandy's eyes widened. "I can't believe you're talking to me like this."

My heart was thumping wildly in my chest. I'd never talked to Brandy like this, and it felt good. "I'm telling you how it is, and I should have done this a long time ago.

"In the future, you can schedule visitations with me ahead of time. You showed up in the middle of the holidays, and we have plans." I needed to come up with one to get Hanna back. I couldn't be distracted by Brandy and whatever bullshit she brought with her. "Ember needs stability, and so do I."

I'd lived in fear of Brandy showing up and making demands for so long that I'd become deeper entrenched in my routines. I was afraid to do anything out of the ordinary. I didn't want to upset the delicate balance. But now, I saw myself as the rock in this situation, and I was letting Brandy knock me off the edge every time I let her see Ember and stay in my house. I gave her money as an act of desperation. The fact was, Brandy disrupted our lives, and she wasn't good for Ember.

Ember was more upset when Brandy left than she was before she came. The fact that Ember was able to articulate her misgivings now couldn't be ignored. Brandy's presence wasn't good for my daughter, and it was my duty to protect her.

"What are you saying?"

I stood, raising myself to my full height. "You need to find somewhere else to stay tonight."

"But you always let me stay with you. Does this have something to do with Hanna?" Her voice was small.

"I guess it does, but it's something I should have done a long time ago. What you're doing, what I've allowed you to do, isn't healthy for Ember or me."

"Any court will allow me to see my daughter. Judges favor mothers."

I chuckled without any humor. "That may be what you've heard, but not in this situation. The facts are that you abandoned Ember a long time ago, and I've been raising her on my own. I'm going to marry Hanna one day"—Brandy gasped—"and we're going to be a family. I can't have you showing up, trying to hurt anyone I care about anymore."

"I'll take this to the courts if I have to."

I moved toward the door. "You do that."

"If you give me money, I'll go away. You'll never have to see me again."

"We both know you'll be back as soon as the money dries up." I opened the door. "Next time you want to see Ember, call me, and we can discuss a good time for us."

The more I talked, the better I felt. It was like there was this weight that had been lifted off my chest, allowing me to breathe easier and stand taller. Brandy was an albatross I should have tossed a long time ago.

"You can't mean this. You'll change your mind," Brandy said as she stepped onto her porch.

"I already called a car for you." It was actually Knox, but she didn't need to know that. I'd texted him after I said goodnight to Ember, and he was all too happy to help.

When I saw him pull up in his truck, I said, "Have a great Christmas."

Then I waved to Knox and shut and locked the door. I knew Knox would ensure she was escorted off the property and that the gate was shut and locked behind her for the night. She wouldn't be bothering us anymore this evening.

# CHAPTER 20

## HANNA

When I arrived home, my mom enveloped me in a hug. "Are you okay?"

I blinked away the tears at the comforting gesture. "Of course. Why wouldn't I be?"

"I thought you were staying with Sebastian?" Mom asked, with a glance in Dad's direction. He didn't like that I was living with Sebastian, even if it was as Ember's nanny and not something more.

"Ember's mom needed the guest room," I said as Dad took the bag from my shoulder. "There's only one available."

I only witnessed their interactions for a few minutes, but it was like Sebastian was a shell of a man when Brandy was around. He gave in to her demands, letting her dictate how things would go, and I hated it.

"So, he just kicked you out? Aren't you helping him?" Dad asked, his voice gruff.

My heart pinged because Dad was protective of me. As much as I hated his backward ideas on living with a man, he wanted the best for me. "I'm not happy about it."

Mom led us into the living room. "I'll make some tea."

I didn't tell her I preferred coffee because when I was home, drinking tea was something I did with her when we had important conversations.

Dad sat across from me in his recliner, lowering the volume on the TV. There was a football game playing. "Are you okay?"

I smiled as best I could. "I will be."

Dad nodded. "Do I need to have a talk with him?"

I let out a breath and attempted to smile. "I've got it handled."

Dad scowled. "You're going to talk some sense into him?"

"That's the plan. In the meantime, Ember's mother is staying at the house, and I won't do anything to come between them." Ember needed her mother, as we all do. Although, I wasn't so sure that the woman on the porch had Ember's best interests in mind.

My phone buzzed with an incoming text.

**Sebastian: Can we talk?**

My heart rate increased, but I refused to get my hopes up. He probably felt badly that I was displaced, but that wasn't what I wanted. He needed to stand up to Brandy and stop letting her dictate his life.

**Hanna: I'm with my dad right now.**

I sent him the message and then set my phone aside.

"That him?" Dad nodded toward the screen.

"Yes."

"You like him."

My heart stumbled. "What are you talking about?"

"You've been friends forever, but you like him as more than that." He stated it so matter-of-factly, as if he'd always known the truth.

I nodded because the lump in my throat made it difficult to speak.

Dad leaned forward so that his elbows were on his knees;

the roar of the crowd in the game on the TV was a comforting background noise. "Does he know how you feel?"

I nodded. "He does."

A muscle ticked in his jaw. "And he still kicked you out?"

"You know it wasn't like that. Not exactly. Brandy showed up without any warning, and apparently, she's used to staying at his house. I'm sure it's easier for Ember, and I doubt she can afford other arrangements." It wasn't about me, or at least that's what I'd been trying to tell myself. But the hurt was still there, a constant physical ache in my chest.

"You're making excuses for him."

"I love him, Dad." I hadn't told Sebastian how I felt, but it was easy for my feelings to grow and expand into a romantic love. I had a feeling they'd always be present, just under the surface. These last few weeks were amazing, and it allowed me to let go of any reservations and just feel.

"Does he feel the same way about you?"

"I think so."

Mom bustled in with two cups of tea. "Are you giving her a hard time? Can't you see she's hurting?"

Dad leaned back in his chair. "I know she is. I just want her to be aware of what's happening."

"I'm aware. I can take care of myself." I wasn't sure what my plan was. Sebastian said he wanted to talk, which was a good sign. But I couldn't stop thinking about Brandy staying in the guest room and being in the cabin. Were they spending time together now? Would she make a move on him because she was worried about me and wanted to mess things up for us?

I wouldn't put it past Brandy to do something drastic to get Sebastian's attention. I was confident he didn't want her, but the image of them together didn't sit right with me.

Mom patted my knee. "Hanna's always been a strong girl. She'll be okay."

"Thanks, Mom."

Dad leaned back in his chair and crossed his arms. "It's not that I don't think she'll be okay. I just want to—"

"Protect her," Mom finished for him. "There's nothing wrong with that, but she's a grown woman. She's harbored feelings for this man for a long time. They have history. A friendship. This is something she needs to deal with on her own. She doesn't need you getting into her head. This is between her and that young man."

I appreciated Mom's support, but my mind was elsewhere. "I wish he'd deal with Brandy differently. Not let her disrupt his life like he does."

"Maybe he will make changes," Mom said, with her positive outlook on life.

"I hope so." The thing was, it had to come from him. I couldn't be the one who told him to make a change.

"We're happy to have you home for a few days. But what are you going to do about your living situation?" Mom asked.

My heart sank. I didn't have an apartment or a place to go to. I was living with my parents again.

Dad tipped his head in my direction. "You can stay here as long as you need to. We're here for you."

"Thanks, Dad." I got up and hugged him. There was nothing like coming home to the love of my parents. They always had my back.

I pulled away and stood. "I'm going to bed early, and I hope that tomorrow will be a better day."

"I'm going to need some help to bake cookies tomorrow," Mom said, sipping her tea.

"Count me in," I said with a smile as I kissed her cheek. "Good night."

I grabbed my overnight bag and went upstairs to my room. I shut the door, taking in the familiar posters on the wall, the pink-and-white ruffled comforter, and the desk littered with various honor roll certificates and awards.

My parents hadn't changed anything since I left, and it was a little unnerving. I could close my eyes and pretend I was back in high school, harboring a crush on my best friend.

The only difference was that I knew what it was like to be with him, and it was so much worse. I loved him, and I wasn't sure how I'd get over it if we broke up. On the other hand, if I stayed, things with Brandy would need to change.

But I couldn't make demands. Sebastian had to realize all those things for himself, and I wasn't sure he would. He'd always given in to Brandy, hopeful she'd come back and be in Ember's life. But I saw her for what she was: an opportunist who played on Sebastian's goodwill to get what she wanted. As soon as he gave it to her, she'd be gone, and Ember would be hurt.

My heart ached for Ember. I didn't want that for her. She needed stability and love. Not someone who showed up to get money from her father. Eventually, Ember would realize what was going on, and it would hurt even more.

Ember had her father, her grandmother, her uncles, and now me. I just hoped Sebastian could see all of that.

I changed into pajamas, brushed my teeth, and climbed into bed. I felt like a little girl again under the ruffled comforter. I wanted to be in Sebastian's bed, sated after a night of lovemaking, looking forward to spending the holidays together.

Now I was sleeping in my childhood bedroom and ruminating over my past mistakes. I'd come full circle, and I didn't like it.

~

The next morning, I woke disorientated. I was used to waking in Sebastian's arms, and the bed felt small, too small.

When I opened my eyes, everything came flooding back to

me. The wonderful evening with the Monroe family, Sebastian kissing me behind the display, and then Brandy showing up.

I wanted to say she destroyed everything, but she didn't. It was Sebastian's reaction, or lack thereof, to her appearance that prompted me to gather my things and leave. I couldn't be in the same house as Brandy.

Not when she'd always hated my presence. It was like she didn't want Sebastian, but I couldn't have him either. He was supposed to be single forever. If I stuck around, I wasn't sure how she'd react, but it wouldn't be good for Ember.

I'd always take care of that little girl. If removing myself was the best thing for her, then I'd do it, no matter how much it hurt.

The last text on my phone was the one from Sebastian asking to talk and me putting him off because I was talking to my father.

**Hanna: Are you sure that's a good idea? Maybe you should concentrate on Brandy's visit and Ember.**

**Sebastian: I told Brandy she couldn't stay here anymore.**

What did that mean? Had he kicked her out or told her that she couldn't stay at his cabin in the future? The difference mattered to me.

**Sebastian: Will you be home today? We'd like to bring you something.**

My heart twinged. Was he giving me my present now? Before Christmas? So that he didn't have to deal with me anymore? Would he be spending the holiday with Brandy?

I knew he didn't want Brandy, but the thought of her living in the cabin, sleeping in the guest room, and eating breakfast with them was too much. Like Brandy said, they were Ember's family. I wasn't.

**Hanna: I'll be baking with Mom for most of the day.**

**Sebastian: See you soon.**

I worried about what he was bringing me the rest of the

morning while I showered and ate breakfast, then rolled out the dough with Mom. My stomach knotted tighter and tighter as the day drew on.

When the doorbell finally rang, I jumped.

"Is it for you?" Mom asked, her brow raised.

My stomach churned. Was this the beginning of the end of our relationship? "I think so."

"You'd better get it, then," Mom said, sprinkling flour on the dough.

I washed my hands, dried them, and slowly made my way to the door. I wiped my sweaty palms on my jeans and turned the knob.

Ember stood slightly in front of Sebastian, and they both looked too good for words. Ember wore a pretty holiday dress in red velvet with black ballet flats. In her hand, she held an envelope. My name, Hanna Roberts, was written in gold.

"That's beautiful. Did you learn calligraphy?" I asked her, remembering I'd bought her a set last year, hoping I'd get to do it with her.

"This was the first time I tried it."

I took the envelope from her and examined the letters. "This is good. Really good. I'm impressed."

"Thank you."

Sebastian rocked back on his heels. "I think you'll want to look inside the envelope."

I carefully opened the flap and slid out heavy card stock paper with gold writing. *Ms. Hanna Roberts, will you do us the honor of joining us on a carriage ride on Christmas Eve, December 24, at 5:00 p.m.? Yours truly, Sebastian and Ember Monroe.*

My eyes blinked back the tears that threatened. "I'd love to join you."

My heart was beating rapidly under my palm, and I didn't know what it meant. I didn't even know if Brandy was staying at the house, and I was too scared to ask.

Sebastian grinned, and Ember cheered. "I knew she'd say yes."

I wondered if it was another one of his elaborate dates. If I could expect a carriage ride and a private meal, a dance, or more time at the ice rink.

Ember stopped jumping in the air and wrapped her arms around my waist. "I miss you, Hanna."

Before she could say anything more, Sebastian said, "We'll see Hanna tomorrow night, remember?"

They exchanged a look, as if they'd planned this before they arrived.

"There's one more thing," Sebastian said as he jogged down the steps and toward his truck parked at the curb.

"We miss you," Ember whispered again, as if she didn't want her father to hear.

"I miss you, too," I said, just as Sebastian returned, carrying a wreath with a huge red velvet bow. "That's beautiful."

"For your door," he said, adding a hook to the door and hanging it.

"That is very sweet of you."

"Dad, the flowers," Ember hissed.

Sebastian shot me an apologetic look and held up his finger before he headed toward his truck again.

I enjoyed the back-and-forth with Sebastian and his daughter. I'd lived with him as our relationship went from friends to lovers, so we didn't have a chance to date. And that's what this felt like.

Sebastian made his way back up the sidewalk with a bouquet of red and white flowers in his hands, and for the first time, it registered that he wore a wool coat over dress slacks and a button-down shirt. He handed the vase to me. "These are for you."

I inhaled the scent of the roses. "Thank you. I love them."

He rocked back on his heels. "We didn't go on a real date.

I've never knocked on your door, brought you flowers, or dropped you off on your porch at the end of the night. And I'd like the chance to do that."

"What are you asking?" I asked, as my heart fluttered uselessly inside my rib cage.

"Would it be okay if I picked you up for the carriage ride tomorrow night?" Sebastian asked hesitantly, as if he wasn't sure of my reaction.

"I'd love that."

Sebastian winked at me. "Dress warmly. I hear there's a chance of snow."

Just the thought of it snowing on Christmas had tingles popping up all over my body. "I'm looking forward to it."

"See you tomorrow," Ember called as she skipped toward the truck.

Sebastian leaned in, and I sucked in a breath. He smelled like spice and evergreen, everything I'd come to love. But he merely kissed me on the cheek; the scrape of his stubble on my face sent a tingle down my spine. As he drew back, he asked, "Are you okay?"

I smiled, my heart fluttering in my chest. "I will be."

He cupped my cheek. "I can't wait to see you tomorrow night."

I pressed my cheek into the palm of his hand, unable to form words. I was still worried about Brandy's arrival and what her presence meant for me, for us.

Sebastian lowered his voice but kept his gaze intent on mine. "Brandy isn't staying with us. Knox escorted her off the property last night, and I haven't heard from her since. I told her she wouldn't be allowed to show up like that again. I'm going to an attorney after the holidays to have papers drawn up for custody and visitation. I never took care of that, and I'm regretting it now."

Relief flowed through me like rain on a hot spring day, and my entire body relaxed. "I'm so proud of you."

"It's something I should have done a long time ago." His expression was filled with regret. "I'm sorry I hurt you."

I swallowed over the lump, not sure how to respond to this version of Sebastian. The one that was honest and decisive. I liked it.

"I'll see you tomorrow?" At my nod, he turned and jogged down the steps to his truck, where Ember was already waiting inside the cab.

Dad joined me at the door. "What was that about?"

"Sebastian brought us a wreath and flowers," I said as I went inside and closed the door.

Mom took the vase, murmuring about how beautiful the flowers were, and placed them on the mantle.

"Apparently, Brandy isn't allowed to stay at the house, and he's going to have legal papers drawn up to define their arrangement," I said, still a little blown away by Sebastian's appearance, his gifts, and his intentions.

"That's great news," Mom said over her shoulder as she continued to fuss with the stems.

"A few years too late," Dad grumbled.

Mom stepped back from the mantle to admire the flowers. "He's doing the right thing. Let's give him a chance."

Dad turned his gaze on me. "If he hurts you again—"

"You always have my back." I hoped that Sebastian would be in my future. I didn't need someone to protect me, but it sure felt nice.

# CHAPTER 21

## SEBASTIAN

Walking away from Hanna without verifying that we were okay was hard. But I'd done what I came to do. I gave her a few gifts, explained that Brandy wasn't staying in my cabin, and invited her to the carriage ride tomorrow night.

Now I needed to plan the perfect make-up date. Or at least I hoped that was what it would be. She had to forgive me. Otherwise, why had she accepted my date proposal? I didn't let myself contemplate the other possibilities. That she wanted to tell me in person we can't be together.

"She said yes," Ember said from the back of the cab, and my heart stutter-stepped.

What if I proposed to her tomorrow night? What if I laid everything out there at once, my feelings for her and my intentions for the future? I'd be laying everything on the line, asking for her to accept or reject me.

I met her gaze in the rearview mirror. "I think you're on to something."

"I am?" Ember asked as I pulled away from the curb.

"How do you feel about me asking Hanna to be in our lives permanently?" I asked, my body bracing for her response.

"Do you mean, like, live with us?"

"I want to ask her to marry me. I don't want to leave anything to chance. We should tell her how we feel and give her the chance to move forward with us, together."

"Would Hanna be my mom?"

"That's up to her. You have a biological mother, and Hanna would be your stepmother if we got married."

"Could I call her S'mama?"

I chuckled at her play on stepmom and mom. "You can talk to her about what she'd prefer. But I haven't asked her yet. What if she says no?"

"She won't," Ember said with the confidence of a seven-year-old.

"How can you be so sure?" I asked, my nerves getting the best of me. It was a nice idea, but was it the right move at this stage of our relationship? I wasn't even sure we had a relationship to preserve. I might have messed everything up last night.

On the other hand, I couldn't imagine Hanna not being in our lives. The thought sent a wave of pain through my body.

"I just know," Ember said simply as she looked out the window.

Do kids have some sixth sense about these things? Or was I being foolish? I called Knox over Bluetooth, and his voice came over the speakers. "Hey."

"You have some time to help us prepare for this date tomorrow?"

"Of course. You'll be a miserable bastard if you don't fix things with her."

"I'm on speakerphone," I reminded him.

"Sh—Sorry."

I chuckled at his not-so-quick save. "Can you meet us in town?"

"Annapolis?"

I met Ember's amused gaze in the mirror. "That's the town we live near."

"What for?" Confusion was evident in his tone.

"I need a ring." My voice rang with confidence I didn't feel.

Knox let out a breath. "Are you serious?"

"I've never been more serious about anything."

"You think she'll forgive you?" His tone was dubious.

I thought back to how she looked at me when I explained what had happened since last night. I'd uncharacteristically acted quickly on removing Brandy from my home and the farm. Talking to an attorney and drawing up papers was a serious move. But I couldn't figure out how she felt about it. Was it too late, or had she been soothed by my actions? "I don't know. This just feels like the right thing to do."

"You have to follow your intuition."

I instinctively knew that Brandy staying in the cabin wasn't right. Everything that followed from there was a natural occurrence. Every move I made felt right, and I wasn't about to stop now. "I feel good about this."

I felt rather than saw Knox nod at my response. "I'll meet you there. You need someone to watch Ember?"

"She's going to help." I wasn't sure how much help she would be, but I wanted her to be involved in every step. I wouldn't keep her in the dark about my relationship with Hanna. I wanted her to feel part of this family we were building.

Ember beamed in the back seat.

When I hung up with Knox, she asked, "Can I pick out the ring?"

"How else will I know which one to choose?" I asked her, and she clasped her hands together in excitement.

We drove the short distance into town, finding a parking spot near the jewelry store in town. I didn't have a family heirloom to offer Hanna, but it would still be special.

"Do you have to ask her dad's permission?" Ember asked when we'd parked.

Her uncles routinely teased her about dating, and how I'd never grant any guy dating her permission to marry her.

"Shit," I said as I threw the truck into park. "I hadn't even thought of that."

"Language," Ember reminded me from the backseat.

"I'm sorry. I wasn't thinking." I was screwing this up. I couldn't show up at Hanna's house, not when she was staying there. I'd ask Knox what he thought. I'd never thought about proposing to anyone before. Not even when Brandy told me she was pregnant. I always thought of marriage as this huge commitment I wasn't ready for.

But now, it seemed like the next logical step. I didn't need to think about it or consider the possible ramifications. I was in love with Hanna, and that's all that mattered.

I wanted to show her what she meant to me and my intentions for the future.

A knock sounded on my window.

I rolled down the window.

Knox raised a brow. "Are you having second thoughts?"

I got out of the truck as Knox moved to the rear door and helped Ember down. "Should I talk to Hanna's father first? Get his blessing? I've never thought about proposing to anyone before. I don't know what the rules are."

We headed toward the jewelry store on the corner. "There are no rules for this sort of thing. You can do whatever feels right. Do you feel like you need to ask his permission?"

"I don't feel like I need to, but I think it would be nice to talk to him first."

Knox opened the door. "Let's look at rings. Then you can tackle Hanna's dad."

When the worker asked if she could help us, I said, "I'd like to look at engagement rings."

"We have a room where you'll be more comfortable." She led us to a back room and brought out an extra seat for Ember.

"My name is Denise," she said, and we introduced ourselves. "What kind of ring were you thinking of?"

"I don't know."

Denise showed us images of the popular cuts, and I pointed out the ones I liked.

Then she brought back options for us, and I appreciated that she didn't overwhelm us with a ton of them at once. We narrowed down the carat, clarity, and then finally, the specific cut. My hunch was that Hanna wanted something simple. She worked with kids all day, doing arts and crafts. I didn't think she'd want something huge that got in the way.

When I showed Ember and Knox the one that I was drawn to, they both smiled and said they loved it.

"This is the one?" the woman asked.

"That's the ring." I felt that deep in my soul. Hanna was the one for me, and this was the ring I could envision on her finger.

"She'll love it," Knox said as the woman left.

"I hope so." Suddenly, I was nervous. I never made impulsive decisions like this.

"You're not having second thoughts, are you?" Knox asked.

"I'm freaking out a little. You know I like to analyze things before I take a step like this. There's probably a conversation we're supposed to have about how many kids we want, where we want to live, and our finances." Any time I read articles about what to discuss with your partner before marriage, I always thought I'd be the one who followed each recommended step. But here I was, buying the ring before knowing if she'd say yes, as if we were on the same page.

"I think you have to go with your feelings when you propose. Does this feel right?"

"Definitely."

"I think you have the financial stuff covered. No one's more fiscally responsible than you."

When the woman returned with the velvet box and the bill, I knew in my heart this was the right move. We'd known each other since we were kids. I knew Hanna wanted children, and I did, too.

Knox shook his head when Denise wished me good luck, and we headed for the door. "I mean, you already built the cabin, and she's living with you, so you're covered there."

We laughed, the tension and uncertainty lifting. The rest of the process was easy. If I just followed my feelings, everything would be okay.

Outside, I took Ember's hand, and she skipped along beside me. "Am I going to be a big sister?"

"One day." That day was closer than it had ever been before, and it didn't scare me. I was content. I still had to ask Hanna to marry me, but I knew I was making the right move. That no matter what happened, I hadn't held back.

Ember rambled on about whether she wanted a little sister or a brother. When she was safely tucked into the back of the truck, I shut the door.

Knox clasped my shoulder. "Thank you for letting me be a part of this. I'm proud of you for taking this step."

"You don't think it's crazy or too soon?"

"Timing doesn't matter. Emmett proposed to Ireland after a few weeks, and then they were married shortly after that. You know how slow he is to make a decision. I think when you know, you know. There isn't a need to wait. Besides, we're not getting any younger, and life is short.

My father's face flashed in my mind. "You're right."

"If you love her, then that's all that matters."

I nodded, overcome with emotion.

"You need any help with the date tomorrow night?" Knox asked, and appreciation for my family washed over me.

"I think I've got it." Initially, thought I needed Knox's help, but now I wanted to do it on my own.

Knox grinned. "Good luck. I'm proud of you. You're finally taking the steps to make your family whole."

As Knox walked over to his truck, I wondered if that was true. Was I making my family whole? Thinking about Hanna living with us, my ring on her finger, marriage, and maybe more kids felt right, but more than that, it felt complete.

I'd drifted along the last few years, just trying to survive as a single dad, thinking I had to do things a certain way or refrain from dating and finding someone to share my heart and life with. But now that I'd put myself out there, I could see so much more for our future.

I didn't want my brothers' help with the date, but I'd take Ember's input. I wanted her to feel part of this.

"What do you think about ice sculptures?" I asked her in the rearview mirror as we headed to our next destination.

"They're cool. But I think you should keep it simple."

"I was thinking about creating a winter wonderland, though," I said, knowing she'd want the same.

"Yeah, that sounds good."

~

I spent the last twenty-four hours planning the carriage ride and what came after. I hoped it wasn't too much. I wanted to wow Hanna but not overwhelm her. At the end of the day, it was about us and not a production. I tried to keep that in mind, but it was hard.

I wanted to give Hanna everything. I wanted her to feel like the most important person in the world to us.

I hoped I'd accomplished that. I waited with Mom at her house. Everything was set up. Ember was watching TV, and I was pacing endlessly.

"You're going to wear a path in the wood floors," Mom chided.

"What if she says no?"

Ember rolled her eyes and sighed. "She's not going to say no."

I stopped my pacing so I could see her face. "How can you be so sure?"

Ember shrugged. "Hanna loves us."

That might have been true, but even love had its limits. What if having an ex hanging around was too much for Hanna? What if my reaction to Brandy was a deal-breaker? What if everything I'd done to fix the situation wasn't enough? What if I was too late?

"Stop it. I can practically see your brain smoking from here," Mom said.

"I can't help it." Everything was done, and we had nothing to do but wait for the time I needed to leave to pick up Hanna.

My fingers trembled as I ran them through my hair.

"I think you have to remember what you feel for Hanna and know that it's enough. You can't control other people and their reactions, but you can put your feelings out there and know that whatever happens is meant to be."

"I feel like we're meant to be."

"Then why are you so nervous?" Ember asked, sounding older than her seven years.

"I don't know. Maybe because I've never put myself out there like this before?"

Mom nodded. "You've always been cautious, so slow to make a decision. It was a good thing when your brothers were jumping impulsively from one thing to the next. I didn't need to worry about you. But it has made it difficult for you to make decisions over the years."

"I know I'm doing the right thing; I'm just worried that she won't think so. That it will be too soon or too much."

"I don't think there are rules about love. If it's the right time, she'll say yes. And if you feel in your heart that it's right, then it is."

"So, you're saying I should stop worrying about how she'll react?"

"Yes."

"Dad, it's time." Ember nodded toward the clock.

I moved closer to her and dropped to my knees in front of her. "I'll pick her up and take her on the carriage ride. Knox will bring you for the proposal."

Ember rolled her eyes. "I know. We've talked about this."

"Just making sure." Before I stood, I asked, "You know I love you, right?"

"I know." Then she smiled. "You've got this, Dad. There's no way she'll say no."

I stood and ruffled her hair. "Thanks for the vote of confidence."

Kids could make things so simple. They brushed the extraneous things out of the way and focused on what mattered.

"Love you, Mom," I said as I kissed her cheek.

Then I was out the door, the air cooling my overheated body. I thought about what I felt for Hanna and let those feelings engulf me. Our feelings were what mattered. As long as I was acting within those parameters, I'd be fine.

I drove toward Hanna's parents' house, hoping it was the last time she'd stay the night. I knocked on the door, holding another bouquet of flowers for Hanna.

Her father opened the door and stepped onto the porch.

"Is everything okay?"

"I think we should talk," her father said, sending my heart galloping in my chest.

I let out a breath. "I love your daughter, and I'm going to ask her to marry me tonight. I thought about asking for your blessing, but—"

"You're going to propose anyway."

I cleared my throat, wondering for the umpteenth time if I was making the moves. "That's right. I love Hanna. I have for most of my life. Recently, it's morphed into something bigger than us. I want her in my life. I want to build a life with her. I hope you're okay with that, but I won't ask for your permission."

His face remained stoic. "What about this business with the ex?"

"I told Hanna that Brandy wasn't welcome to show up unannounced and that she wasn't welcome in my home anymore. I'm also talking to an attorney in the new year to get things settled officially."

"That sounds good."

"I know I've made mistakes in the past. I've held back from Hanna when I should have been leaning in. But I know what I've got in her, and I'm not willing to let her go. I want to make her mine."

"Then I guess there's nothing to say but good luck."

I let out the breath I'd been holding. "You're not upset?"

"How could I be? A deserving man is asking my daughter to marry him."

"Thank you, sir. I appreciate your vote of confidence."

"I didn't say she'd say yes. I just said I approve, and it's about time."

"I'm sorry?" I blinked at his blunt admission.

"You two have been dancing around each other for years. I'm glad you finally made the move. I think you'll be very happy together." He touched my shoulder, holding my gaze.

"I hope so." I didn't think I needed his blessing, but it sure felt good to have it.

"I know you will be."

The door opened. "Dad?"

Hanna wore leggings, boots, and a red sweater, with a puffy

coat over it. She was dressed for the cold, but she might as well have been wearing an evening gown. "You look gorgeous."

Hanna's cheeks turned pink. "Thank you."

"These are for you." I handed her the bouquet, and she inhaled the scent. "They're lovely. I'll just put these in a vase."

Hanna disappeared inside again.

"No offense. But I'm hoping to not have her home on time tonight, or at all," I said to her father, and he let out a large guffaw.

"Is that right?"

I'd taken a risk that Hanna's father was okay with us being together, and I'd been right. Her parents probably saw what we'd been avoiding for years. They just wanted Hanna to be happy.

By the time Hanna returned, we were talking about business on the farm.

"Are you ready to go, or do you want to spend the evening with my father?" Hanna asked dryly.

I grabbed her hand and kissed the back of it. "I want to spend it with you."

"I'll leave you two to it." Her father disappeared into the house, shutting the door behind him and leaving us alone.

"Are you ready for your carriage ride?"

Hanna grinned. "More than."

I led the way to my truck, helping her inside and shutting the door. This evening was ours, and I'd let go of any misgivings. I knew in my heart that Hanna felt the same way for me that I did for her. I might be moving quickly, but I had a feeling she'd appreciate it after years of indecision.

# CHAPTER 22

## HANNA

Sebastian knocking on my parents' door and handing me a bouquet of flowers was surreal. It was everything I'd wished for when I was a teenager, and even as an adult. For so long, I wanted Sebastian to pursue and choose me.

It felt good. I knew we had some things to discuss. I wanted assurance that Brandy wasn't just going to keep popping into our lives, but I had a feeling we'd weather the storm better in the future.

Brandy wouldn't surprise us because we were rock-solid in our relationship. Nothing could shake us, certainly not the person who continually abandoned Ember.

"What are you thinking about?"

I sighed. "The last few days. What it means for us going forward."

"I was hoping to wait until the carriage ride to talk about this, but what I said to you yesterday is how I feel. Brandy has had too much leeway in my life. I'm making moves so that she can't just show up on the property again, much less my front porch."

I let out the breath I felt like I'd been holding since I saw that woman and Ember had called out, *"Mommy."*

"I'm sorry. I didn't react the right way that night. I was shocked that she was there, and I shouldn't have been. This is the sort of thing she does."

"It's a hard situation. You want Ember to see her mother."

"Yeah, but not like that. She can't just show up and surprise everyone. That's not okay. I realized how much it affected us."

"I was so afraid of moving forward with you because I've grown to hate change. And I think it was because I don't like the way it feels when Brandy shows up unannounced and then disappears a few days later. If I don't handle it well, then what's going through Ember's head?"

"It can't be good for her," I said, taking a chance that my opinion was welcome.

"My thoughts are the same. I try to do what's best for Ember and weigh it against having a relationship with her mother, but I don't think this is the best way. Sometimes, I think it would be best if Brandy didn't come at all."

I reached over and took his hand in mine, my heart going out to him. "I can understand that."

Sebastian shook his head. "The coming and going, the attention, then lack thereof, is confusing for a child."

"You're a good father, Sebastian. You're doing the best you can."

He glanced over at me before signaling to turn into the farm. There wasn't a line of cars tonight, so there was no one at the gate to greet us.

When he pulled past the gate, he stopped and got out to close it. When he returned, he said, "Everyone who wants a tree should already have one. I don't want to be interrupted."

Pleasure slid through me, settling in my chest. "That sounds nice."

He parked at the main house, where a carriage and two horses were off to the side. "Are you ready for this?"

"I can't wait," I said with a grin.

We met at the side of the carriage, where he gave me a boost onto the seat.

"There are blankets and hot chocolate," Sebastian said as he moved to greet the horses before joining me.

"You don't need to talk to your mother or your brothers?"

Sebastian flashed me a smile. "Not tonight. It's just me and you."

I settled into the seat, arranging a throw blanket over our laps.

I hooked my hand through his arm and snuggled closer. The first time we took a carriage ride, I was falling for him, but now I was in love with him. I was in so deep with this man; I just hoped we were on the same page. If he wanted to pump the brakes and go in a different direction, I wasn't sure what I'd do.

I wouldn't settle for anything less than moving forward with him and Ember. I wanted a life with them, a family, and a future.

"I want you to know I'm happy to answer any questions you have about Brandy and the plan going forward. I made some decisions while you were with your parents, but I want you to know that going forward, we'll discuss them together. I always want to hear your input. You're as much a part of this as Ember and me."

"Thank you for including me." My throat tightened at the unexpected gesture. I wasn't sure of my role. I'd always been around to care for Ember, but I'd stayed out of his decisions when it came to her mother.

The horses moved forward in a slow gait, the air cool around us and the stars visible in the sky. Twinkling lights lined the path. We passed Emmett's house, then Heath's. "Where are we going?"

"To the pond."

"Does Talon still have lights floating in it?"

"We're going to find out," Sebastian said, but his expression was a little uncertain.

Was he worried about something? Maybe he wasn't sure if I was okay with reconciling. "I appreciate that you made changes, but I want to make sure it's what you want, and you're not just doing it for me."

"It's for me and Ember. I don't want you to feel disrespected, but I could see how Brandy's actions weren't helping us. Ember's well-being is always my first concern."

"Of course, it is." I squeezed his arm to show my support.

"I think your being there helped me see how crazy it was that I let Brandy pop in whenever she felt like it."

"You've given her money in the past. Is that what she wanted this time?"

"I told her she wouldn't be getting anything from me. I need the money for Ember. I want to save for her college tuition and make sure she has everything she needs to thrive. I can't do that if I'm constantly siphoning money to Brandy."

"Brandy's not your responsibility."

Sebastian glanced down at me, the passing lights reflecting in his eyes. "You and Ember are. I want to make both of you happy."

We approached the pond; I could see lights reflecting on the surface. Sebastian turned the horses so that they followed the path around the pond. When we reached a spot that he'd set up for us to stop, he pulled the reins, and we got out.

"What's all this?" I asked him as he led me to the pile of blankets and pillows. There was even a basket of what I hoped was food. I had been too nervous during the day to eat much.

He helped me settle onto one of the large cushions on the ground.

"I didn't ask my brothers for help. Everything I planned for tonight was my idea."

"I wouldn't have minded if they helped." I loved how close they were.

He stood stiffly. "I wanted you to know how I felt and what my intentions are going forward."

The seriousness of his tone had my heart skipping a beat. I didn't think he'd go through all this trouble to tell me he didn't have time for a relationship, but now, I wasn't sure. Sebastian was an interesting combination of one step forward and two steps back.

He knelt on the ground next to me. "I was going to wait until after we ate for this, but I can't wait any longer."

"Sebastian?" I asked, a little confused as to what was happening.

"I can't wait another minute to tell you how I feel. I love you, Hanna. I think I have for most of my life. It may have been a little different when we were teenagers, but it's morphed into something larger than life now that we're adults. I want a future with you. I want to live with you in my cabin on the farm. I want to raise Ember with you, and any other children that you might want."

I sucked in a sharp breath. Was he proposing? I hadn't expected this. I'd have expected we would live together for a year or two before he'd even think of getting engaged.

He pulled a black velvet box out of his pocket, and my heart stopped. "Hanna, will you marry me?"

I think I was surprised by his question and the sparkling diamond he'd opened the lid to reveal to me. "Are you sure?" I asked, my hands shaking as he slid the ring onto my finger.

"I've never been surer about anything. I love you and want to build a future with you. I want you to be my wife."

"I want that, too." Then I was scooped into his arms, straddling his lap as he kissed me. The rest of the world fell away as I got lost in him.

Eventually, he softened the kisses and pulled back.

"I can't believe you want to get married." I felt elated, happier than I'd ever been.

"You think it's too soon?"

I took stock of my feelings, the exhilaration at his question, the joy at his expression of love for me. "Not at all. I just thought it was too soon for you. I wasn't expecting it."

"Those are the best kinds of surprises."

"I have to agree," I said, as I admired the simple diamond ring he'd chosen for me.

"I wanted to be alone tonight, but I also wanted to include Ember. I wanted you to know that she helped me pick out the ring, along with Knox."

"That's sweet."

The sound of a golf cart moving over the lane reached our ears. "I asked Knox to bring Ember so that she could be part of this."

"That's sweet." Happiness bubbled inside of me.

"You don't mind?" Sebastian asked.

I shook my head. "Of course not. I want to share this with her, too."

When the golf cart pulled up to us, Ember hopped out. "Did she say yes?"

Sebastian grinned. "She did."

Ember surprised me by hugging both of us. We were laughing and crying when Knox said gruffly, "Congratulations. You deserve this."

Sebastian stood, disentangling himself from me and Ember. They embraced, and Knox said, "I'll leave you alone."

"Thank you," I said to Knox, "for everything."

"Anytime," he said with a grin as he took off in the golf cart.

Ember grabbed my hand so she could examine the ring. "It's so shiny."

"It's the lights." It added a magical quality to the evening.

Music began to play from speakers that must have been on the poles he'd added.

"Will you dance with me?" Sebastian asked us.

I took his hand, the other settling on his arm, while Ember stood between us. She stepped onto his toes and wrapped her arms around his waist. It must have been something they'd done many times before, because she didn't hesitate to move into position.

We swayed with the music. I couldn't be as close to Sebastian as I wanted, but it was perfect. All I ever wanted was to be part of this family, and now I was.

"I love you," Sebastian said.

I grinned, my cheeks hurting from the cold and the joy emanating inside me. "I love you, too."

Just as he leaned down to kiss me, Ember popped off his feet and ran to the blankets to bury her head in them. "No kissing."

Sebastian grinned. "You better get used to it because I won't be able to resist kissing Hanna all the time, now that we're engaged."

Ember groaned as his lips met mine, and everything around us faded away.

"Are you done?" Ember asked, her fingers splayed in front of her eyes.

"For now," Sebastian said to her, never taking his eyes off me. "Let's eat. After dinner, you're sleeping over at Addy's house."

"Oh, that's right." Ember tore through the basket, pulling out food and setting it on the blanket.

"If that's okay with you," Sebastian said, his hand cupping my cheek.

"It's more than okay with me." I loved having Ember around.

I wanted her to feel a part of the engagement, too, but I also wanted some time alone with Sebastian. I wanted to feel his love without any distractions.

I knew going forward there would be nights when we couldn't have this, but I'd relish it when it happened. There might be more kids and disruptions in our future, but we'd weather them together.

We ate dinner, then danced some more. The evening was so beautiful, between the lights on the water and the ones around our cozy seating area; none of us were ready for the night to end.

When the golf cart reappeared, Sebastian didn't seem to be surprised.

"Come on, Ember. Addy's been waiting for you."

Ember hugged Sebastian, and he held her tight to him. "Be good."

"I'm always good," she huffed as she moved to hug me. "Love you."

Tears stung my eyes as I held her tighter. "I love you, too."

Then Ember climbed into the passenger seat of the golf cart, and Knox took off with a wave and a wink. "You two be good."

We watched them drive away.

"Please tell me we're not going to have any more surprise visitors tonight? Your family isn't going to show up for a surprise engagement party, are they?"

"That's a good idea," Sebastian teased, and I smacked his chest.

"I love that you included Ember, but I want to be alone with you tonight."

Sebastian eased me to my back and hovered over me. "I want that, too. No one else is supposed to show up here. I think they know what's happening."

"Oh, yeah, and what's that?"

"I'm making love to my fiancée, the love of my life, and my best friend."

"Are you saying that nothing has changed?" I asked him, my heart soaring.

"You'll always be my best friend. I didn't think it was possible to love you more, but I do. It's like we've been holding back all these years, afraid of our true potential. And once we unleashed the love, it was all-encompassing."

"I love that. I love you."

Sebastian settled his long body over mine, and I relished the weight of him pressing me into the blankets. Despite the cold air, I was warm all over.

He whispered words of endearment as he worshipped me and my body. When he entered me, I gasped at the sensation of him filling me, knowing that I'd have this forever. It wasn't a fleeting moment. This was our forever.

We hadn't left anything to chance. We'd gone after what we wanted and gotten something more than we could imagine.

When stars burst beneath my eyelids, I reveled in the feeling of his warm skin against mine. He threw a blanket over us and kissed my temple. "I love you more every second."

"Me, too."

I couldn't imagine a more perfect proposal. There was excitement about the life we'd share, combined with the heat of the moment. There was so much love. I could finally trust in forever.

# EPILOGUE

## HANNA

When I arrived at Talon's workshop, he had his protective goggles on, and what I assumed were noise-cancelling headphones. I moved to stand where he could see me.

He was a large man, like his brothers, with well-defined muscles and a beard. He was the Monroe brother I knew the least about because he wasn't around often. He kept to himself, using the excuse that he was working.

His forehead creased when he finally looked up to find me. He turned off the machine he'd been working with, lifted his goggles to his forehead and slid his headphones off, letting them rest around his neck.

"What can I do for you?" Talon asked. His voice was raspy, as if he hadn't spoken in a while.

Sebastian mentioned that he was a bit of a recluse, working in his shop and forgetting to eat and sleep when he was in the middle of a project.

"We were scheduled to meet this morning to talk about the blog." When he didn't acknowledge our standing appointment, I continued. "Marley tasked me with writing about each brother, and you're next."

He angled his head to the side. "Was that today?"

"This is the time and date we discussed."

Talon sighed. "Fine. Let's get this over with. What did you want to talk about?"

This was where I faltered a bit. Would readers be interested in his work, or something else? He didn't seem to have much of a personal life, so I couldn't use the same angle I had with Sebastian.

"Sebastian said your cabin was the first to be built?"

Talon leaned against the table, crossing his arms over his chest. "I needed a workshop, and I always knew I'd stay on the farm. It made sense to go ahead and pick my spot on the property."

"Why don't you tell me about your typical day? Your schedule, what you do, and then we can talk about how you come up with your ideas."

"I don't really have a schedule. I get an idea and then work on that. When I've made considerable progress, I'll remember that I'm hungry or tired, and I'll take care of those needs." He shot me a wry look. "I'm not like Sebastian. I don't live by my routine."

"Is that an artist thing?" Sebastian would lose his mind if his life was ruled by inspiration.

"I take commissioned pieces to pay the bills, but I prefer to create whatever I'm motivated or inspired to make. I also like making things for the farm, like the light display."

"That must make it difficult to see other people or be involved in activities?"

Talon's brow furrowed. "This is the only thing I'm involved in."

I loved my job and working with children, but I couldn't

imagine it being my only thing. Maybe I thought it was weird because I'd never met an artist before.

"Why don't you start from the beginning. How did you get noticed by these magazines?" I gestured at a nearby table that was piled high with architectural and design magazines. He'd been featured in several.

Talon shook his head. "In high school, my shop teacher, Mr. Beyer, encouraged me to work after school on whatever I was led to do. That's when I created my first simple light fixture. Mom needed better lighting in her kitchen. So, I made these pendant lights. At Mr. Beyer's insistence, I shopped them around to various shops in the area. I didn't think they were good enough, but he thought I was on to something. Then my designs became more elaborate. People used them in dining rooms and entranceways." He opened one of the magazines and flipped the pages to his spread of pictures.

"They're really neat." I couldn't come up with a word for the pieces that would do them justice. They were made out of metal, and a few incorporated wood into the design. They were different from anything else I'd ever seen, clearly on trend enough to be noticed by design magazines. "And that's so great that your teacher supported your dreams."

"I wouldn't say this was my dream. I enjoyed creating things, and he convinced me that it would be helpful if I could get paid for my passion."

"That makes sense."

"Annapolis gets visitors from all over, and eventually, word spread. I was getting more and more commissioned pieces. Then the magazines started calling."

"I bet that kept you busy."

"I make a few for the shops I have contracts with, and I only take a few other commissioned pieces. Lately, I've been making the holiday light sets that you see around the farm."

"Which do you prefer to make?"

He considered my question for a few seconds. "I like to help my family. It's the one thing I can contribute. I'm not good with numbers like Sebastian, and I don't help babysit my nieces."

I loved that he referred to Addy and Ember as his nieces. "I'm sure they appreciate you being here."

Talon grunted and waved in the direction of the pieces lining the wall. "This is my contribution to the family. It's not enough for everything they've done for me. It's the least I can do."

"Can you tell me about the pond?"

He winced.

"I'm curious what prompted you to create the lights in the water and how you did it."

His expression turned thoughtful. "You'll notice there's no pattern to the lights. I was experimenting with methods on how to create the structure under the water. But I didn't get it right. I'm still working on it."

"Is that why you haven't shared it with the family?" I asked gently, hoping he'd confide in me.

Talon's jaw tightened. "It's not ready yet."

He kept his creations private until they were deemed ready for viewing. Maybe he was a bit of a perfectionist.

I heard the rumble of a truck outside, and a few minutes later, Sebastian came inside, with Ember skipping ahead. "Uncle Talon!" she cried, as he scooped her into his arms. "Where've you been hiding?"

"Nowhere, silly," Ember said as she gazed down at him, and tugged playfully on his beard.

She wasn't put off by his surly moods like her uncles were.

Talon rubbed his beard against the delicate skin of her neck, and she giggled.

The display warmed my heart. In a professional capacity, he was successful, but I couldn't say he was happy or fulfilled.

Sebastian draped an arm over my shoulder. "Did you get what you needed?"

I pursed my lips as I watched Talon interact with Ember. "I've learned a bit."

"That's good." Then he leaned in to whisper in my ear. "He's a tough one to get to know."

"So, it's not just me," I murmured.

I wasn't sure how I'd get what I needed for the article. Everything he'd told me was already included in the various magazines that had already been written about his work and his origin story. I wanted a new angle that would interest the farms' customers and local residents. But I wasn't sure what it would be.

I couldn't write about how lonely he seemed. But my heart went out to him. I wanted him to have what his other brothers had found—love.

But it wasn't a surprise that he was the last one to be single. He kept to himself and focused solely on work. If one of his family members wanted to spend time with him, they had to seek him out.

Sebastian turned his attention from me to Talon. "How was your date with Holly?"

"What are you talking about?" I asked Sebastian, sure he was stirring up trouble.

Talon slowly lowered Ember to the floor.

"Apparently, Talon won a date with Holly at the auction," Sebastian explained to me.

My mouth dropped open. "I didn't know that."

"I couldn't let Teddy win her. Their Christmas tree farm is our competition. I don't know what they were doing at the auction anyway."

"Their sister, Daphne, was a bachelorette. They were just there to support her." Then to me, Sebastian said, "Teddy is Daphne's oldest brother. Their family owns Pine Valley Farms."

"They had no business bidding on Holly. She may not be a Monroe—" he broke off, seemingly struggling to find words, "but she's one of us."

"Because she works here, she can't date someone from a competing Christmas tree farm?" I couldn't stop myself from asking.

His muscle worked in his jaw, and I surmised that he didn't like her dating at all. "I know everyone wants to know what's going on with me and Holly, but I'd appreciate it if you'd give us some privacy. I'd like to settle things between us, and I can't do that if everyone is pushing us together."

My heart contracted in my chest.

Sebastian moved closer to him and lowered his voice. "I'm sorry. I shouldn't have given you a hard time. It took guts for you to bid on her."

Talon shook his head. "She wasn't happy about it."

"I'm proud of you for taking that step, for trying to clear the air. You've got my support." Sebastian touched his shoulder, and Talon nodded tightly.

"I appreciate it."

Everyone was curious about the demise of their relationship, but it was between Holly and Talon. I just hoped they could resolve whatever the issues were between them and become friends.

It was my love for Sebastian that had me hoping that all the Monroe brothers could have their happily ever after.

# BONUS EPILOGUE

## SEBASTIAN

I woke up to Ember jumping on the bed. "Santa was here!"

I scrubbed a hand over my face. It felt like I'd only been asleep for a few hours. We were up late, assembling a dollhouse and wrapping presents.

"It's Christmas!" Ember said, jumping on her knees at the end of the bed.

"Merry Christmas, sweetie," Hanna croaked.

Ember's movement slowed. "Are you coming? There are presents under the tree."

"Did you go downstairs?" I asked her, feeling slightly more awake as I pulled myself to a seated position.

Guilt crossed her face. "Maybe."

"You know you're not supposed to go downstairs before us." I tried to add censure to my tone, but it fell flat.

"I had to see if Santa came," Ember leaned in to whisper, as if he were still here and she didn't want him to overhear her.

"You didn't start without us, did you?" Hanna asked as she rolled over on her side to face us, an amused expression on her face.

Ember angled her head to the side. "Of course not. I've been waiting for you to get up."

My lips twitched. "You waited by jumping on the bed?"

Ember shot me a disgruntled look.

I held up my hands as if to ward her off. "Give us a few minutes to get dressed, and we'll be ready to open presents."

"Yay!" Ember cried as she hopped off the bed and raced toward the stairs, where I knew she'd sit on the top step to wait for me. That had been our tradition in the past, but this year, our morning would include Hanna.

Hanna looked so inviting—her hair mussed, her cheeks pink from sleep—that I couldn't resist leaning over to kiss her on the lips.

This is what I'd dreamed about, waking up to Ember's excitement on Christmas morning and spending the day with my girls.

When I pulled back, I said, "Merry Christmas, *fiancée*."

She bit her lip. "I'll never get tired of you calling me your fiancée. Merry Christmas."

"You better get tired of it. Otherwise, we'll never get married." Despite my overly cautious nature, I didn't want a long engagement. I wanted to call Hanna my *wife*.

She reached across the rumpled blankets to touch my hand. "I'd marry you tomorrow if I could."

I raised a brow, my heart picking up the pace. "Are you serious?"

Hanna moved so that her hand curled around my arm, her breasts pressed against my elbow. "We could have a nice, simple wedding on the farm. We wouldn't need much preparation."

My dick thickened in my briefs, Christmas and our wedding momentarily forgotten.

"Are you coming?" Ember asked, and I shook my head, lamenting our lack of privacy in the mornings. I had visions of making love to my fiancée today, but it would have to wait. "We need to get dressed. Let's table this discussion for later."

I kissed her one more time, knowing today would be full, between my brothers coming over soon to watch us open presents, a family dinner at the main house, and a bonfire at the end of the night.

I texted my brothers as we got dressed and brushed our teeth. I stalled long enough that the doorbell rang as we went down the steps.

Ember ran to open it.

Talon stood at the door with a red velvet bag flung over his shoulders.

"You wore your pajamas," Ember said as he moved inside.

Talon dropped his bag, lifted her into his arms, and kissed her cheeks.

He had a soft spot for Ember. "You told us to wear them, remember?"

Ember looked down at him from her perch on his hip and touched his beard. "I wasn't sure you would."

Talon shrugged, but I knew the truth. He couldn't deny her anything.

"Uncle Talon, Santa came." Ember's voice still had a hushed quality to it, as if she couldn't believe it was true.

I lamented the day when some punk at school would tell her there was no Santa Claus because mornings like this were magical. I'd treasure these memories.

Someday, Emmett and Ireland would stay home to open presents with their own kids, just like Sarah and Knox.

"Show me these presents, Miss Ember."

Ember pointed the way, whispering something into his ear, and Talon grinned at her. It warmed my heart that he was here, enjoying the day with us.

"I love that your brothers come over on Christmas morning,"

Hanna said, and I drew her into my arms, kissing her more thoroughly than I had in our bed.

When I pulled back, Hanna asked with a smile, "What was that for?"

"It's the first of many presents."

"Mmm. Spending Christmas with you, Ember, and your family is the best present of all."

"I have to agree," I said as the doorbell rang for a second time. "That must be Emmett and Ireland."

"Get the door. I'll make sure Talon and Ember hold off on opening presents." I grabbed her wrist and kissed her lips one more time before letting her go with a wink, a promise of more to come.

I opened the door wide, grinning when I saw that it was Emmett and Ireland and Marley and Heath. "Come on in. It's a full house."

Our quiet morning gave way to laughing and excitement. But I wouldn't have had it any other way.

Ireland and Marley greeted me, giving me a hug and a, "Merry Christmas," before following the noise into the living room.

Emmett pointed to Talon's red bag. "I think it's moving."

"Why would it be—" But there was a lump in the bag moving around, and then a black nose appeared at the opening.

"Talon," I called to him, my heart fluttering in my chest.

Talon rushed toward us. "The breeder who gave us the other pups called to see if we wanted another one. I was going to keep her for myself, but—" Talon held his hand out, and the puppy moved further outside the bag. "Hanna mentioned that she and Ember wanted one."

My mouth was dry.

"What's taking so long?" Hanna asked as she appeared at my side. Her hands flew to her mouth. "Is that a—"

My jaw tightened. "It's a puppy. Apparently, you asked for one."

She blinked, her eyes suspiciously wet.

"Did someone say puppy?" Ember rushed to join us, Marley and Ireland not far behind.

There was a chorus of "awws."

Ember fell to her knees, and the puppy climbed into her lap, bumping her chin with his head as she squeezed him. "Can we keep him, Daddy?" she asked as she looked up at me, and the pup licked her face, sending her into a fit of giggles. She fell onto the floor, and the puppy stood on her chest, kissing her face while Ember giggled and squirmed. "Can we keep him? Please, Daddy?"

"I don't know how you can say no to that," Emmett observed, and I shot him a look because that was his favorite word.

He merely smirked.

I couldn't wait until Ireland was pregnant. I could see him being protective and sweet, worried about child-proofing his house and ensuring everything was perfect.

Hanna stilled. "For the record, I said we'd love to have one, but that you—"

"Wanted one, too," I said with confidence, as I plucked the yellow puppy off of Ember and cuddled him in my arms.

"Everyone else named their puppies after Santa's reindeer," Emmett began, and Ember's eyes brightened when she asked, "Can we name her Dancer?"

The puppy was prancing around Ember as if she wanted her to play. "I don't see why not. Besides it seems to fit."

"Prancer or Dancer," Hanna said as everyone's gaze shifted to the puppy.

Ember hugged the puppy. "She's a Dancer."

"And she's perfect," Hanna said as she touched his downy fur.

I scooped up the puppy and moved into the living room so

we could sit by the tree, Ember in front of me, her presents from Santa forgotten.

"We're keeping him, right?" Ember asked as she knelt in front of us, her hands running over the puppy's fur.

"How can I say no?" I asked her, amused when the puppy crawled from my lap to Ember's. I knew all the arguments in favor of a dog because I'd researched them all. This puppy would be good for Ember. She'd learn responsibility and how to love and care for someone who needed her. But most of all, she'd be a normal girl with a puppy.

She might not have a family in the traditional sense, but she wasn't lacking in love. And there was no way I could deny her the joy of a puppy at Christmas.

I wasn't sure how we could top this for next year, but I had a while to figure it out.

"You can thank your favorite uncle," Talon said, his voice full of pride as he sat on the couch.

"You're not the favorite," Heath countered, and they were off, arguing about which uncle was Ember's favorite, and I sat, my arm around Hanna while my family laughed and joked around us.

I couldn't imagine a more perfect morning. Not until Ember crawled into my lap, the puppy still in her arms. I kissed her cheek and then Hanna's lips.

"Can we open presents now?" Ember asked, bringing my attention back to the pile of presents under the tree.

I smiled, my heart full. I'd have alone time with Hanna tonight after Ember was asleep, and I couldn't wait. "Let's do it."

I hope you loved Hanna and Sebastian's story! Holly and Talon's romance is next in *Endless Hope*. ***This Christmas, I'll finally make her mine.***

Do you enjoy grumpy mountain men? Read the Mountain Haven Series 40% off.

## BOOKS BY LEA COLL

The Monroe Brothers

*Runaway Love*

*Finding Sunshine*

*Reviving Hearts*

*Trusting Forever*

*Endless Hope*

*Forbidden Flame*

**Ever After Series**

*Feel My Love*

*The Way You Are*

*Love Me Like You Do*

*Give Me a Reason*

*Somebody to Love*

*Everything About You*

**Mountain Haven Series**

*Infamous Love*

*Adventurous Love*

*Impulsive Love*

*Tempting Love*

*Inescapable Love*

*Forbidden Love*

**Second Chance Harbor Series**

*Fighting Chance*

*One More Chance*

*Lucky Chance*

*My Best Chance*

*Worth the Chance*

*A Chance at Forever*

**Annapolis Harbor Series**

*Only with You*

*Lost without You*

*Perfect for You*

*Crazy for You*

*Falling for You*

*Waiting for You*

*Hooked on You*

**All I Want Series**

*Choose Me*

*Be with Me*

*Burn for Me*

*Trust in Me*

*Stay with Me*

*Take a Chance on Me*

Download a free novella, when you sign up for her newsletter.

To learn more about her books, please visit her website.

## SPECIAL EDITION BUNDLES

## ONLY AVAILABLE ON LEA'S SHOP

***If you prefer to read by trope:***

Brother's Best Friend

Childhood Crush

Contractors

Enemies to Lovers

Fake Relationship

First in Series

Forbidden Love

Friends to Lovers

Grumpy Meets Sunshine

Hot Heroes

Office Romance

Second Chance Romance

Single Dad

Single Mom

Single Parent

Sports Romance

***If you prefer to read series:***

All I Want

Annapolis Harbor

Ever After

Mountain Haven

Second Chance Harbor

***If you prefer to read paperbacks:***

All I Want Series

Annapolis Harbor

Brother's Best Friend

Childhood Crush

Enemies to Lovers

Grumpy Meets Sunshine

Hot Heroes

Office Romance

Second Chance Harbor

Single Mom

Sports Romance

# ABOUT THE AUTHOR

Lea Coll is a USA Today Bestselling Author of sweet and sexy happily ever afters. She worked as a trial attorney for over ten years. Now she stays home with her three children, plotting stories while fetching snacks and running them back and forth to activities. She enjoys the freedom of writing romance after years of legal writing.

She currently resides in Maryland with her family.

Check out Lea's books on her shop.

Get a free novella when you sign up for Lea's newsletter.

Printed in the USA
CPSIA information can be obtained
at www.ICGtesting.com
LVHW091938060224
771006LV00002B/459

9 781961 939608